Alien Blood Wars

HEALING DANCE

SAMANTHA CAYTO

Healing Dance
ISBN # 978-1-78651-849-1
©Copyright Samantha Cayto 2019
Cover Art by Cherith Vaughan ©Copyright August 2019
Interior text design by Claire Siemaszkiewicz
Pride Publishing

HEALING DANCE

Dedication

This book is dedicated to all of the wonderful people at Pride Publishing, not the least of which is my awesome editor, Jamie, as well as all of my readers for their unfailing support and patience with me while I was battling cancer.

Prologue

Wales, 1647

Dafydd knew what he was doing was wicked. Hiding behind bushes as he watched the Parliamentary soldiers bathe in the pond was a sin in God's eyes. *A man who lieth with another man was an abomination worthy of death.* Didn't he hear that often enough in church? And two men in the village had been castrated and hung not three years ago for buggery. He might not have dared to act on his depraved desires, but he was still risking his immortal soul and his life by indulging in this temptation to watch naked men.

And yet he couldn't stop. Each time that he'd sworn he wouldn't do it again, he'd ended up right back at this spot. Small as he was, the thick bushes hid him from view as he spied on the men. They came to wash off the sweat of the day each evening. With the sun lowering in the sky behind him, he could see everything without being easily seen in return. All those wet muscles gleamed with the water that sluiced off them. When the men shook themselves like dogs, their cocks and balls swung, catching his gaze and holding it captive.

The variety of how men were built amazed him. Some dicks were long and thin, while others were thick and short. One man in particular had the best of both kinds — long and thick in equal measure. They were all delicious to see and so very different from the skinny little thing hanging between his own legs. Saliva pooled in his mouth and shivers danced along his skin at the notion of what those men could do with what God had given them. He held only the faintest of ideas, based on the whispering of other boys and his limited imagination.

The men themselves put on an instructive show on occasion. Apparently a bit of grabbing and pulling one another was okay, like he did for himself. Going into his twelfth summer, his cock had come alive. He'd known what do from watching his older brothers in bed, tugging at their dicks, milking them like cows' udders. Not that the church sanctioned such, either. But a little sin was acceptable, and if that were true, why not this, as well?

He reached under his tunic to take hold of his shaft. It had sprung up the moment the men had arrived. The anticipation of the show was enough to make him hard. Seeing the men now dipping into the water brought him close to climax unaided. When he yanked a few times on his foreskin, he came with a muted gasp that left him breathless. Then he wiped the signs of his sin on the grass beneath his knees, never taking his gaze off the men. If he waited a few minutes, his cock would rise again.

The sound of hoofbeats behind him caught his attention. Heart in his throat, he turned to see who was approaching. A tall man with black hair and pale skin cantered toward him on a magnificent beast of a horse. A spike of true terror hit Dafydd, freezing him for a few seconds. He knew that man. Everybody did. Not Welsh, nor English, nor even Scottish, he was a new lord just to the north. People whispered that he had been a Royalist before allying with Parliament, not that switching sides was rare. Many had in the course of the civil war. Dafydd and other common folk hardly knew or cared who ruled. It was never good for them, regardless.

This foreign lord, though, was different. No one trusted outsiders, and this one was whispered to come from a far off, barbaric place. Rumors abounded at his cruelty. No one who crossed him lived for long, and death was never quick. Anyone dragged into his castle wouldn't be seen again, taken to a hideous fate that rivaled anything other powerful men inflicted upon their enemies. The fact that he rode about alone was testament to how frightening he was. No one else dared to do such a thing. The man was fearless like the Devil, which was reason enough to steer clear of him.

Dafydd was nothing to this man, and yet being caught spying on the soldiers would spell his doom. Forcing breath into his lungs, he launched himself from his hiding place and raced away. He was quick for his size. Everyone remarked on it. He pumped his legs as fast as he could, growing fright and the sound of the horse's hooves speeding him along. His feet were tough from his lack of boots, so he didn't even try to pick his route carefully. All he could think of was reaching the outer edge of the village and the meager safety it would provide. Likely no one would come to his aid. At least there would be places to hide.

The foreign lord got closer, for there was no way to outrun a horse. A laugh rang out, skittering up Dafydd's spine. He ran faster, lungs and muscles burning with each step. Without even knowing it for sure, he ran as if his life depended on it. Then the horse was upon him and fingers latched on to the back of his tunic. For a few seconds, he flew, arms and legs flailing in the air. The lord had monstrous power, lifting Dafydd as if he were a strip of cloth. Dafydd shrieked, not caring how much he sounded like a girl — and a terrified one at that. With a dizzying rush, he found himself slung face-down across the lord's thighs.

A hard slap hit his rump as laughter floated above him. "What a pretty catch. And here I thought I was only out for a breath of fresh air."

The horse kicked up to a gallop. Dafydd would have slid off if not for the firm hand holding him in place. He closed his eyes and gritted his teeth at the miserable ride. It was nearly impossible to breathe with his stomach slamming against what felt like stone. How many times had he fantasized about being carried away by a strong, handsome man?

It was never like this.

The sickening and perilous ride came to an abrupt end when they entered the forest. The lord reined his horse in, but before Dafydd could catch his breath, he was spun around again. This time, when his vision cleared, he was sitting astride and staring right into the lord's violet eyes. *So beautiful. So cruel.*

The lord pinched Dafydd's chin, moving his head this way and that. "Hmm, very fetching, the prettiest thing I've seen in a long while. And it just so happens I've been looking for a new fuck toy." The man's Welsh was flawless, yet with an accent Dafydd had never heard before.

Foreign devil.

The lord leaned in, his strangely-colored eyes raking Dafydd like a scourge. "You enjoy looking at naked men, do you? What a wicked, wicked boy you are."

When Dafydd tried to shake his head in denial, the hold on his chin increased, hard enough to make him whimper.

"That's it, slut. I like hearing how much you hurt." He grinned, showing a full set of teeth, white and gleaming. Sharp.

Dafydd whimpered again. "Please, M'lord."

"Please, what, cunt? Do you want me to show you what a man can do to a pretty boy who shouldn't wander too close to temptation?"

Dafydd tried to free himself from that punishing grip. He had to get away. If he could only slip down, the forest would give him cover. This wasn't what he wanted. Something terrible was going to happen if he didn't escape.

His efforts were for naught. There was no breaking the man's hold. Instead, he was lifted and turned as if he were nothing more than his sister's rag doll. Now he faced away from the man and with his tunic riding high on his thighs, his exposed crotch mashed against the rough saddle. The lord clasped his hand around the back of Dafydd's head and forced him to bend over the horse's neck. His tunic was rucked up more to expose his bare ass. He closed his eyes while he clenched the horse's mane. The familiar smell of the animal was his only solace.

He didn't know what was coming, not truly, and yet he wasn't really surprised when something thick pushed against his ass. He could tell just by the feel that this was unlike anything he'd seen before. It was too big and oddly cool, a battering ram pushing past the globes of his buttocks. He clenched his hole instinctively, even though he knew it was useless.

There was no fighting this man, this lord, this devil. When the club breached his hole, it went all the way in with a hard, brutal thrust. Dafydd screamed in agony before begging with words that made no sense. There was no mercy to be had…or beauty or pleasure — only pain that didn't lessen as the man plundered Dafydd's body. This was what came of his wicked desires, God's wrath visited upon him. He knew then that his life was over, no matter if he kept breathing.

He was forever broken.

And yet the violation of his ass was nothing. A few seconds later, sharp teeth sank into the side of his neck. The pain of it was quickly overtaken by the revolting sensation of his blood being drawn out of his body. He stretched his mouth wider in a silent cry of terror. His mind shut down, sinking into oblivion, unable to face the horror that a monster had truly claimed him.

.

Chapter One

Boston, Modern Day

Dafydd turned his head just in time to avoid getting soapy water in his eyes. "Idris, what did I say about splashing?"

His son gave him a toothy grin and lifted his hand to do the forbidden act again. Dafydd reached over the side of the tub and took hold of the baby's wrist. He was careful to keep his touch light — not enough to hurt, merely to contain.

"I said 'no'. Stop being such a chopsy boy or bath time is over."

Idris looked at him, his violet eyes assessing, as always. Even at his young age, he was calculating how much he could get away with. His growth spurt had been troubling, although not unexpected. He should have still been a wiggly bundle of soft skin and small bones…if he were human. He wasn't. Instead, he'd grown to toddler-size — and with his father's monstrous intelligence in the bargain.

And his evil inclinations.

No, he couldn't think like that. It was too early to tell what manner of boy, then man, he might grow into. He didn't have to become like his brothers, a shadow of their alien father's nature. There was a chance — a good one, if he were to believe his current hosts — that Idris would mature into whatever manner of man Dafydd raised him to be. He'd never been given the chance to influence the twins. This time would be different. Maybe if he showered this son with love, he could dispel whatever bad thing lurked in his blood. He might have done the same with Bran and Cadoc, regardless of the manner of their conception, if he'd been permitted.

The mere thought of his other sons and what he'd been forced to do with one of them caused his vision to blur. For a few seconds, he didn't see Idris sitting in a bubble bath. He saw Cadoc's wide-eyed look of surprise before his face and body crumbled into dust. His heart squeezed in an echo of the grief that had overtaken him at the time. He wouldn't have thought he'd have any capacity to love his sons, yet he had.

He mentally shook himself. There was no value in dwelling on it. His life went on and so did this newest child's. There was a chance for him to make things right, to raise a hybrid to be a good citizen of this world, not a monster. He'd taken the first step by putting aside the forced pregnancy and the way he'd loathed it. Idris wasn't to blame. He knew, and mostly felt, that.

Idris blew a raspberry before saying, "Otay, Dada. Duck!"

Dafydd gave his son an approving smile before releasing his hand and reaching for the New England Patriots rubber duck. Idris squealed in delight as he took it and plopped it into the water. The boy was an odd mixture of abilities. His understanding of language was excellent, as was his vocabulary. But he had what Harry referred to as speech impediments, reflective of the way his body was growing rapidly. He was also a bit clumsy. This was all normal, his hosts assured him. He had to trust them on that. Other than being used as a punching bag at Dracul's encouragement, Dafydd had had no real hand in raising his first two sons.

"How is bath time going?" Lucien, Harry's husband, asked the question from the doorway of the large bathroom.

Dafydd tamped down his irritation. He didn't like being monitored, even unobtrusively as Lucien typically did. He understood their concern. Having first rejected Idris then killed Cadoc, Dafydd's intentions toward the baby were a little suspect. When he was being fair-minded, he could see their point of view.

"Fine," he replied without taking his eyes off his son. "No one's drowned yet."

He winced. *Now who's being the chopsy boy?*

He looked over his shoulder. "Sorry. Not funny, I know, and I need to watch what I say in front of the baby."

After grabbing the bottle of shampoo, he squeezed a dollop onto his palm and began to work it into Idris' thick hair. He could feel Lucien's gaze on his back then heard him come into the room to stand next to him.

"I'm sorry if it feels as if I'm your jailer." Lucien had a lovely voice, soothing, and a quiet way about him that put Dafydd at ease.

"No, that's fine. It doesn't. Not really, like." He glanced up. "I'm doing all right, though, yeah?"

Lucien smiled. He was such a pretty man and appeared to be so happy to have been changed in a way that had allowed him to bear Harry a son. Dafydd had hated that whole thing and was glad to be rid of that ability. Harry had kindly cut the unnatural womb out of him. Although he had never been actually able to detect the thing within him, he still felt better now. His body had changed back to the state he wanted and he'd never been healthier in his life.

"You're doing very well, indeed. I'm here to help, Dafydd. That's all."

No, it wasn't, but Dafydd held his tongue.

"You know," Lucien continued, "I was hopelessly out of my depth caring for Demi his first couple of years. Harry was of little help, having had no experience, either. We figured it out as we went along. I hope my experience can be of use to you."

"For a certainty. Rinse now, Idris."

This was the tricky part. Nobody wanted soap in their eyes, so the boy naturally kicked up a fuss as Dafydd tried to sluice water down his head using a cup. He shielded the boy's face with his other hand, but when Idris' movements got stronger, Dafydd lost his grip. Down the boy went backward into the water, his slick skin too hard for Dafydd to keep a hold on.

For a brief moment as Idris' face went under, Dafydd flashed on another time and place. Only it was he who was looking up as a smug Dracul held him under until his lungs burned and his panicked thrashing sent water spraying around. He'd been stupidly rebellious in the beginning, too young to truly understand that fighting outright would earn him nothing but pain. The near-death experience had broken him more than any rape or beating had, more than having the blood sucked out of him.

"Oh my God!" He grabbed the slippery baby and hauled him out of the tub. He clutched the squirming body tightly to him for fear of dropping him back in, or on the floor. Idris' outraged wail made Dafydd hug all the tighter.

"It's all right, Dafydd." Lucien quickly wrapped a towel around the baby, forcing Dafydd to loosen his grip. "He's fine, except you're squeezing him. Ease up."

The man's calm tone and sure movements helped pull Dafydd back from the emotional cliff he'd been careening toward. Damn, every time he thought he was okay, something happened to prove he wasn't ready to be a real father to Idris.

"Here, take him. Please," he added, as he pushed Idris into Lucien's arms, although with his heart pounding and his nerves on edge, he didn't feel the least bit capable of civility.

Lucien, bless him, was quick to comply. He pressed Idris against his shoulder and rubbed his back through the towel. "Everything's fine," he crooned. Whether it was only to soothe the baby or Dafydd, too, was hard to tell.

Didn't matter, either. Dafydd pushed back his loosened hair with a shaky hand. "Thanks for that." He stuttered out a breath. "I'm that tired, I guess. Do you mind putting him down for the night?" He swallowed hard. "I know I should. It's only…"

Lucien flashed a smile. "It's all right. I understand and am always happy to help." He jiggled a fussy Idris with practiced ease. "With my own son grown, you know I'm desperate for time with yours."

"Yeah." Dafydd edged away and toward the door. "And you're better at it than I ever will be." Familiar panic was rising inside him, eager to get out and send him spinning out of control

"Don't say that. It's only a matter of practice. You're too hard on yourself. You'll get there."

"That's kind of you to say. I wish I had your confidence." God, how was he managing to carry on a conversation given the screaming in his head? *Oh, right, practice*, as Lucien had said. Living with a monster for centuries made it easy to be one thing on the inside while showing a different face to the world.

"I'll be back in a little while," he said, then turned to race from the bathroom.

There was just the one bedroom for him and the baby, so he couldn't stay there while Lucien put the boy down for the night. He needed air and privacy, and there was only one place for him to find that.

He opened the door to the hallway, peering in both directions before stepping into it. Not enough time had passed for him to shake the ingrained habits of checking out his surroundings and being on the look-out for big, scary men who would drag him back to where Dracul had set him. He wasn't a prisoner anymore — or so everyone kept saying. He wasn't sure he believed it. Trust was something he'd lost long ago.

He hurried down the hall then punched through the door leading to the stairwell. The pounding beat of the club could be felt all the way to his floor. A faint amount of music floated up as well. Although he liked listening to it when he could, the idea of going down held no appeal. There were too many men who looked at him with hungry eyes. He'd tried a few times and had run back to the relative safety of his room within minutes.

So, solace was above him and of his own making. He reached the roof quickly and pushed open the door with some trepidation. There was typically no one up there, although sometimes the scariest of the men he lived among — Val — would stand around, smoking a cigarette and checking out the night sky. Dafydd breathed a sigh of relief when he confirmed that was not currently the case.

He had no interest in enjoying the view himself. Not yet. Instead, he made straight for the stash he'd created behind the great big whirring thing that made the building cool. Crouching, he grabbed the bottle first and popped its lid. Small white pills rattled around inside, although not enough for his liking. He frowned as he tapped one onto his palm, already planning how he'd cage more from Harry. It was only a light tranquilizer — for his nerves, as he still slept poorly. The doctor would understand, and if he didn't, maybe Dafydd could find a way to be extra nice to him as an incentive.

No, don't be daft. That's not how things are done here. You can't offer to suck his cock for favors.

Besides, Harry wasn't his only option. There was another with dark brown eyes, only not quite the same shade as his own, and slightly curly brown hair, again different than his. Ric, the human doctor who had refused to let him die. His vehemence on that point had almost made Dafydd laugh, even during Idris' horrible birth. And there had been strength in the man as well, a power that came from something other than brute strength — confidence, perhaps, although wrapped in an amazing gentleness. He'd put Dafydd at ease, never wavering from his certainty and remaining calm in the face of Dafydd's storminess.

The man had effortlessly brought out things in Dafydd that he'd tried to keep buried — a desire to live, not the least of which, but also a nascent sense of hope. There were reasons to keep living, including now raising Idris. With quiet persistence, the doctor had forced Dafydd to see parts of life that he'd tried to block out. It wasn't only a desire to keep breathing and be a father. No, the man had persuaded a much more surprising part of Dafydd to rise from the depths of his soul — desire. Dafydd had thought it dead and buried, desecrated by Dracul's brutality. And yet there was a disturbing spark, a tug that made Dafydd remember long-ago fantasies and guilty spying on men bathing in a pond.

Alarm had him dismissing his own thoughts.

I don't want him. I don't want any man ever again.

Although if he needed to make the doctor think otherwise, he could do it — for the pills, nothing more. If it became necessary — which it wouldn't. Harry would help him. There was no need to go to Ric, even though the man came with alarming frequency to check up on him and Idris.

Putting the worry aside, he closed the bottle then popped the pill into his mouth. He chased it down with a swig of brandy wine that he'd picked up next. No, they called it only 'brandy' in the here and now. Oh, but that was fine stuff, sliding down his throat with a smooth burn, if that were a thing. He only knew that it was very dear, and he felt slightly guilty in having pinched it from the bar's storage room, except that the leader of this group of aliens, Alex, was as rich as Dracul had been. The man could spare a bottle or two.

Taking another slug, he slid down with his back against the low edge of the building and looked up. It was a warm and pretty night. The stars here looked much as they did back home. He tried to appreciate only their beauty and forget that monsters lived up there and sometimes came to Earth to steal stupid boys and turn them into slaves.

Ah, and there he was again, getting maudlin. The past was best buried. He had a good future to look forward to, if only he could pull his shit together. The pill helped and so did the spirits. Warmth and peacefulness infused his body, making his muscles lax and letting his worries go.

Yes, this was what he needed. Idris was fine with Lucien. Once down, the babe slept straight through the night. He didn't need Dafydd fussing over him. No one would miss Dafydd if he sat there for a couple of hours, easing his pain and gazing at the stars. His brain already felt fuzzy, his panic in the bathroom a distant memory. More brandy would make it even better. He took another long swallow and stuttered out his breath.

It was so peaceful with only the sounds of the city intruding. He liked them, actually. Having spent so long in isolation, it was good to know he wasn't buried away somewhere. Life teemed around him yet couldn't get close. He was safe on that roof. Another pill would blur his thoughts and fear even more, but no, he had to conserve those. He frowned at realizing he'd quickly forgotten how few he had left.

More brandy. That was what he needed. Plenty of that was available for the taking. He just had to be careful not to drink too much. Idris was extra hard to deal with when Dafydd woke with a heavy head. That was hours away, though, so he could have a bit more.

Another sip, more star-gazing and he could almost forget the demons that plagued him.

* * * *

Moving from emergency medicine to pathology had been the right decision. Ric reaffirmed that thought every day as he walked into work. While the ED had been filled with people and constant controlled chaos, the medical examiners' domain was quiet and precise. It had been a big leap to switch his career path, but ever since alien vampires had turned his world on its head, he found the peace of the pathology lab a welcome change. He didn't need the excitement of treating trauma victims in the hospital when he got plenty of stimulation hanging with his new friends.

And that was the truth of it. What had started out to be clinical assessment of the supernatural had morphed into the personal. Quite unintentionally, he'd become emotionally attached to his subjects. He cared what happened to Alex and his unusual family and was dedicated to helping them as much as he was his own species. Moreover, since his adventure in Wales and beyond, he'd fallen in love with someone he shouldn't have.

Dafydd.

He said that name inside his head more times during the day than he could count. It was like thinking of sex – unplanned, unbidden and unwarranted. Throw in 'inappropriate', as well, given what the poor man had been subjected to not only for years but for *centuries*. PTSD didn't even begin to cover what Dafydd must be experiencing, especially after having killed his own son. All without therapy, too. Ric had dared to broach the subject with Harry, the alien doctor who had probably forgotten more than Ric would ever learn about medicine. The man had been emphatic in his response. Alex would never allow yet one more human in on their secret, and without that piece of the puzzle, what good would therapy be? Dafydd had to let out all the demons or there would be no way to help.

So despite Ric's commitment to pathology, he'd started learning what he could about psychotherapy in the hope of helping Dafydd cope with his trauma. He'd visited as often as he'd dared, and although the man was making progress—accepting his baby being an amazing step—Ric knew there was instability lurking under the surface. Dafydd was the proverbial powder-keg, ready to blow at any time. If Ric could help even in a small way, it would be better than nothing. Everyone would benefit from his being able to intervene.

All of which was possibly only a big rationalization for his spending time with the guy, but so what? Lots of good things happened because people convinced themselves to do the right thing for the wrong reason. As long as Ric never acted on his attraction to Dafydd and kept their relationship strictly clinical, it would be fine. He just had to keep himself under tight rein and stop his thoughts from going into inappropriate directions—no thoughts of Dafydd's beautiful body on display, no more dreams of Dafydd naked and under him, moaning his name, clutching him tightly as Ric dove into a hole that welcomed him because he knew how to give pleasure and not pain.

He tripped over his own feet, sloshing his grande hot latte with coconut milk over his finger. *Yeah, that's exactly the kind of shit I have to knock the fuck off.*

"Hey, Paz?"

Grateful for the distraction, he waited for the coroner, Vincente, to catch up with him. "Good morning, sir."

Vincente slapped a clipboard with a file attached to it against Ric's chest. "Here's your first task of the day. A DB sent over from the ED at Saint B's."

Ric grabbed the file. "Yes, sir." He knew without looking at the information that whatever it was, the coroner considered it low priority and not the least bit interesting. That was the kind of autopsy work the man passed along to Ric. He wasn't exactly the mentoring type. Vincente was more the 'you take the shit work off my hands' sort of boss.

"Pretty straightforward. This guy fired his gun during a drug-related confrontation of some kind and died from multiple shrapnel wounds when the gun exploded in his face."

Ric frowned. "That's unusual."

"Not when the gun is made out of crappy products and a 3-D printer." Vincente shook his head. "Dumbass."

Ric's interest perked up, and in his mind, he was already making a call to Trey Duncan. Even if there was no alien angle, the cop would want to hear about this.

'If anything unusual comes your way, I want to know.'

"I would think that would make this a high-profile case." Ric was surprised Vincente didn't want it for himself. "3-D gun printing is illegal."

The coroner shrugged. "The case *is* a big deal. I think the FBI is already flying people in. How and where he got the weapon is hot stuff. But the autopsy is going to be pretty cut-and-dried. Of course, if you find anything important, you let me know ASAP."

"Yes, sir." Ric watched his boss walk away. He juggled the items he held in order to open the file to study it as he headed to the room where the body was being stored. By the time he'd finished reading the report and had the guy on a slab, he was sure that Vincente had been right. There was nothing surprising about how the man had died. As he peered down at the body, making his initial visual assessment, he could see the pieces of plastic embedded all over his face, neck and torso. One had nicked the carotid, so no mystery about the cause of death. The hand holding the gun had been shredded right up to the elbow. There were no other signs of injury.

"Why did you go for a crappy plastic gun when metal ones are so easy to buy on the street?" he asked his patient. "Was it cheaper? I wouldn't have thought so."

He knew the reasons why the printed guns were appealing. They were relatively expensive to make but could be done under the radar of law enforcement and were capable of getting through security without setting off a metal detector. *It makes sense if you're a terrorist.* For a local criminal, however, it seemed like something harder to get, pricier, and ultimately a weird choice for a local criminal engaged in drug dealing.

"Well, let's see if you have any secrets to share with me, huh?"

He started taking pictures of the corpse, first clothed then nude, careful to put everything he removed into an evidence bag. He conducted a visual exam of the external parts of the body while dictating his notes into a hand-held recorder. Vincente had fancy, hands-free equipment for that, but Ric preferred the low-tech option. He noted some old scars on the man's torso and thigh, evidence of a frequently violent life, even for one who was in his early thirties. When he was ready to open up his patient, he put on his protective gear. Then he got to work.

For a little while, he managed to banish thoughts of a pretty Welshman from his mind.

Chapter Two

Lux was never quiet at night, regardless of the day of the week. Given that it was Friday, Ric wasn't surprised that the place was really hopping. He'd actually had to wait a few seconds to get in because there was a short line in front of the doorkeeper. When it was his turn to show his member card, the go-go boy merely flashed him a smile.

"You go on, Dr. Ric. I don't need to see anything other than your gorgeous face to know you belong here. Catch me later for a lap dance, why don't ya."

Putting his card away, he gave the boy a quick grin and a nod. "Thanks, Shawn. I might do that."

He wouldn't and they both knew it. While he appreciated the beauty of the young men who worked at the club, he'd found the experience of actually having one gyrating over his crotch very embarrassing. Never particularly aggressive in his dating life, he couldn't quite pull off any kind of bravado in the face of being catered to by the eager, flirty dancers. Besides, although he knew the boys were there by choice, treated well and that they were allowed to keep every penny they made plus drawing salaries with freaking health benefits, for God's sake, he couldn't quite shake his feeling that he was exploiting them. He'd seen too many victims of abuse to be comfortable with it.

As he walked into the club proper, he noticed the bouncer, Val, stood holding up one wall, as per usual. His legs were crossed and his hands were jammed into his front pockets. The casual pose didn't fool Ric, nor should it have done so for anyone. The guy was primed to launch an attack in a millisecond. His assessing gaze swung to Ric. Val nodded once, the man's version of an enthusiastic human bear hug and back thump, before continuing to scan the first floor.

Ric waved in greeting, knowing it went unseen, and headed straight toward Trey Duncan's table. The two of them had formed a tentative bond, both being humans accepted into the aliens' cohort. Plus, they shared another trait that was rare in this environment — poverty. Well, strictly speaking, they were middle class, but in a place filled with gazzilionaire members, Ric felt poor. His membership was a gift, and one that he would have used sparingly but for the draw of seeing Dafydd. He was out of place in this luxurious environment where men paid God-knew-what for the privilege of sexy fun twenty-four-seven.

He tried not to fuss with his clothing as he weaved his way around better-dressed men. His Tommy Hilfiger outfit, from his button-down shirt to his neat slacks, seemed hopelessly staid compared to the flashier brands in the room. He felt like his grandfather. Plus, his wardrobe came from the outlet store in Kittery, Maine, so hardly this year's fashion. Still, he blended in better than the cop, who sat at his reserved table dressed in his Levi jeans and some snarky T-shirt. Then again, what did Duncan care what he looked like? He had the love of his life perched on his lap, nuzzling his neck, while he sucked down a bottle of beer. *Lucky bastard.*

First Duncan then Demi shifted to focus their attention on him when he arrived at the table. "Hi, Dr. Ric." Demi treated him to a pretty smile that held no invitation whatsoever. The hybrid had finally snared his man, and he was the very picture of bliss.

"Hey, Paz," the cop added before draining his bottle and standing. He set Demi on his feet. "Sorry. No time to get comfy. I promised Alex we'd chat as soon as you arrived."

"No problem." Ric swiveled his head to look for Val. The guy hadn't moved. "It's not going to be an all-hands one?"

Duncan shook his head. "Nope. There's no obvious connection to what they're concerned with, so this is more of a social call than anything else. If it turns out to be more relevant, then..." He shrugged.

Yes, this was their life now, always pondering whether something bad happening around them was purely the same human nonsense that people had been perpetrating on themselves since the dawn of time or something related to aliens being marooned on Earth a thousand years ago. The purported demise of Dracul—the mutinous and murderous traitor from Alex's crew—hadn't eliminated the threat, either. At least one of the bastard's sons was out there still, as well as a few minions. Trouble could pop up at any moment. They'd all been reminded of that only a couple of months ago.

Demi pressed a kiss to Duncan's cheek. "This sounds really boring, so I'm going to go hang with Mackie and the boys if that's okay with you?"

Duncan returned the gesture and said, "It's fine, and remember, you don't have to get my permission to do anything."

"I like getting it," Demi replied with his trademark smirk and a flashing of the simple ring on his finger. "*Remember*?" he added in a teasing tone.

Duncan rolled his eyes. "Right. Off you go, then." He helped Demi on his way with a smack on the ass that made the boy's eyelids droop.

Ric couldn't hide his grin. "Seems as if you two are settled into domestic life."

"Faster than I can keep up with sometimes. Come on. Alex said to come to his penthouse."

Ric followed the cop through the crowded room and over to the elevators. "Have you set a date yet?"

"No." Duncan's tone was firm. "That's not happening for a few years. I don't care how long he's been alive or what his fake birth certificate says, Demi is way too young to get married. I haven't even introduced him to my family yet. My mother is going to have a heart-attack as it is over his baby-face. She's going to think I'm robbing the cradle, which I kind of am."

Ric figured the cop was overestimating his own ability to hold out and seriously underestimating how determined Demi was going to be to move matters along.

Duncan pushed the call button for the elevator. "Plus, there's college then medical school. Even if he doesn't elect to go the full route, it's going to take years."

The doors slid open and they stepped inside. Duncan scratched the back of his head after pushing for the fifth floor. "And the really weird thing is that the boy who used to give his fathers fits by being rebellious has become totally submissive to me. *Docile*. It's freaking me the fuck out, to be frank."

Ric leaned against the elevator wall. "Perhaps he thinks that if he's a good boy, you'll change your mind about waiting." Based on what he knew of Demi, he wouldn't put such a strategy past him.

"Maybe." Duncan jammed his hands into his front pockets. "If it's an act, it's a good one. A really good one," he added under his breath and in a way that made Ric realize part of Demi's obedience included fun things of a sexual nature.

Duncan heaved out a breath. "Anyway, he's going to be disappointed if that's his game." The man's tone conveyed some uncertainty, however.

They exited on Alex's private floor and both waved at the security camera. By the time they'd made the short trip down the hall to the suite, they found Alex straightening his clothing while sitting on the couch. His boy, Quinn, sat between the man's outstretched legs with his head resting on one of Alex's thick thighs. The boy didn't try to hide the fact that he'd just given a blow job. Both greeted them with lazy smiles. Plus, one of Quinn's arms lay across that same thigh. Alex flicked his tongue around a corner of his lips. It was that obvious proof of bloodsucking that gave Ric discomfort, not the sex. Like many, if not most humans, he'd grown up with scary stories of vampires. It was the hardest thing about his new friends to get used to.

He wasn't sure he ever would.

"Come in, gentlemen, and make yourselves comfortable," Alex called out and gave a wave of his hand. "May I offer you refreshments?"

"No, thanks." Both Ric and Duncan spoke the same words at the same time, and went to sit on two of Alex's big, comfy chairs.

The luxury these aliens lived in after centuries of amassing wealth staggered Ric. That was also something he didn't think he'd ever become comfortable with. If there came a time in which the whole world learned of the aliens' existence, and if Alex and his crew tended toward exhibitionism, their lives would make for spectacular reality TV.

Alex carded his hand through Quinn's hair. "What news do you bring from the front lines, gentlemen?"

Duncan gestured toward Ric. "You first, Doc."

Ric settled into the cloud-like softness behind his back and wondered briefly if he might fall asleep from the amazing pleasure of the chair. "Well, pathologically speaking, I don't have much to report. I did an autopsy this morning on a young and very stupid man who died when his 3-D printed gun exploded on him. A shard of plastic cut an artery, causing him to bleed out. If he'd lived, it would have been with one less hand and most of the arm."

He shrugged. "That's it, but I contacted Duncan because I figured it fell into the category of the unusual and therefore possibly problematic, from your point of view."

Alex nodded. "Yes, thank you. I agree with your assessment. Anything out of the norm is always worth an extra look." He turned to the cop. "I assume this has been picked up by the feds."

"Yeah. This whole printing-guns-out-of-plastic phenom has everyone shitting their pants. Regardless of what the law says, anyone who looks hard enough is going to find out how to do this. And unlike, say, making a nuclear bomb, once you have the plans, the material is easy to come by."

Like Ric, Duncan settled more into his chair. "What's odd about this, though, is who had the weapon and what he was doing with it. I mean, why would some low-level offender, with a rap sheet that could paper your walls for drugs and gang-banging, use this thing to take down a rival?" The cop shook his head at his own rhetorical questions. "It doesn't add up. Old-fashioned metal guns are cheap and easy to get. Why bother with this new tech?"

Ric chimed in before Alex could respond. "That's what I was wondering. It seems a strange choice for the kind of man I cut open. Given his clothing and overall condition, he wasn't someone living well." A thought struck him. "Unless of course it was a free sample."

Both Alex and Duncan turned sharp gazes on him.

"Say *what*?" the cop asked.

Ric shrugged. "I don't know. I was just thinking of how pharmaceutical companies give free drug samples to doctors to try out on their patients. If it proves effective, eventually the patients start paying for it." He pulled at one ear. "It's controversial but it works, and many really effective drugs end up being used like that and helping people."

Duncan narrowed his eyes. "Sounds like what drug pushers do out on the street."

"Yes, well…I'm a pathologist now, so it's not going to be part of my practice. It's only that a 3-D printed gun in the hands of this work-a-day criminal, if you will, strikes me as being similar."

"That's an excellent point, Doctor," Alex said. "An intriguing idea, don't you think, Sergeant?"

"It has some legs." Duncan laced his fingers behind his head. "The question remains, though, why this particular guy?"

"Anthony Marcello," Ric supplied, because no matter what the guy had done, he'd been a person with a name and a family, and his life had ended far too soon and much too brutally. It was important for him to remember that the bodies he cut open had once been living, breathing human beings.

Duncan hummed. "Tony Two Claws, as he was known on the streets, according to his record I accessed this afternoon."

"What an utterly ridiculous nickname," Alex scoffed. "Honestly, you humans…"

"It's because he had a connection to Maine." Dropping his hands, Duncan sat forward. "You know, lobsters?" He snapped his thumbs and forefingers together.

"Ah, yes. They are delicious." Alex licked his lips with almost the same delight as he had when they first came in. "Emil must have some in the kitchen."

Quinn snorted. "It's the butter you love. Honestly," he added to the room at large, "lobsters are just conduits for the butter."

"You insult my palate, dear boy." Alex patted his lover on the head. "Can you do some further digging on the matter, sergeant, without raising any suspicion?"

"Sure, no problem. I'll see what I can find out. Hopefully, it's just typical human shit, not that such an answer isn't sufficiently scary."

"Indeed," Alex agreed. "In the meantime, why don't you both enjoy the club for the evening — the entire weekend, of course, if you're not on duty." He focused his gaze on Ric, and that intensity was a little hard to take. "I hope you know that you are truly welcome to use the club as much as you'd like."

Ric resisted the urge to squirm. "Yes, sir, I do." Which was not quite accurate, but he figured Alex shared the human need to hear what he wanted and not necessarily the unvarnished truth.

Alex's gaze hardened for a moment. "Hmm. I imagine you're hungry. I know I am. Let's go see what Emil has brewing in his kitchen."

It was on the tip of Ric's tongue to say no, that he'd eaten already, then he thought better of it. There was someone who frequently took his meals there, someone he was desperate to see, even if he tried to deny it to himself. *Does Alex know that? Is that what's behind the invitation?*

He couldn't tell by the man's expression, but Quinn was more of an open book. As Alex helped him to his feet, the boy popped his eyes at him and gave a quick shake of his head. Alex merely distracted him with a kiss while gently nudging him forward.

"Duncan?"

"Yeah, I'll come with. Except I'm going to scare up Demi instead of going to the kitchen."

Ric let the three others pass before bringing up the rear. He tried not to get excited at the possibility of seeing Dafydd, but his heart and dick had other ideas. One started beating rapidly as the other stiffened as much as his tight pants allowed. *Thank God my shirt is untucked.* Still, he crossed his wrists in front of him as he followed his friends to the elevator.

Alex snapped his fingers. "Oh, I almost forgot to mention that Malcolm and Brenin are on their way over for a visit."

Stepping into the elevator, Ric stood to one side to let Alex push the button for the lower level. "Is anything wrong?" He wondered as he asked whether seeing the boy he'd suffered with and helped escape Dracul's terror would upset Dafydd or be just the thing to perk him up.

"Not to my knowledge. I gather they need a break from the rehabilitation of the poor souls we rescued from Dracul's castle. At least, I assume Brenin does."

"It did seem like a lot for him to take on when he was still recovering from his own ordeal."

"When's their flight due in?" Duncan asked.

Alex chuckled. "You'd think they'd fly, wouldn't you? But no, Malcolm is bringing them in his yacht — the good one, not that trawler we used for our journey to Wales. They're due to arrive on Sunday. I imagine they've spent the last two weeks or so on a kind of honeymoon. They've certainly earned the rest."

Ric thought back on what the two men had done, the lion's share of the work in the assault on Dracul's castle. And all of that had been after Brenin had been brutalized for months at the evil creature's hands. Yes, he could certainly agree that Brenin at least needed some time off.

So long as his arrival didn't set Dafydd's recovery back, Ric was all for the visit.

* * * *

"No, Idris, the potatoes go into your mouth, not on your face."

Dafydd merely got one of his son's typical impish grins in response to the mild rebuke. Then he reached out toward the plate with his chubby fingers and did the same thing all over again.

Putting the spoon down, Dafydd sighed. "All right then, do as you like. You're getting a bath before bed anyway."

He was counting the minutes before Idris' last meal of the day, his sixth, was over and he could be washed and tucked into his crib. The baby ate more than a human, thanks to his rapid growth, so even though it was well past any normal child's bedtime, they were still at it. Beyond the cozy kitchen, the sounds of the club in full swing were audible. They held no allure for him. Nothing really did, other than his special place on the roof. He longed to be there now.

"Hey, Idris, giving your father trouble, are you?" Emil, the chef — the sight of whom didn't cause as much fright in Dafydd as it once had — came sauntering over.

The big man picked up the spoon and filled it with mashed potatoes. "Open up, kiddo. The airplane is coming in for a landing." He made all kinds of whirling noises and moved his hand in funny circles before pressing the spoon against Idris' lips.

The baby loved the antics and dutifully ate the food as intended. He kicked his legs against the highchair, waved his arms and giggled. It took no time for Emil to empty the plate of mashed up bits of dinner. It seemed that everyone was better at taking care of Dafydd's son than he was. He told himself it didn't matter, that his feelings for Idris were a jumbled mix of horror, duty and love. *What difference does it make if I never get the hang of raising this child?*

It does. Somehow, despite everything that I've gone through, from forced conception to near-deadly delivery, it does.

"Thanks for that," he said to the chef, forcing himself to look the man straight in the eye. It was hard, always hard, to go against Dracul's vicious lessons.

"Oh, it's nothing. It's easy for me to swoop in at the last minute after you've done all the heavy lifting."

It surprised him still how much everyone here seemed to care about his feelings. Before he could muster a suitable reply, footsteps told him someone was coming. Three people, actually. Over the centuries, survival had taught him to recognize the sounds the men around him made. Being force-fed Dracul's blood had also given him some useful advantages, including enhanced senses. Those effects remained, even with the diet of blood having stopped.

There were Alex and Quinn — naturally, as they were almost always together. The human boy's ease with his man gave Dafydd some comfort, as well. Actions spoke louder than words. If there was anything to fear in Alex, surely the boy who warmed his bed would show it in his expression and movements. He shot them an acceptable nod of greeting before refocusing on who trailed behind them. It was this third person who caught his attention the most.

Ric.

He was always sure to call the man by his title of doctor, but inside his own mind, the first name popped up. He couldn't help it, no more than he could prevent his heartbeat from stumbling at the sight of the man entering the room. A flash of heat infused his body before he suppressed it. This perverse reaction was ridiculous. Dr. Ricardo Paz was a man, for all that, and Dafydd wanted nothing to do with males of any species. He forced his expression to become neutral, as if seeing the doctor had no effect whatsoever.

Nevertheless, Ric's reaction held no reticence. His face lit up when he caught sight of Dafydd. "Hi there." He called out the greeting from across the room. Although his gaze swept around to encompass everyone, it homed in on Dafydd.

"Hello." Politeness dictated he respond and maintain eye contact, even though he wanted to drop his gaze, grab Idris and bolt away from this strange temptation.

"How are you doing?" Ric came directly toward him as Emil moved away.

Alex asked the chef something about lobsters, which made the man laugh. The three of them — Alex, Emil and Quinn — headed into the walk-in refrigerator.

"God, he's gotten so big," Ric added, gesturing toward Idris.

Dafydd managed to shift his gaze back to his son. He picked up a napkin and scrubbed away the mess on the baby's face. "Yes, little monsters grow fast." He froze and forced a smile to his face. "Sorry, that's your dada making a stupid joke." He continued with his cleaning.

Ric sat down on the other side of the highchair. "I don't think he understands quite that much."

Dafydd flicked his gaze at the man. "Don't underestimate him. I don't." He pulled the tray away, unhooked the straps and hauled Idris into his arms.

The weight of the child as he settled him on one hip, the warmth of the small body, so reassuringly human, set him through a series of emotions that he'd become used to. There was a shot of revulsion, quickly overridden by a fierce sense of protectiveness, a dash of pragmatism and finally a spark of love that was growing with slow determination. The dizzy array of feelings galloped through him in a second, leaving him somewhat unsteady, as usual. There was really only one way to tamp down the wild emotional ride.

His thoughts strayed to the rooftop, which led him to eye the doctor. Should he bring up the topic of medicine? *No.* His stash wasn't that low and Harry hadn't refused to give him more — yet. Besides, he didn't like how his life with Dracul had made it second nature to plan and scheme about how he might exploit a man's weakness to get something he needed. He was disgusted that his first thought upon seeing someone who'd been nothing but kind to him was how to play him.

He really should leave. Ric deserved to have an entertaining night at the club. He didn't need to hang around with someone who was anxious to get away. It was on the tip of his tongue to say good night, when the doctor spoke.

"How are you doing?"

Dafydd looked briefly into those kind, deep-brown eyes. He read concern there, genuinely so. "I'm that fine. Truly," he added when those eyes conveyed doubt.

"Are you having any lingering pain?" This was a question he asked each and every time, as if somehow remaining Dafydd's doctor mattered to the man.

"None whatsoever. You did a good job of it, Doctor."

"Ric," came the gentle reminder, as always.

Dafydd ignored the correction. "You're here for a spot of fun, I imagine. Friday nights are busy, but there are lots of pretty boys out there who'll show you a good time."

He winced inwardly. Now why had he gone and said such a stupid thing as that and with a tone that sounded very much like he hoped the opposite would happen? It was none of his concern what the doctor got up to.

"Oh, um, I came to speak with Alex, actually. Nothing's wrong," he added quickly, because Dafydd hadn't been able to keep alarm off his face.

It was silly, really, but he didn't feel safe, not with Bran and Petru loose in the world. "Truly?"

Ric nodded. "Yes. Just some human shit, that's all. Except—"

"What is it, mun?" Dafydd couldn't help asking.

Idris let out a squawk, telling him he was squeezing the boy too hard.

Ric held out his hand. "Sorry. I didn't mean to frighten you. I was only wondering if you knew that Brenin is on his way."

Dafydd frowned. "I do, yes." He thought Lucien had mentioned something about it that morning, but with his head fuzzy and Idris fussing, he hadn't paid much attention. "He's all right, though?"

Ric smiled and nodded. "Fine. Alex says he and Malcolm are taking a break. A vacation. A holiday," he amended.

"Oh, yes."

Not that Dafydd had the faintest idea of what the concept really meant, nor did he care. Back in the days before Dracul, people didn't do such things. But for that hideous fateful day, he would have more than likely spent his whole life within the confines of his little village and thought nothing of it.

"I'll be that glad to see him again."

"Will you? I mean, do you think it will trigger bad memories?"

Dafydd almost laughed at the idea that any one person or thing could conjure up the awfulness of his life, as if he didn't remember every day what horrors he'd been through. Brenin was, if anything, a bright spot, a reminder of the one time he'd managed to successfully thwart the monster. But the look of concern on the doctor's face forced him to swallow down the impulse.

He made his lips turn into some semblance of a smile. "No. It really will be good to see him. I hope he's doing well."

Ric's face lit up in a genuine smile. Such a handsome man he was, not that Dafydd noticed such things anymore. "Good. If it turns out not to be the case, please remember that I'm here if you need to talk to someone." He paused. "You have that phone Alex gave you, right?"

Dafydd nodded. "I have like three numbers in it and yours is one of them. I expect I'll be fine, though. No worries, hey?"

Ric stepped closer to him, close enough that Dafydd could smell the perfume he was wearing, although unlike in the old days, it didn't mask anything foul underneath. The man's natural odor was clean and fresh. It reminded Dafydd of the meadows he used to scamper in as a boy.

"I do worry, though, Dafydd. Very much. Please at least text me if you're feeling… I don't know, anything that bothers you, day or night. Do you know how to do that?"

"Sure. Demi showed me how." He stared down at the top of Idris' head, unable to look the man in the eye. "I won't need to. I'm fine, like I said."

He tried to make the lie convincing, but when he dared to look at Ric, he could see that the man wasn't fooled. He felt both dismay and relief and wondered if, in his dark moments up on the roof, he'd ever dare to reach out to this man for help.

Chapter Three

"The skyline looks so different from this approach." Brenin stood by Malcolm's side in the center cockpit as he steered his magnificent yacht carefully into Boston Harbor.

"Och aye, we've only ever seen it from the air. This is even prettier, dinnae you think?"

Brenin heard the forced cheer in his lover's voice and his constant guilt ate at him. This was all his fault — the lazy trip across the Atlantic, even when there were a million matters to attend to back home, the way Malcolm was tiptoeing around him, trying not to startle him, always peering at him to glean Brenin's mood. It seemed to change by the hour, sometimes cheery, other times sad, and occasionally chopsy enough to set his own teeth on edge.

How can he stand me? Brenin was heartily sick of his own volatility.

Making himself lay a hand casually on Malcolm's arm, he said, "It is, yes. I do hope Alex doesn't mind us dropping in like this."

Malcolm took his eyes off the water for a second to smile down at him. "Dinnae fash yourself over that, laddie. Alex's door is always open to his family. He's like a gran in that regard. And I bet Emil's got milk and cookies out already. They like nothing more than company, the lot of them."

"Val, too?"

"Well, maybe not him. But Mackie for sure, I'm thinking."

"Yes, it will be nice to see him again. All of the boys, really." He cuddled up closer to Malcom's big, hard body. There was comfort there, and more, so long as he was the one to initiate the contact.

Malcom made no move other than those necessary to steer. He'd become attuned to Brenin's needs in a way that was almost heartbreaking. After such a good start, where the man had showed Brenin the joys of two men sharing passion, things had changed. It was hard for Brenin to accept Malcolm's overtures without some hesitation. At first he'd thought he was hiding it. Then it had become clear that Malcolm had noticed. The man rarely touched him without a lot of visual warning and moving slow enough for Brenin to object.

To make up for his ridiculous sensitivity, Brenin tried as often as he could to show that he still loved the man and wanted him.

He dropped his head against Malcolm's arm. "It will be good to see Dafydd again, too, of course. I hope he's coping well." The irony of his statement, given his own turmoil, wasn't lost on him. Malcolm, naturally, didn't point it out.

"I only ken that he's taken to caring for Idris, as I've said. Alex has been short on details. I expect Dafydd will be pleased to catch up with you. He may not feel as if he can talk to any of those around him."

Brenin thought of the doctor, Ric Paz, and wondered if that were true. No one had said anything about the man, except that he'd helped them bring down one of Dracul's sons a couple of months before. News that Dafydd had been the one to kill the hybrid had been particularly terrible. No matter what the junior monster had done, he'd still been the man's son. Regardless, Brenin didn't need anyone to tell him how the doctor felt about Dafydd. He'd seen for himself the way the doctor had looked at Dafydd while they'd remained at Malcolm's castle.

Home, he reminded himself, and he did love it and the people there. "You think Darling, Cook and Doc MacPhee are truly all right on their own with that hellion in particular?" The hybrid they housed was a trial for both his human father and the rest of them.

Malcolm chuckled. "They're fine, laddie. Dinnae fash yourself. With help from the village, they're barely going to miss having us. Put aside any concern, please. For my sake?" He glanced down and the worry in his eyes squeezed Brenin's heart.

Brenin rubbed his cheek against Malcolm's bare arm. Here in their own little world, they both wore summer-weight kilts and nothing else. He hated the idea of having to dress normally once they docked.

"I promise to have fun. No worries. We can be proper tourists, something we couldn't do before."

"Aye, that's right. I don't know the city myself, so it will be fun to explore it together." There were a few seconds of silence before he added, "I want you to be happy, Brenin."

He closed his eyes and sighed. "I know. And I am. I'm just tired, I think, from all the work. It has been harder than I expected. You were right about that, but what else could we do? Those poor men and boys need us."

"Aye, you're a kind-hearted laddie, that's for sure, and I love you for it. I love you, Brenin. You know that, don't you?"

"Of course. I love you, too. Let's put our cares away and enjoy our time in…Beantown, is it?"

"Aye, that's what they call themselves, although why they boast of something you can have every day for breakfast is beyond my ken."

Brenin giggled. It felt good to experience genuine mirth. Now, if only he could get back to the way they were before, where Malcolm's touch was all he craved and the horrors of Dracul were behind him.

They kept the banter to a minimum as Malcolm entered a slip in the Black Falcon Terminal with a sure hand and deft skill. He was a marvel by any estimation, and Brenin was proud to be his lover. A cruise ship was docked right next to them, waiting to head out somewhere fun and warmer than Boston. That was what this dock was normally used for and Malcolm, naturally, had bribed his way in when other spots were either taken or too small for his ginormous yacht. A bunch of people stood by the rails, staring down at them. Brenin didn't miss the way many pairs of eyes stayed glued to Malcolm's every movement, first when he'd been bare-chested, then later as they disembarked. Even wearing a T-shirt, he cut a drool-worthy figure as he flashed a fair amount of long, muscular leg through his kilt. The scars he bore from their battle in Wales only added to the man's rugged beauty.

They walked onto the dock in nearly identical clothing, and lest anyone think somehow that they were brothers, Brenin reached out to clasp Malcolm's hand. It helped to steady his sea legs, as well, and with the sun shining hot and bright on them, his emotions lifted. He basked in the feeling, knowing that they could change at any moment. He was so volatile these days.

For the moment, though, he was nothing but happy. He waved at the cruise ship passengers and pressed closer to Malcom as they headed for the street. Val was waiting for them, the big, scary man with the Mohawk and badass everything else leaning against the side of his SUV. His gaze was obscured by sunglasses that probably cost more than a week's worth of wages for the average dockworker. His jacked arms were crossed and his expression gave away no sign that he was pleased to see them. That wasn't true for his husband, Mackie. The red-headed changeling had been waiting in the SUV, undoubtedly taking advantage of the air conditioning. He was out of the vehicle in a flash before they got within twenty feet of it and he skipped over to them.

"Brenin!" Mackie plowed right into him and wrapped him in a hug. "I missed you!"

Brenin grunted at the impact. The guy really was getting stronger than he knew. *This can be me if I want it.* It was too early in his relationship to make such a decision, however. Malcolm certainly hadn't pressed the issue.

He did his best to return the gesture of affection without losing his grip on Malcolm's hand. "Me too, Mackie. Thanks for coming to meet us."

Linking with Brenin's free arm, the boy said, "'Natch. It's the least we can do. You left all your stuff onboard? Does that mean you're staying there during your visit? Ooh, can we have a sleepover?" Mackie was a whirlwind of words.

"I suppose we could," he said, focusing on the last question, "if it's okay with Malcolm."

The man squeezed his hand. "Of course, laddie. Whatever you want."

"Dangerous words, MacLerie," Val offered as they reached him. He uncrossed his arms and gave them a curt nod before opening the back door. "If you let the boys have a party on your pretty yacht, it could end up going the way of the Boston Tea Party or the Andrea Doria."

"Oh, Val." Mackie swatted his husband's arm before jumping into the passenger seat up front. He turned immediately to peer back at Malcolm. "I promise we'll be good. We just want to catch up. Oh, oh" — the guy practically bounced on his seat — "do you know about Demi and Trey going through Demi's manhood ceremony or whatever, then becoming engaged to be engaged?"

"Mackie," Val chided as he slid in behind the wheel, "put your sweet ass on the seat and buckle up."

Mackie huffed but did as he'd been told. It didn't stop him from craning his neck as Val pulled away from the curb. "Now that we're not in the middle of the war, you definitely have to play the tourist. You've staying a while, right?"

The sheer force of energy emanating from Mackie was overwhelming after the calm of the ocean trip. It reminded him of the noise and chaos back at the castle. From where he sat, Brenin slipped his hand across the seat to clasp Malcolm's once more. The warm look the man shot him in return eased Brenin's nerves.

"We'll stay as long as you like," Malcolm replied. "There's no agenda for this trip — at least, not any that I know of. Val?"

"Probably not," came the disturbingly vague reply.

Brenin leaned forward a bit, his heart tripping with worry, despite Malcolm's calming touch. "Is there trouble again?"

"Nothing you need to be concerned about. It's just human shit, most likely."

That wasn't very reassuring at all. Before he could ask a follow-up question, Mackie interceded.

"Val, stop. Please. Brenin's on vacation." He craned his neck once more to look at him again. "Pay no attention. I'm beginning to think these guys can't stand the idea of peace and quiet." He settled back into place.

Brenin didn't say anything, nor did he look at Malcolm, even though he could feel the man's gaze on him. There had been a time when Brenin hadn't expected trouble, either. After all he'd been through, the idea that problems lurked constantly around every corner had become ingrained in him as well. He didn't like being that way, but it was proving hard to shake.

He chose to ignore the prick of fear and changed the subject. "How's Dafydd? And Idris?"

"They're both doing really well. I mean, killing Cadoc was super awful for Dafydd, but I think it's what caused him to start taking care of the baby — who, by the way, has grown to toddler size. You won't recognize him."

That seemed unlikely, given how much alien blood was coursing through the baby's veins. Alien physiology was indelibly tattooed on Brenin's brain. "I bet," he said, because it was the obvious and socially acceptable response.

He shifted his gaze to stare out of his side window. The Boston streets were crowded with tourists and locals alike. He could easily tell the two groups apart based on what they were wearing. Given that it was late afternoon, the roads were also clogged with vehicles.

Val navigated with skill and calm, maneuvering the SUV among the cars as if it were a scooter.

"Dafydd's doing really great," Mackie reiterated. "He'll be glad to see you and I bet he'll come to the sleepover if we ask him."

"Yes, we should," Brenin said, because again, it was the acceptable response.

He had his doubts, though, about both Dafydd's state of recovery and his willingness to indulge in such a silly, modern activity. *If I'm having this much trouble recovering from a few months with the monster, how much harder is it for Dafydd?* His countryman had been enslaved for centuries. One didn't simply put aside hundreds of years of physical and mental torture in just a couple of months. Well, he'd see for himself and perhaps he and Dafydd would be able to help each other.

As if sensing his thoughts, Malcolm squeezed his hand and leaned over to say, "Don't put pressure on yourself, laddie. Whatever you want or dinnae want is fine. You ken?"

Turning to smile at his lover, Brenin nodded. "Yes, of course. I'm excited to be here. Really, Malcolm. I just hope you won't be bored. I mean, what are you guys going to get up to while we boys party away on the boat?"

"Och, not much, I dinnae suppose. Probably sit around drinking and catching up. We're a boring lot, for all that."

"Speak for yourself, Highlander," Val said.

Mackie huffed. "Now, Val, I forbid you from having too much fun while I'm not there. I know what entertains you, and so long as I'm unavailable, you are doomed to a celibate and vanilla night."

"We really need to work on those definitions of Master and slave, Mackie. You're getting awfully bossy."

That set off a playful exchange between the married couple about their BDSM contract and their marriage vows. Because they were so obviously in love and only teasing each other, Brenin let the words wash over him without concern. He would have gone back to people-watching if Malcolm hadn't claimed his attention once more.

"It will be good for you to see Dafydd, won't it? He's someone you can perhaps talk to about…whatever."

He saw the concern in the man's eyes and he would have said anything to ease it. "Of course. No worries."

Malcolm shot him a quick smile. "None at all."

And they both knew that was a lie.

* * * *

Malcolm reluctantly let go of Brenin within minutes of entering the club, following Val toward Alex's office while Mackie highjacked Brenin in another direction. He kept his gaze on the pair for as long as he could and told himself he was being a ninny. Brenin was not only safe in this place, it was a chance for him to find emotional support from young men who understood him.

"What's doing with the kid?" Val dropped that bomb of a question with the same casual ease as asking about the weather.

Malcolm jerked his head in the man's direction and frowned. "What do you mean by that?" His tone was sharper than was warranted, and even knowing that, he continued to glare at his old shipmate and friend.

Val held up a hand in a peaceful gesture. "Don't get your kilt in a twist, MacLerie. I simply meant that he seems…I don't know, fragile, maybe." He shrugged. "More so than the last time I saw him. Not that I know squat about humans, but Mackie has made me more attuned to boys' emotions, I guess."

Malcolm sighed. "Sorry. It's a fair question and one I wish I could answer for you. The sad truth is he's having trouble adjusting to the turn his life has taken. I blame myself. I was too sure of my own power to get him past his ordeal and didn't listen to Doc MacPhee when she warned me early on that he was going to have his ups and downs. Add to that the strain of rehabilitating Dracul's slaves and, well…" He shrugged again.

They'd reached Alex's office, finding Emil and Harry already there, so he snapped his mouth shut. With their extraordinary hearing, all three of them surely had heard what he'd said in the corridor, so their reunion was more perfunctory than usual. A few mutual nods, the one he gave Alex deeper and more respectful as was due his captain, and that was that. Emil offered him a glass of ice-cold lemonade and a plate laden with sugar cookies. Unlike humans, his kind didn't take the passage of time as seriously. For him, it was as if he'd seen these men mere days ago and not weeks.

"Thanks for this, Emil," he said as he slid into a vacant chair. "My stores aboard ship aren't nearly as fine, and neither Brenin nor I are particularly talented in the kitchen." He took a long swallow of his drink, because he was thirsty and it allowed him to avoid any discussions for a few more seconds.

Harry didn't allow it, however. "Is Brenin having trouble?" He peered intently at Malcolm, kindness showing through his eyes.

There was no helping it. He'd have to voice his concerns and hope that his friends, as well as their human companions, could help. Brenin's well-being was the most important thing, far more than any inadequacies his bruised ego might feel.

"Aye," he admitted. "He's become moody and skittish, I suppose is the right word for lack of a better one. I find I'm walking on eggshells around him."

He didn't add in the concern about touching the boy, or how when he did without Brenin expecting it, he'd catch a flicker of something in his eyes. It was more than fear, too. Revulsion, perhaps, and the idea that Brenin might be repulsed by him cut deeply. He couldn't quite bring himself to talk about it in front of everyone. Maybe he'd talk to Harry later in private and get his take on what to do.

The doctor nodded thoughtfully. "I'm not surprised. Humans process trauma over long periods of time and in unpredictable ways. What does MacPhee say about it?"

Malcolm bit off half a cookie, because damn, they smelled heavenly and tasted even better. He missed Cook's daily treats and looked forward to the culinary pampering that Emil could offer in her stead.

"Much the same," he answered around his mouthful. "She's tried to talk to him, but he's not very forthcoming."

From where he sat sprawled behind his desk, Alex weighed in. "I don't suppose a young man who was kept as a sex slave is all that comfortable relaying his experience to a woman."

"Aye," Malcolm agreed. "She said as much. Her advice was that he needed a specialist, too. She's a wonder with fixing bodies, but head problems are not her specialty. Unfortunately, we can't have Brenin relating his experiences to anyone else without all of our secrets being spilled."

"We have the same problem when it comes to Dafydd," Harry said. "That boy needs counseling that I'm not equipped to provide."

Malcolm washed his treat down with more lemonade. "What about that other doctor, Paz? Is he any help?" If he was, perhaps he could have a go at Brenin.

Alex grimaced. "Afraid not. He's gone from emergency medicine to exploring cadavers, a useful career change for us possibly, but no help for this."

Malcolm's brief, small hope died.

"He likes Dafydd, though," Emil offered. "The love and devotion of a good man might be enough to get Dafydd past his life with Dracul and the killing of his son."

"Och, aye?" Malcolm shifted his gaze to the chef. "I can't say I'm surprised by that. He did spend every moment with him while they were still at my castle. That could be of help, then."

For Dafydd, but it did nothing for Brenin. And brooding over it wasn't going to solve anything, either. He decided to change the subject.

"What's this about trouble Val alluded to on the ride over?"

"I said it was human shit...probably," the man amended before stuffing an entire cookie in his mouth.

"As you say, probably. You really are terrible at nuance, man." He looked to Alex for some clarity.

Their leader scratched the underside of his chin. "Val's right. It's likely nothing to do with us." He gave Malcolm a brief summary of the 3-D printed gun situation.

Malcolm drained his glass, and before he could think to ask, Emil brought the pitcher of lemonade over and refilled it. Malcolm nodded in appreciation.

"Humans do seem intent on destroying themselves," Malcolm mused. "They think of something then blunder ahead with it and damn the consequences." He mulled the information over for a few seconds. "Gunrunning was ever a sideline of Dracul's. He loved putting weapons in the hands of fractious people."

"Except that he's dead," Val reminded him.

Is he?

It was the question that had been rattling around Malcolm's head ever since that night in the bastard's castle when Malcolm had seen the fucker drop into the cistern. He'd raced down to the pool of water in search of evidence that the fall had killed him, knowing there would be nothing left to find. Death turned his kind to dust. Malcolm didn't need anyone to remind him of it. He saw the signs of it every day when he looked at his own face and chest where his adventure in Wales had left permanent grooves in his skin. He didn't mind the beat-up appearance, and Brenin had assured him that it gave him a more rugged look. He wasn't so sure of that. Perhaps those scars reminded the boy of his own ordeal.

Shaking off his inner turmoil, he refocused on the less personal issue. "Petru would have kenned the ins and outs of the arms sale business — and Bran, as well, I shouldn't wonder. Either of them could have easily picked it up after they fled Wales."

"It's possible, of course," Alex allowed. "But we also run the risk of jumping at shadows. We've fallen into this trap before in centuries past, where we inserted ourselves in what ended up being purely human matters. We meddled and changed outcomes simply because we mistakenly thought Dracul was already doing so." The man shook his head.

Aye. Alex had always worried about being too much like Dracul, to the point of chastising himself where it wasn't warranted.

"Dinnae fash yourself over it, sir. I for one am happy to be visiting the United States of America instead of another Commonwealth country." He winked and went back to concentrating on his delicious snack.

"Hmm," was Alex's only response. Then, "Duncan is coming in later this evening. We can reconvene and discuss whatever new details he has. With any luck, the FBI that has flown into town to investigate will have found the human behind this nonsense and we can simply enjoy your visit. Do you want to go to Brenin? They're all up in my suite."

Malcolm considered the offer. He missed his boy easily and deeply when they were apart for even a short period of time. But his wants and needs weren't important. Brenin deserved some space, especially as they'd been in each other's pockets during the journey across the Atlantic.

"No, thank you, sir. If it's all the same to you, I'll just sit here and stuff myself full of lemonade and cookies. I'm sure the lads want to have their time to catch up."

"Of course. You're welcome to camp out here for as long as you like. I've finished my work for the day and could use the company, what with Quinn being off with the others." He rubbed a hand down his thigh, a sure sign that he missed having his boy sitting on his lap.

Malcolm wiggled his ass as an exaggerated way to get comfortable. "That's grand, then." He held up the last bit of cookie. "Any chance of more of these, Emil?"

The chef tsked. "Of course. You'll spoil the wonderful dinner I have planned, though."

"Never. I have a bottomless pit for a stomach, as you well ken. And eating is one of my favorite ways to pass the time."

He may as well indulge himself in that vice, as he very much feared his time with his lad was limited and getting more so with each passing day.

Chapter Four

"It's so great for all of us to be together again—and for happy reasons." Demi was a bundle of excited energy that rivaled anything Mackie was capable of.

Since entering into his official adulthood and extracting both a ring and a promise from Duncan, the hybrid had become increasingly upbeat. Dafydd focused his attention on the boy, as he often did. It boosted his courage and hope for the future with respect to his own child. *This is what Idris can be if I try hard enough to make it happen.* His inner voice didn't bolster his mood as much as he would have liked. He was determined, however, not to wallow in fear and pessimism. It helped, as well, that his child wasn't with him. It was always easier to find encouragement when he wasn't weighed down by the unrelenting reminder that the baby provided about his origins.

Although his thoughts were on Demi, his gaze wandered constantly over to where Brenin sat curled up in a big chair. Alex's living room was large, giving the boys plenty of room to spread out. While Dafydd appreciated being included in the gathering, he wasn't comfortable sitting close to anyone. He'd snagged the far end of the sofa for himself. It gave him the ability to keep track of everyone in the room without the possibility of someone sneaking up on him from behind.

Will I ever be rid of that worry?

Probably not. It didn't really matter anyway. He appreciated the new life he'd been handed. So long as he was aware of his surroundings and had his stash up on the roof, he could survive well enough. He wondered if Brenin had the same sense of comfort. He saw the moment the boy had entered the room that he, too, was struggling with the 'after'. Their lives would forever be marked by the 'before' of Dracul and the 'after' of him. It was a daily trial. He could tell instantly that Brenin was suffering from it because there was the same look in the boy's eyes that Dafydd saw every day in the bathroom mirror. He wanted to talk to Brenin about it. Perhaps they could offer some comfort to each other that the others could never do, despite their good intentions.

"It's heather, can you see?" Demi had his ring right in front of Brenin's face, oblivious to how uncomfortable he was making him with the closeness.

Brenin leaned as far back as his chair would allow. "Very nice, indeed. Engaged to be engaged, you say? Is that a thing here in America?"

"It's a thing in Demi's mind," Quinn replied, but with a quick grin that conveyed he was teasing his friend.

Demi huffed and threw himself back into his own seat. "Duncan is being noble. He wants me to get on with my studies and mature…or something." He rolled his eyes. "It's only a matter of me wearing him down.

Don't make any big plans for next spring. I'm counting on a late-May wedding." He eyed Brenin again. "I don't suppose you could talk Malcolm into crossing over again in his yacht? A shipboard ceremony would be awesome."

Brenin looked at his lap and said, "I expect Malcolm would do practically anything I ask of him."

The melancholy in the boy's expression and tone were all too obvious to Dafydd.

Do the others see it? Do they hear it? Can they even understand it on any level?

His heart—what was left of it—ached for his friend. They'd spent very little time together in the grander scheme of things, yet they knew and understood each other better than the other boys ever could.

"Awesome!" Demi grabbed a grape from the fruit-and-cheese plate Jase had laid out. After tossing it into the air, he caught it with his mouth. "Now I don't have to worry about getting a venue. Kitty can DJ and Emil will cater, of course."

"Of course," Jase echoed. "Don't eat too much. You know that Damien is working on a traditional clambake for tonight. It's for the entire club, but our food will be served up here. There'll be steamers, lobsters, corn on the cob, potato salad and rolls." He ticked off each item on his fingers. "Oh, and Boston cream pie for dessert."

Demi dismissed his concern. "As if I could fill up on this snack food. Trey says I'm too thin anyway. I could use some fattening up."

The off-hand comment sent a frisson through Dafydd. "He's controlling what you eat?" He blurted the question out before he could stop himself. Dracul had always been the gatekeeper of Dafydd's food, although for the monster, it was about keeping Dafydd slender.

'I don't want you getting fat, slut.'

His breath caught. For a moment, it was as if the voice had come from somewhere outside him. He darted his gaze around the room, expecting he would find Dracul lurking in a dark corner. Something of his panicked response must have shown in his face.

Demi leaned forward. "It's okay, Dafydd. I didn't mean anything. It was a joke. That's all."

Dafydd swallowed down his silly fear and managed an anemic smile. "Yes, certainly. I should get back to Idris." He started to rise, although he was lying through his pathetic teeth. It wasn't his child that he wanted to hurry off to. It was the roof.

"No, stay," Demi said. "Please. You know my father loves watching the baby, although I don't know why, given his experience with me." He rolled his eyes and grinned.

Mackie, Quinn and Jase all chuckled and giggled, sounding forced to Dafydd's ears. They were trying so hard to include him and make him feel welcome. It was a waste of effort, for all that it was kindly meant. He was never going to fit in. He wasn't sure he wanted to.

"I know." Dafydd stood anyway, the lure of the peace waiting for him on top of the building too hard to ignore. "Still…"

"You'll be back for the clam bake, though, won't you?" Quinn asked. His earnest expression was such that Dafydd didn't want to disappoint.

"I will, yes, so long as Idris isn't fussing."

"We don't mind if he is," Mackie said. "Honestly, he's — you know — adorbs."

"And Dr. Paz is joining us," Jase tossed in, not quite as casually as he might have thought. "Along with Trey and Anderson," he added.

But the boy had achieved his intended results. Dafydd's heartbeat quickened at the thought of seeing the doctor again. Damn, he hated his own reaction. He didn't want to *want* to see the man.

"Oh?" He shrugged, trying for nonchalance. "That's nice for him, I suppose—being at the club, I mean."

His anxiety mounting, he knew he had to get out. Fast. Skirting his way around the chairs closest to him, he headed for the door.

Then he stopped and turned toward Brenin. "We'll catch up later, yes?" He felt responsible for the boy in a strange sort of way. His own troubles aside, he wanted Brenin to have the chance to regain his life, at least.

Brenin nodded. "Sure, mun. I'll see you later." The way he couldn't hold even Dafydd's timid gaze spoke volumes.

Determined to be of help, Dafydd resolved to find a way to get Brenin alone at some point. Later that night, perhaps. It was a good reason to force himself to come to the party. If he concentrated on helping someone else, he could shove down his own problems and pretend he didn't have any.

* * * *

"Hey, Ric."

He turned to see one of his former colleagues come out of the condo building. He'd forgotten that she'd bought a unit in the same place he had in Charlestown. "Hi, Delia."

He waited at the bottom of the stairs for her to reach him, then they did that half-hug, air-kiss thing that was so popular with their generation.

She grinned at him while repositioning her shoulder bag. "We miss you in the ED. How are things in the land of the dead?"

"Quiet."

She barked out a laugh. "Besides that. I hear Vincente is as cold as his corpses."

"Well…he's not the cuddly sort," he allowed, not wanting any negative comments to get back to his boss. Doctors were terrible gossips. "The work is interesting, though."

"I suppose there's some symmetry to it. Some of the people we treat unsuccessfully in ED end up with you, huh?"

Ric thought of the young man shattered by his new-fangled gun. "Yes, that's true."

Delia snapped her fingers. "Oh, we almost had another one for you this morning. A kid came in during the wee hours with plastic sticking out of his eye, among other places. We managed to save the kid, although not his sight. It reminded me of a few days ago, when the outcome was very different."

That perked up Ric's interest. "You mean another exploding gun?"

"Yup." She shook her head. "Like we didn't have enough gun violence to deal with… Now we have to worry about that."

Ric opened his mouth to ask more questions. He didn't get the chance, because an SUV rolled up to the curb, driven by Duncan and carrying Anderson in the passenger's seat. They were his transportation for the big party at the club, at Duncan's insistence, even though the Boston public transportation system was convenient.

"Oh, sorry. This is my ride."

Delia's eyes popped. "Huh! Gay men have all of the luck. *Two* hot guys?"

Ric flashed her a grin. "They're only friends. Good to see you, Delia."

"You too." She waved as he got into the car before turning to walk down the sidewalk.

"Who's that?" Anderson asked before Ric had even buckled up. "She's pretty."

"I thought you were already occupied," Ric said by way of answer.

"I'm not saying I'm interested, merely curious."

Duncan shook his head as he pulled away. "Careful, Karl. I'm pretty sure Kitty can snap you like a twig if she has a mind to."

"Yeah," Karl sighed. "That's one of the things I love about her."

"Well, as you asked," Ric said, "that was Dr. Delia Verona. She had some interesting information about another emergency patient suffering from the shrapnel of an exploding gun."

"We've heard." Duncan's tone was matter-of-fact, yet grim. "I'm going to give everyone an update in Alex's office before we chow down at the clam bake. You know MacLerie floated into town this afternoon," he added, glancing at Ric through his rearview mirror.

"Oh, good to hear." He wasn't sure he was truly happy with the visit. It all depended on how it affected Dafydd's mental health. Seeing Brenin again would either be a good thing or a bad one. There was no way to predict which it would be, and Ric felt helpless anyway. He couldn't aid Dafydd if the guy didn't allow him to.

The ride was mostly a quiet one and once they arrived at the club, they made straight for Alex's office, when Ric would have preferred to seek out Harry or Lucien for an update about Dafydd. No, what he really wanted was to find the man himself. He hoped to see him at dinner yet didn't dare ask anyone about it directly. His feelings for the Welshman were both complicated and too private for him to tip his hand in any obvious way.

"Ah, gentlemen, come in," Alex called out the moment they came into view. "You remember Malcolm, surely."

The alien Scotsman rose like a statue from Easter Island, large and imposing, his expression inscrutable even with a flash of a smile. And he wore an unusual combination of a T-shirt, kilt and heavy black boots. As smitten by Dafydd as Ric was, he couldn't help but admire the raw sexuality of the man on a purely primitive level, battle scars and all. He shook Malcolm's hand when it was his turn and found himself pinned by the man's stare.

"When you have a moment, Dr. Paz, I'd like a word, if you dinnae mind?"

"Certainly. And please call me Ric, remember?"

"Ric, then. I'll find you later."

That was all that was said, yet Ric could tell there was genuine concern lurking behind the man's eyes and words. It made Ric wonder if something was wrong with Brenin. It was either that or an issue with the human slaves Malcolm and Brenin were trying to rehabilitate. Although, if that were the case, Dr. MacPhee was more than capable of handling it, at least based on what Ric had seen of the woman. If Brenin was the problem, Ric was eager to help, if only because it meant he and Malcolm shared a common predicament. They both loved one of Dracul's victims and were anxious to heal them.

The room was filled with all of the alien men, plus Kitty and the vet, Logan. It made for a cramped space, but it was probably the most private location in the club other than the basement. Ric found a sliver of room on the arm of the couch and settled down. Duncan and Anderson also squeezed into spots. Val shut the door for privacy, no doubt. None of the boys were there, which was just as well. They were all strong and brave, yet they also deserved some time free of worry. Ric understood the desire of every man in the room to shield the ones they cared for. There might not be anything noteworthy anyway, not by the aliens' standards.

Alex nodded toward Duncan. "Sergeant?"

The man cleared his throat. "So, here's the story. We've now had two incidences in which a 3-D printed gun has exploded during use by drug-dealing gang members. One was a personal vendetta situation in which the gunman died. That one we already discussed. The second incident occurred earlier this morning during a robbery of a convenience store. That perp lived, although he's in rough shape and, to my knowledge, hasn't been properly questioned yet. This information is all fifth-hand, if you will, because it's an FBI investigation and neither I nor Karl rank."

"I just heard of this myself," Ric added, repeating what Delia had told him. "I assume that his survival will eventually lead to our knowing who is behind this." He looked at Duncan when he said it.

"Maybe. Both of these guys were low-level criminals in the grander scheme of things. One thing we do know, however, is that they were part of the same gang."

"So, they got the guns from only the one source," Val said.

"Probably," Duncan allowed. "It's too early to tell."

From where she lurked in the corner, Logan raised her hand.

Alex swiveled his chair in her direction. "You have something to add?"

Logan lowered her hand and stared at the floor. "Yes, sir. Word is the guns came from Maine." Although the woman had been given a room at the club, making her in theory no longer homeless, she did still spend a lot of time out on the street. That was according to Emil, who constantly worried about her.

Duncan nodded. "That ties in with what we know about Tony Two Claws. And it's weird enough to generate gossip. I'm not sure the FBI will have acquired that kind of intel. They're relying on Boston PD's local CIs, which means the flow of information is spotty. You're my best confidential informant, that's for sure," he added with a grin toward Logan. "I'm lucky in that."

The woman shrugged and shrank back into her corner. "That's what I hear, anyway, for what it's worth."

"Does that tell us anything about who's behind it?" Ric asked. "Does it help in figuring out whether this has anything to do with your kind?" He winced at his own word choice. It sounded so racist. "Alien-driven, I mean. No offense." *Jesus.*

"No need to worry about the thickness of our skin, Doctor," Malcolm assured him. "It is the million-dollar question and I, for one, am hard put to say one way or t'other."

"Karl and I will keep our ears to the ground. The FBI might be able to get something out of this second guy that will clue us in better. In the meantime, assuming the weapons are being manufactured or smuggled in from Maine, I think we can rule out a major city like Portland. There's too much activity there, especially around the harbor, to use it as a place of import or export. They'd want something more low-key."

Anderson added, "Plus, I'd say we can assume it's somewhere in southern Maine. There would be no reason to make distribution harder than it needed to be by hauling stuff for hours down the Maine state highway system."

"Okay, since we're playing what-if," Val said, "I've already pulled up my files on what we know about Dracul's weapons dealing. He did use a small coastal town about ninety minutes from here as a smuggling point years ago. Putnam's Cove."

Ric perked up at the mention of the place. "I've been there." When everyone swiveled their gazes on him, his cheeks heated. "It's very gay-friendly and quicker to drive to than Provincetown."

MacLerie frowned. "Sounds like a lovely place to visit, but why would anyone smuggle in these computer-printed guns when making them can be done anywhere? It's just a matter of materials, isn't it?"

"And that's the issue," Duncan replied. "The material is easy to obtain, but the quantity necessary if you were to go into mass production can raise red flags if anyone is looking. Before countries started cracking down on publishing and possessing the plans themselves, there were some notable opportunities taken to crank out a lot of them. Parts of Europe and Australia in particular had problems. If Dracul had already gotten in on the act, maybe one of his boys is simply picking up where he left off and getting the weapons into this country."

Val nodded. "It fits his pattern with more conventional weapons."

"I don't know," Anderson injected. "It still doesn't make any sense to me. The 3-D printed ones have to cost more than a metal gun. Why would a relatively low-level guy like Tony Two Claws and this other idiot have them?"

"Marketing." This came from Logan, whose head was up once more. "It's big news on the street because they're just regular guys. Word gets around, creates a buzz. Everyone wants one if those guys have them, like a pusher giving away free drugs."

Duncan turned toward Ric. "You nailed it, Doc. That was his theory a few days ago," he added to the room at large.

Yes, it made sense, and Ric was rather proud to have thought of it himself, except… "Who wants to peddle something that's so obviously bad for its user?" he asked. "You won't get many orders for a defective product. I know people say that all publicity is good publicity, but surely not in this case."

MacLerie hummed. "I bet that's not part of the plan. Poorly made, is it? They handed out free guns only to find out they'd cut a corner and the fucking things are literally back-firing on them?"

"Excellent points, gentlemen," Alex agreed. "It doesn't tell us any more about whether this falls under our purview, but would anyone be surprised to find out that Petru or Bran, more likely, tried to pick up the ball and fumbled it?"

"No, not all," Emil answered, and everyone else nodded.

Ric couldn't agree because he didn't know as much as the others in the room. He had heard murmurings about how Dafydd's twin sons were pale shadows of their alien father — and thank God for it. It was probably why it had been relatively easy for them to bring down Cadoc's short, brutal reign as the king of the boy prostitutes in town.

"So, we what? Wait and see?" he asked.

Malcolm shrugged. "Not necessarily, Doc. We could take my yacht up the coast for a wee holiday and have a poke around. I promised Brenin we'd see the sights here in Boston, but nothing says we can't also find a bit of fun elsewhere first. Is there a port for me to dock in?" he asked Val.

"Fuck if I know...but I'll find out," Val amended when his friend glowered at him.

"Many thanks." The almost-Scotsman turned his attention to the one who made all of the decisions. "What do you say, Alex? The boys are having a sleepover, as they call it, on the boat tonight. We could easily take off as early as tomorrow if I can make arrangements at this Putman's Cove. There's no need for hotel rooms, which are like as not hard to come by."

"It would be nice to go somewhere without the sure knowledge that it was a call to battle," Emil said. "Jase could use a treat, and his classes have ended for the summer."

"Same with Demi. And given the short drive, I can join you when I'm off duty," Duncan added.

Ric felt a spurt of envy at the casual way the cop could assume he'd be welcome.

Anderson shot a look at Kitty. "We could hold down the fort as usual, right?"

The woman's icy demeanor thawed slightly and only for a second when she answered. "Sure, we can. I don't like Maine anyway. There are too many tourists down here at this time of year. Up there, it's a nightmare."

Alex slapped his palms on his desk. "Well, it's settled then, I suppose. We take a nice little vacation and hope that's all it turns out to be." He stood. "Shall we go upstairs and eat?"

"I'll go check on how Damien is doing." Emil weaved his way around everyone to leave first.

Ric got up along with the others, happy to be included in the festivities for the evening, yet worried about whether he'd see Dafydd at all.

Malcolm came up behind him and clapped him on his shoulder. The big hand jolted him enough to make him grunt. "You'll do the same, then, will you, Doc?"

"Sorry?"

"Come up when your day of work is done. I'm sure Duncan will give you a ride if you need one."

"Oh, um, that's a kind offer, but…" He wasn't sure what to say. He wanted to be where Dafydd was.

As if Malcolm could read his thoughts, he added, "I'll make sure Dafydd and the baby come along. It will do him some good, I figure, plus Brenin could use some time with his friend. I think they're the only two people on the planet that can understand how each of them feels."

Ric paused and looked up at him. "Is Brenin having problems? Is that what you wanted to speak with me about?"

"Aye." Malcolm pulled him aside so that all of the others could pass them and move on. "I think he's struggling a wee bit." Then the man sighed heavily. "That's not true. I *ken* he's struggling *a lot*. I'm at a loss as to how to help him."

Ric felt for the man, his expression and obvious distress a mirror for his own. "I understand. It's…um, the same with me and Dafydd."

Malcolm's expression softened. "Aye, I thought as much. We're two peas and that's a fact. What do we do, is the question? I'm hoping you have some suggestions."

Ric hated dashing the man's hopes, as well as his own, so he gave them both false ones. "I'll see what I can do."

Malcolm landed his hand on Ric's shoulder again, like a thunderbolt. "Good man. Now let's see what all the fuss is about with this clam bake. Lobsters are big bugs, as far as I'm concerned. Nothing like salmon. Still, when in Rome…"

Ric offered a smile and fell into step beside him, and if his heartbeat ticked up a notch at the idea of seeing Dafydd, so what? It was okay to have some faith that life would grant him his most fervent desire. Otherwise, what was the point of moving forward at all?

Chapter Five

Despite its size, Alex's suite was crowded with the family, as Brenin supposed one might call it, ranged around eating the delicious meal Emil and his sous chef had prepared. For his own part, Brenin sat pressed against Malcolm's side. He felt both comforted and guilty that the very size of the crowd made it easier for him to be with the man he loved. There was no chance of intimacy happening at the moment, which meant he didn't have to remind his body that Malcolm's touch was nothing to fear. It was something to welcome, yet the demons lurking deep inside him were lately forgetting that part.

"Have you had enough to eat, laddie?" Malcolm's slightly cool breath wafted over him, familiar and triggering at the same time. It reminded him of how Dracul had panted on him as he'd pounded into Brenin's sore and battered body.

He pushed the memory away and forced a smile to his lips as he looked up. His gaze slid, as per usual, to where scars marred Malcolm's masculine beauty. *He got those saving me.* The reminder helped quell his anxiety, so he stared at those marks instead of into Malcolm's eyes.

"I have, yes. It's a bit messy, though, isn't it?" He held up the buttery fingers of one hand close to Malcolm's lips.

It had the intended affect. Malcolm flicked out his tongue to lap at them before leaning closer to suck them in. As he licked the fingers clean, his eyes flashed with need and his pupils dilated with arousal. The touch sent a shiver through Brenin, testament to how constantly at war he was with his own mind and body. His cock hardened and he didn't need to check Malcolm's lap to know he'd affected his lover the same way.

But Malcolm, ever kind and sensitive, didn't push the matter further. Instead, he released Brenin's fingers and went back to finishing his own plate of food as if nothing untoward had occurred.

Brenin tried to do the same and found that nerves had filled the rest of his stomach. He put his plate on the coffee table and sat back. He snuggled closer to his man and made a conscious effort to relax before putting his hand with its still-wet fingers on Malcolm's thigh. He could feel the man's muscles twitch through the plaid.

"Are you coming back to the boat with the rest of us tonight?" Brenin wasn't sure what he wanted the answer to be.

Malcolm snorted. "My yacht is a big vessel to be sure, but even so, I can't imagine surviving a night with you boys partying. Alex has offered me his guest room, and I've accepted it." He paused meaningfully and put his own plate beside Brenin's. "Unless you want me to be there?"

Brenin weighed what was the best answer and decided to go for the truth. "No, that's fine. You're right that we'll likely stay up most of the night, dancing and gossiping." He snorted. "We might even braid each other's hair or some such nonsense."

Malcolm tugged a stray lock and tucked it behind Brenin's ear. "Being a highlander, I heartily approve of that. I'll miss you, though. You ken?"

"Yes." He slipped his hand up under the man's kilt. The weather being warm, they were both commando. He had no trouble finding Malcolm's semi-hard cock in the folds of cloth. He clasped it slightly. "We should say a proper good night before I go."

Malcolm put his hand over his with the kilt between them. "A kind offer to be sure, but not necessary."

Brenin flicked his gaze up. "I want to." He licked his lips before adding. "Please."

Malcolm's heated gaze penetrated him. "Nothing would make me happier, if it's what you want."

"It is." He was perhaps too quick to reassure. Determined to bring them both pleasure on his own terms, he glanced around for an expedited solution to their need. "Come on."

Jumping up, he let go of Malcolm's dick in order to grab his hand. Then he guided his lover across the room and headed toward the guest bathroom off the kitchen area. No one paid them much mind, probably because some of the other couples were already cuddling in prelude to making more intimate good-byes. As they passed Val and Mackie, the alien was hooking a leash onto his boy's collar. The glassy look in Mackie's eyes told even an inexperienced lad like Brenin that the submissive was heading down into what he called subspace.

"Come on, boy," Val said as he yanked on the leash. "Let's go play before you trash poor Malcolm's pretty boat."

Malcolm chuckled, although he didn't pause to respond. As he always did, he let Brenin lead him to the where and the how of their sexual encounters. The loo was almost as big as Brenin's bedroom had been back when he was a normal boy living an ordinary life. After tugging Malcolm in, he quickly shut and locked the door. Then he closed the lid of the toilet and gestured to it.

"Sit there." He wasn't surprised by his breathless tone. He was as aroused as his lover, his hard dick tenting his kilt in the mirror image of Malcolm. This was the constant dichotomy of his life, the wanting and the fearing at the same time. The only way through it was to take command and please himself. Somehow, whatever he did was enough for Malcolm—or so the man said. And he did a convincing job of it. Brenin had to believe, though, that a man as virile and commanding as Malcolm chafed at the constraint.

Malcolm sat as ordered, practically quivering with desire. Brenin didn't make him wait. He knelt and shoved the man's kilt up to his waist, exposing the rampant cock that glistened with pre-cum. The sight of it always caused saliva to pool in Brenin's mouth as he concentrated on how tasty it was. He pushed himself between his lover's legs, which parted like the Red Sea, and took Malcolm's dick and balls in each hand while lowering his mouth.

The initial burst of tangy, salty cum hit his tongue and he paused for a second to savor the taste. Lobster had nothing on the treat that was Malcolm. Brenin moaned around his mouthful, taking the shaft in as far as he could. This was no act on his part, either. He did love giving blow jobs — when it was his choice. There was a power in it, making his man shake and groan as he was now. He was in control. Malcolm would only come when Brenin decided he was allowed to. If he thought the guy was getting ahead of matters, all he had to do was squeeze the base of the thick cock and that would put a stop to it. He loved, as well, Malcolm's grunts of frustration when he did so.

Not that they played that game this evening. Knowing they had little time before spending the night apart, neither of them wanted to draw this encounter out. At least, Brenin didn't, and he could read Malcolm's moods quite well now. The man kept his fingers wrapped around the folds of his kilt and not on Brenin's head. It was those little touches, how he thought ahead of what might please Brenin or upset him, that reaffirmed Brenin's love for him. There really was no question about that. It was more the problem of chasing away the lingering effects of Dracul's brutality that kept getting in the way.

He wouldn't think of that now, however. Instead, he feasted on the cock, using his lips and tongue to lavish it with attention. He moved his hands along the smooth shaft and swollen balls in a coordinated rhythm that he'd honed in the last couple of months. He knew what he was about, and knowledge was its own kind of power. Each time, he tried to swallow more of the silky hardness, knowing he'd never manage to deep throat someone as thick and long as Malcolm. His fingers met his lips, though, about halfway and he counted that as a win.

Malcolm stuttered out a breath. "Och, laddie, what you do to me."

Encouraged, Brenin smiled around his mouthful of cock, sank down as deep as he dared and swallowed. At the same time, he squeezed the balls and loosened his grip at the base of the shaft. Cum flooded his mouth in the next instant, but he was ready for it. He opened his throat and let it slide down, pulling back only when he felt as though he might gag. And still, he kept sucking and swallowing until Malcolm's entire body went lax and barely a drop remained in Brenin's mouth.

He let go of the shaft slowly, sliding his tongue around every inch he could reach to lick it clean. When he was done, he sat back on his heels and heaved a big sigh. "All right, then?" He smiled at his own question, the look of bliss on Malcolm's face all the confirmation he needed.

Malcolm opened his eyes a sliver. "You took my very breath away, as you well ken, laddie. The only issue I have now is, how do I reciprocate?"

Brenin understood that it was important to his man that he not go wanting. And with his kilt hanging off his standing dick, it was hard to argue he wasn't in need of tending to. He considered jerking himself off with the sight of Malcolm sprawled in front of him as inspiration, then decided that wouldn't be nearly satisfying and might give Malcolm the idea that he truly didn't want his touch. That was not the case.

So he stood, his passion making him more graceful than he would have expected, and hiking his kilt up past his straining cock, he shuffled between Malcolm's thick, splayed thighs. He didn't need to say anything, and the silent communication somehow amped up his arousal. With their gazes locked, Brenin lined himself up with Malcolm's lips, which opened slowly, widely, welcomingly. When the head of his dick entered Malcolm's mouth, he shoved it all the way in.

Malcolm was ready for him, the way Brenin knew he would be. Unlike Brenin, he had no trouble swallowing the entire cock down to the root. His lips pressed against Brenin's pubic bone while tight throat muscles massaged his cock in an undulating wave that made Brenin come with dizzying speed. He gasped as he slammed his eyes shut, and he blindly reached out to grab Malcolm's broad shoulders to steady himself.

He uttered a cry, uncaring who heard. For those brief seconds, where waves of his orgasm washed over him, he was free of all his worries. At that moment, it was only him and his lover, taking pleasure in each other. There were no fears or doubts, no hesitation in the way that he clung to the man who'd given him back his life — the man who'd become his life.

"I love you, Malcolm." Brenin almost sobbed out his declaration. Hot tears sprang up, making him hold on all the tighter and more desperate.

Malcolm worked Brenin's dick until it was dry then released it gently. He wrapped him in a loose embrace and rubbed his cheek against Brenin's chest. "I ken, laddie, I ken. And I'm here for you, always."

Brenin believed him. He did, and yet he couldn't help but wonder, *For how long?*

* * * *

Too many people. Too much laughter. It reminded Dafydd of the kind of sick merriment that had often occurred in Dracul's castle. Back then it had almost always been over some poor soul's degradation, terror or even death. Knowing that this gathering was of a different sort hardly mattered to Dafydd's damaged nerves. Added to that was Idris starting to fuss because of the noise, perhaps, or the lateness of the hour. It gave him a good excuse to leave, except that while he made his hasty goodbyes, it wasn't with his room in mind. He wanted to escape to the roof. Of course he did, weak and pathetically broken person that he was.

"Aren't you coming for the sleepover at the yacht?" Demi asked the question from where he perched on his lover's lap.

This idea of a bunch of boys spending the night together, gabbing and doing God knew what until the wee hours of the morning made no sense to him. What did he know of such things? It was a modern concept, to be sure, and one for those who needn't get up early to toil. Besides, the very idea of going from one small, noisy party to another set his teeth on edge.

He jiggled Idris and tried for a smile when he answered. "No, thanks. I have to get the boy down and I'm not sure how I feel about spending time on the water, truth be told." He wasn't making that part up. His journey from Wales to Scotland was a blur, given that he'd been mostly unconscious for it. What he remembered of it wasn't pleasant.

"I'll be happy to take care of him," Lucien said, coming up.

Oh, but that was a tempting offer, except it came with a string attached that he didn't want. "No. Thank you, all the same. He's my responsibility and I'm that tired, I am. Good night."

He made haste, not wanting to discuss the matter further, avoiding everyone else as much as possible. That included the human doctor. *Ric.* Yes, he was there, as well, and that was no real surprise. Whatever was going on — and something surely was, given how the men had huddled earlier — the doctor was part of their world now. His dark eyes with their obvious concern shining through had sought Dafydd out during the meal. Despite having deliberately sat as far away from the man as he could, Dafydd had felt the weight of that attention all evening. It disturbed him, but not so much as his own wandering gaze. How many times had he sought out Ric, tracking his movements? Just one more good reason to leave.

Relief washed over him the moment he stepped into the hallway. Lucien had followed him out of the suite anyway, though, and caught him by the elevator. Being changelings, they were evenly matched in strength and speed. That was true despite the fact that Dafydd no longer partook of the alien blood, while Lucien almost certainly did. Dafydd kept wondering when he'd lose the good parts of his forced conversion from human to whatever the fuck he was now.

Lucien held out his hands. "Please. I can see you've reached your limit for the day. However well-meaning everyone has been to include you in our social activities, I know it's taxing on you. It bothers me occasionally, I must confess. I get flashes of the time in my life when the sound of men laughing meant nothing good for me."

Dafydd knew there was some story there, yet he hadn't bothered to ask the details. He didn't want to know them. He had his own horrid memories to deal with, and unlike Lucien, no real way to vent. No, that wasn't true. There were plenty of folks who would listen if he asked them to. His mind flashed on Ric again, and he forced the image away.

"I'm fine. Really. Now," he added, "Idris is my responsibility. You do too much as it is."

Lucien kept his arms outstretched. "I do no more than I want. If you push yourself beyond what you're comfortable with, it won't do you or Idris any good." He beckoned, like a siren in the sea.

Dafydd held out for only a second more before handing over an increasingly fussy Idris. The boy settled instantly, as if he knew that Lucien was a better caretaker.

Because he is.

"Thank you." He dropped his gaze. "You're right, of course."

"It is not a failing, Dafydd. You are too hard on yourself. Give it time. You are really doing a remarkable job, considering all that you've been through."

Dafydd said nothing, knowing how wrong the kindly man was about everything. He thought of the bliss that awaited him on the roof and wondered what Lucien would have to say about that if he ever found out. *Not doing so well after all, hey?*

"I'm going to take some air. I'll see you later."

"A good idea. I'll stay with the boy until you get back. No hurry."

Dafydd didn't bother to wait until the man had gotten into the elevator before turning and racing to the stairs. He took the steps two at a time and, bursting through the rooftop door, ran straight to his stash. He popped a pill into his mouth, then fuck it, two, and was reaching for the brandy to wash it down when he heard soft footfalls behind him. On instinct, he whirled around, braced for a blow. His heart beat jack-rabbit fast and he swallowed the pills dry. His body's reaction didn't slow, even as he saw who it was.

"I'm sorry. I didn't mean to startle you." Ric offered up a smile as he approached. "I saw you leave Idris with Lucien and was worried something was wrong."

Dafydd made no attempt to reassure the man. *Everything* was wrong, after all. He merely stood breathing harshly, one hand clenched around the almost-empty bottle of pills, the other grasping the liquor bottle by its neck. His flight-or-fight instinct having been beaten out of him, he stood frozen, waiting for the doctor to do something that he could react to.

Ric stepped closer and frowned. "What do you have there?" He peered down at Dafydd's left hand. "Is that a bottle of pills?"

Dafydd raised his chin in a show of defiance that he knew could land him into trouble. "And what if it is? Harry gave them to me — for my nerves, which are bad, don't you know?"

"I understand." The man's voice was soft and kind, which only served to grate on Dafydd. He wasn't used to kindness and had yet to learn how to accept it with grace and gratitude.

Ric gestured to the left. "That's obviously liquor, though. Are you mixing the two?"

"So what if I am, mun? It's none of your concern."

That shut Ric up for a few seconds. A sorrowful look passed over his face, but Dafydd refused to feel bad about it. "You're right in that it's none of my business, perhaps. I am concerned, though."

He got even closer, enough that his features were easy to discern in the moonlight. "Please, let me be of help."

In a rash act of defiance, Dafydd tucked the pill bottle into his front pocket before opening the brandy and taking a long swallow. He kept his gaze on Ric, nevertheless—a matter of habit. The liquid burned a trail down his throat, making his eyes water. He didn't let up until his lungs screamed for air.

He remained as he was, glaring at the doctor while breathing heavily. Fatigue washed over him, egged on by the medicine and the brandy. His eyelids drooped and he swayed a bit.

"You want to help me, then?" He pulled the pill bottle out and shook it. "I'm getting a bit low on these. Care to get me more?"

Ric closed his eyes and shook his head. "I don't write prescriptions anymore. I'm a pathologist now. Besides, it's unethical, if not illegal, for a doctor to proscribe medicine for friends and family."

"That lets you off in my case. I'm neither to you." Dafydd winced inwardly at his cruelty. *Oh, how well I've learned Dracul's lessons.*

Ric looked at the skyline around them before coming back to stare at him. "I'm sorry you feel that way. I would like to think we're friends. I certainly think of you that way."

Dafydd scoffed. He couldn't help it. "Don't lie to me. I'm not some gullible fool, haven't been for about four hundred years or so." He dared to walk forward until they were a meter away. "I know what you want." He pointedly stared at the man's crotch before taking another swig of brandy.

Now Ric's face crumpled in obvious misery. Dafydd's heart squeezed in sadness and guilt and yet he didn't take the words back. He was afraid that if he started to apologize, he'd devolve into that sniveling, frightened boy he'd once been, begging for mercy. It didn't matter that Ric was nothing like Dracul or that the situation was different. On this occasion, Dafydd did have something to be sorry about. After living so long in the world of a monster, he had lost the ability to interact with someone in a normal way.

Long minutes of silence stretched between them, in which Dafydd wondered why this man stayed in the face of such a bitter dismissal. Finally, the doctor took in then let out a deep breath.

"I do want you." The confession was made in a low voice laced with pain. Dafydd knew that sound very well indeed. "I know it's wrong, but there it is. I won't come again. You don't need my unwanted attention with everything else you're dealing with." He turned to go.

A new kind of panic hit Dafydd, almost literally knocking him over. "Wait! That's it?" he asked when Ric stopped and looked at him with questioning eyes. "I act like a fucking cunt and you just let me?"

"Don't call yourself that!" The order snapped out of the man's mouth with the force of a whip. Dafydd flinched, despite his ill humor. "Sorry. I shouldn't have used that tone with you. I simply meant that—"

"I know." Now impatience overrode everything else. "Although why you should bother to care about how I feel or what I say or what I do mystifies me. It's not about the sex. I know that. There are plenty of pretty and willing boys down in the club. Why do I matter?"

"Oh, Dafydd." Ric reached out for a split second before snatching back his hand. "Sorry. I know I don't say your name right."

"You do well enough, mun." His head swam and he staggered.

Ric was there—of course he was—to catch him and hold him steady. Dafydd stiffened a moment from the touch before relaxing again. There was too much swirling around his system for him to remain anything other than limp.

"I'm that tired," he whispered.

"Come and sit down." Ric's touch and tone were so very gentle that it was easy to allow the doctor to guide him to a sitting position in the very spot he usually occupied.

Ric tugged both bottles and the cap from Dafydd's lax grasp and closed up the brandy. "This is really a dangerous thing to do. How many pills have you taken?"

Dafydd let his head lull against the cement wall. "Two."

There was a sigh. "And I saw you consume a good third of this brandy on top of it. Do you do this every night?"

Dafydd gazed up at the stars. "No. Yes," he amended for reasons that he couldn't understand. "Mostly it's one pill and not so much brandy."

"For how long now? Since you arrived?"

Dafydd shrugged. Thinking was getting too hard. He yawned and, drawing his legs up, rested his chin on his knees. "I told you back in Wales that I needed to die."

"I'll tell you again. No, sir, not on my watch."

Dafydd smiled at the fierceness in the man's reply then closed his eyes. "I'm terribly broken, you see."

"You're alive and you're free. That means there's hope. And you have Idris to think of. You want to raise him, don't you?"

"I suppose."

"I see how you look at him. You love him, Dafydd, I know you do. And that's a wonderful thing. It tells me that you are getting better. Please don't give up on yourself. And please don't trade the prison you were in at the castle in Wales with the one that addiction creates. What you're doing here with these pills and the booze will hurt you in the long run, as surely as what that asshole alien did."

There was the sound of glass clinking on the roof, and he sensed that the doctor had settled down in front of him. "I know that you want to be alone, but it's not safe for me to leave you. I'm going to stay here so long as you do. I'm sorry if that bothers you."

"No, it's fine, I suppose."

"No one else knows you're up here, do they, or what you do when you come?"

Dafydd shook his head, a mistake given how his head swam. "You do, now. Are you going to tell the others?"

"I should, but there's only one pill left, so I'm not as worried that you'll hurt yourself after tonight. I'll keep my mouth shut on one condition."

Dafydd almost laughed. There was always a price to be paid, and for a brief second, he thought the man would ask for something sexual. He should have known him better than that now.

"I want you to go up to Maine with the others. You heard about the trip during dinner, right? You were paying attention?"

"I did, yes, but it's nothing to me. The last thing I need is to go somewhere else. Any place where I'm not being beaten and raped is holiday enough for me." He regretted the glib remark the moment he'd said it.

"I wish I could have killed him," Ric said into the ensuing silence, "which is crazy, I know. What chance would I have against a human soldier, let alone an alien one? I'm just saying."

"Why do you want me to go, anyway?"

"Because it will separate you from this roof and the habit you've fallen into, using medicine and liquor as crutches. You can get out into the sun and Idris can play on the beach. It will be good for you. Trust me, please. I…um, won't come and bother you. I promise."

This was an easy way out. All Dafydd had to do was agree. Harry could always get him more pills and there was undoubtedly brandy and other spirits aplenty on MacLerie's fancy boat. Plus, the doctor wouldn't be there to spy on him. *Just say yes, mun, and be done with it.*

"All right. I'll go…except you should come, too, when you can. It will be good for you, too, won't it?" *Idiot!*

"I will…and thank you." The man's joy was easy to hear in his voice. "It's okay to rest now, Dafydd. You're safe with me. I'll make sure no harm comes to you, especially not from me."

A voice inside him said not to trust the man. Pretty words meant nothing, rare as they were. Instead, he gave into the sleepiness brought on by his indulgences and found it was easy not to worry after all.

Chapter Six

"I think you're absolutely crazy to do this, MacLerie." Val gestured toward the controlled chaos of more than a dozen people making themselves and their belongings comfortable on Malcolm's yacht.

"It's going to be very cramped for sure, but we'll manage. It's a good thing the lads are small. They can easily fit into the bunks of what normally serves as the crew's cabins or on the saloon's couches, if need be. With Duncan showing up from time to time, we may play a few rounds of musical chairs."

"Yeah, but none of we men will want to sleep apart from our boys, so I for one am going to be getting acquainted with the floor, I expect. This yacht may be huge by human standards but our kind fills up a lot of space."

"Och, you're a tough one. I'm not worried about your creature comforts. The lads are already having a fine time, and if that's all that this trip accomplishes, it will be worth it. They deserve the fun."

"You're right about that. The human ability to enjoy themselves with such abandon is one of their more admirable qualities." Val paused, his eagle eyes homing in on Mackie. "I like it when he enjoys himself. He hasn't had enough of that in his short life."

Malcolm clapped his friend on the shoulder. "You're an old softy after all, aren't you, Val?"

Val grimaced and shook off Malcolm's hold. "Only with Mackie. With everyone else, I'm the angel of death…and don't forget it."

Malcolm barked out a laugh. "I wouldn't dream of it." Unfortunately, this trip wasn't entirely for pleasure, and he couldn't lose sight of that fact. "I don't suppose we have any more word from Duncan about the source of those guns?"

"No, but I've pored through the intel I collected on Dracul's early gunrunning. I'd forgotten that I had pinpointed a possible cave system along the uninhabited shore north of the town. Dracul used to bring their boats in there undetected by the humans." He ran his hand down his Mohawk. "Then again, that was pre-World War I. There's nothing to say that spot isn't overgrown with fancy houses now."

"Well, it will give us something to do while the lads frolic on the beach. I expect they'll enjoy that and I know we won't join them in that particular pastime."

Val sneered. "I hate Earth's sun, especially during the summer. No hat or pair of sunglasses is sufficient to block the fucker from giving me a monstrous headache. It's a good thing it will be going on evening when we arrive today."

"I was lucky to find a slip opening up, but as it's not available until later, I intend to take it easy on the helm.

This may turn out to be a fun holiday after all, and nothing else."

Val gave him the side-eye. "You really believe that?"

"In my gut? No. I'm expecting trouble, make no mistake. I'd like to think it's simply a matter of adjusting to the new reality of Dracul being vanquished. My head tells me we've got nothing to fash about, but my intestines are giving me a right hard time."

"It doesn't sit well, does it? Kind of like eating spoiled food or something."

Malcolm chuckled. "Not a bad analogy. And with Petru and Bran out there, a case of mild indigestion is certainly warranted, I'd say."

Their mirth ended when Dafydd approached. It had surprised Malcolm that the Welshman had agreed to join them. He was pleased, because it would give Brenin more chances to speak with his friend, if he wanted. With all the activity since they'd arrived, he didn't think that had happened yet.

"I'm sorry to disturb you, gentleman." Dafydd's meek demeanor was a sad reminder of his hellish life with Dracul. The way he placidly, yet with resolution, held on to his squirming hybrid son was impressive. The babe was almost as big as his father. Poor Dafydd was a man of the middle-ages, short and thin. He was beautiful, too, although Malcolm barely noticed. Nothing compared to his lovely Brenin in his mind.

"Not at all, laddie. How can I help?"

"Oh, I don't need anything, thank you. Rather, I was going to say that Idris and I don't need an entire stateroom to ourselves. We can make do in one of those little rooms with the bunk beds down near the engine room. Demi should have the one Lucien showed me instead, for when Sergeant Duncan joins him."

"That's kind of you to offer, Dafydd, but you and Idris need the space more, I'd say. I've no doubt Demi and Duncan would agree." *Won't being cramped in a windowless place be upsetting to the former slave? He's suffered too much confinement in his life as it is.*

"Brenin, my love," he called out before the Welshman could argue the point. "Won't you come help Dafydd get settled?"

The idea worked. Brenin hurried over, looking more relaxed than he had in a while. Being with all of these happy boys and not stuck in Malcolm's shadow twenty-four-seven was doing him a world of good.

He shot both Malcolm and Dafydd a smile. "Sure thing. Where are your bags?"

"Over there," Dafydd replied with a jerk of his head. He was busy now containing the babe, who'd managed to all but turn himself upside down within his father's embrace.

Out of the corner of his eye, Malcolm saw Val gesture briefly with a flick of his hand. Mackie came skipping up in the next instance.

"Hey, how about I deal with the Tasmanian Devil for you, Dafydd, while you settle in."

Dafydd looked skeptical. "Really? He's being chopsy this morning."

Mackie bounced on the balls of his feet. "If that's a Welsh way of saying he's acting like a toddler, I agree. No worries," he added, holding out his hands. "I've got mega babysitting chops. Come on, little man."

Mackie plucked Idris out of Dafydd's arms with ease and pretended he was an airplane as he whisked the kid away.

"Well, that settles that," Malcolm said. Then, turning to Val, he mouthed, *"Thanks."*

"Come on, Dafydd. Let's get your stuff." Brenin waved for his friend to follow.

"That was clever of you to put them together. It was almost not obvious."

He smacked his friend on the arm. "Och, thanks for that."

"Sorry, I have no filter, as you know. Maybe it was only clear to me what you were trying to do," Val told him.

"You did your bit getting the kid out of the way. I must confess I have my worries there. You should see the kind of trouble the hybrid we took in gives us. A mischievous little bugger, he is. I'm not sure how possible it is to undo the problems both nature and nurture heaped upon these creatures of Dracul."

"Don't say that in front of Lucien, in particular. He'll have your balls for it. He's the one that's taken the brunt of Dafydd's recovery and the care of the brat. What progress you see is his doing.

"I wish I shared his optimism, but I feel as you do," Val went on. "I'm not sure there's any real hope for Dafydd, either. Can a human recover from such a thing? It doesn't seem like it from what I've observed of the guy. Not that I spend much time with him — or any time, really. I can't imagine shooting his own son has made things easier on him, and frankly, I hate to say it, but if I wake up one day to find that he's done himself and the baby in, I won't be surprised."

Malcolm recoiled at the idea. "You dinnae mean that, really?"

Val shrugged. "You know me, always looking for trouble. It's not my call, luckily. And who knows? With

Brenin to talk to and Paz popping in on occasion, the guy might prove me a nervous nelly."

He slapped Malcolm on his back. "I've had as much of this hoopla as I can stand. I'm going to pore over my files on this Putnam's Cove. Do you need any help getting underway?"

Malcolm shook his head. "I've got it covered. Thanks all the same."

As he watched Val walk away, he couldn't help thinking about what the guy had said about Dafydd. What if the boy couldn't overcome his past? And if he couldn't, did that say anything about Brenin and their future? He wanted to change him for very selfish reasons, so that they could live a long life together. Yet even though Brenin had agreed, he hadn't managed more than a few sips of Malcolm's blood so far. And if he ever did bear Malcolm a son, would there always be that worry that he might someday turn on the babe?

It was too much to ponder and caused a hurt deep inside that was pure torture. Besides, he had a job to do. The damn yacht had every modern convenience but it still couldn't drive itself.

* * * *

"What do you think?" Brenin asked the question while Dafydd stood in the middle of the stateroom, taking it all in. He hoped his friend would enjoy his time onboard.

"It's grand, isn't it? More than Idris and I need, like I told your mun, not that he listened. They never do, these aliens." He tossed first one bag, then the other, onto the bed. "I can't believe I've accumulated enough stuff to warrant three suitcases."

Brenin added the one that he carried to the pile and placed the folded-up portable crib on the floor. "It's not only you, though, is it? A lot of this must be for Idris."

"Yes, you're right there." Dafydd sat near the pillows and ran his hand along the comforter. "One thing being enslaved by the monster did was get me accustomed to the finer things in life. This boat is almost as big as the village I was born in." He glanced at Brenin. "How was it you managed with just the two of you on the journey over?"

Brenin shrugged and leaned against the closed door. "Malcolm did most of the work, and you know how fast he can get around, like all of them." He'd run himself ragged trying to keep up with the hybrid back home.

"I do, yes. I find I'm much quicker than a normal human, too, now that I've been given the freedom to go about on my own and test the limits of my good health."

Brenin rubbed his thumb along the seam of his jeans. "Are you drinking blood?"

"No." The reply was short and sharp. "I don't want that anymore and stopping doesn't seem to have done me any harm."

"That's good to hear." It was one of Brenin's fears. Now that he'd started to take Malcolm's blood in small quantities, he worried about what would happen to him if he changed his mind. "I, ah, do feel something of it. Stronger, anyway."

Dafydd's gaze flew up. "You're taking his blood, mun? Did he make you?"

Because he could hear the worry in his friend's tone — and the fury — he pushed away from the door to go to him. "No, he didn't. I swear. It was my choice."

After shoving a bag aside, he settled next to Dafydd. "After it was all over, you know, the battle or whatever, I was so happy. I love Malcolm, and oh, Dafydd, he showed me how it can be between two men. How it *should* be. And it's amazing."

Dafydd stared at the floor. "If you say so."

"I do! I wish you could experience it for yourself."

A visible shudder ran through Dafydd. "Not bloody likely. And anyway, if he makes you happy, why are you so sad?"

Brenin's stomach dropped. "It's that obvious?"

"It is, yes—to me at least. I don't think the others have noticed. Why should they? They haven't gone through what we did."

"Jase did, though, didn't he? And Mackie and Quinn had it rough for a while, I think." They all seemed utterly happy now. *What's wrong with me that I'm not?*

"They suffered only at the hands of humans, though, yeah? It's not the same. At least it doesn't seem like it would be to me."

"Maybe." He wasn't sure that it was as simple as that. Human beings were despicable to their own. The one difference between his own experience and something like what Jase had gone through was the blood sucking. Perhaps that variation was all it took. Or possibly the other boy was coping with the same type of trauma better than he was.

"I thought I was okay," he confessed. "I'd found a way to find pleasure with Malcolm without the shadow of Dracul hanging over us. Then it started creeping up on me."

"What did, exactly?"

"Anxiety, I guess. And memories. I got jumpy and moody. If Malcolm touches me unexpectedly, I practically pop out of my skin. Sometimes for a brief second when I look at him, I see…you know who. It's only a flash of confusion, but it's enough to be upsetting. If it's not me who initiates the contact, I can barely stand it sometimes. I see the hurt and worry in Malcolm's eyes. It makes me feel terrible. I hate that he thinks I don't want his touch."

"But do you? Really now?"

"I said as much, didn't I?" He glowered. "Sorry. I don't mean to snap at you, of all people. You saved my life and have much more to be upset about than I do."

"You don't ever have to apologize to me, *of all people*. And I don't think that's how misery is measured, by who got it worse than another. It's all personal, isn't it? You were tortured by Dracul for months. I was for centuries. So what? After the first few weeks, it's all the same. The shock wears off and the numbness sets in. Hope dies."

"That's not true, not for you. You never gave up. If you had, I wouldn't be here."

Dafydd gave him a wan smile. "Ah, well, planning ways to thwart and escape the monster helped pass the time. Living for centuries can be boring, you know. You're sure you want it?"

"I know I want Malcolm for as long as I can have him. I just don't understand what my problem is. Doc MacPhee gives it a fancy name — post traumatic stress syndrome."

"I've had that thrown at me and all, too. What does it matter what they call it? They can't snap their fingers and make it go away, can they?"

"They would if they could. We're lucky to be part of this family, Dafydd. They are as loyal and kind as Dracul was deceitful and wicked."

"True enough." His mouth formed a thin line and his brows furrowed. "There is something that Harry gives me that helps."

Twisting around, Dafydd grabbed one of his bags and opened a side pocket. He pulled out a small, plastic bottle and shook it like a rattle.

"Pills, then?" Brenin asked with a frown. "Doc MacPhee offered me something that she said might help, but I didn't like the idea of taking anything. Where does it end, that? You're on them for life, maybe."

Dafydd rolled the bottle between his fingers and thumb. "Don't know, and I don't much care. For now, this plus a bit of brandy gets me through."

"I don't think you're supposed to mix that stuff."

Dafydd laughed mirthlessly. "That's what Ric said."

"Dr. Paz? He knows?"

"Followed me, didn't he? Nosey."

"Concerned."

"Whatever. Anyway, he promised not to tell if I agreed to come on this trip. He's going to check up on me, even though he didn't say as much. I should mind more than I do."

"He cares for you. It could be that fresh start you're looking for." As he gave the advice, Brenin wondered how he dared, in the face of his own inability to settle in with the life Malcolm had served him on a platter.

"Who says I am?" With a sigh, he tossed the bottle onto the nightstand. "I'm just trying to get through each day and take care of Idris. It's survival, the same way it was back in Wales, only with less fear and no pain."

That was as good a way of summing up their lives as any, he supposed, except he wanted more than just getting through the days. Most of the time, he had it better than Dafydd was describing, with real happiness and purpose that was only occasionally disturbed by the lingering effects of his captivity. Perhaps he'd been too hasty in rejecting some chemical help.

"Do you... Would you mind if I tried one of those?"

Dafydd's expression turned canny, a distinct change from the normally placid demeanor the man presented. It reminded Brenin of the night he'd escaped.

"I'll share all right, but I need something in return."

Wary, he asked, "Like what?"

"Scotch. There must be loads of it onboard. I couldn't pack anything with Lucien hanging around and helping. If you can get me a bottle of Malcolm's spirits, I'll share my pills with you. I'll give you one a day, even, because the liquor makes it work better," he added in when Brenin started to shake his head.

"It's dangerous, Dafydd, to mix the two. I know it is."

His friend batted the concern away. "I've been doing it for weeks. You have to be careful, mun, that's all. One pill and a couple of slugs of liquor is fine."

Brenin knew it was a terrible bargain to make. He should run right back to Malcolm and the others and tell them. Except he couldn't betray Dafydd that way. The two of them shared a bond that no one else would understand. Not really. Dafydd could have reveled in Brenin's misery back in Wales, happy to have someone else distracting their brutal master. He hadn't, though. Instead, he'd yielded his own careful plans of escape to give Brenin a chance at freedom. It had been an act of compassion and generosity that few in the history of humanity would ever experience. Whatever else Dafydd might be, he was noble in the finest sense of the word. Brenin couldn't bring himself to betray him, even for his own good.

"It helps, you say?"

Dafydd's eyes closed and his face went lax. "Just thinking of it makes life bearable." He opened them again. "It's not forever, Brenin. You want to enjoy being with your mun again, don't you?"

"Y-yes, but…"

"No buts. Try it. If you don't like what it does, then stop."

"Okay, maybe once." A voice inside his head screamed at him that he was making a terrible mistake. It was one thing to turn a blind eye to Dafydd's action, another to join in. Ignoring his own inner warning, he reached for the pills.

Dafydd grabbed his hand. "Not yet. It's too early in the day. Plus, you need to get the Scotch first."

He looked his countryman in the eyes and saw determination and hardness. Again, it reminded him of the night Dafydd had sent him fleeing to save his life. The guy had been right at the time, and Brenin had put aside his fear and blindly followed his direction. It had worked out then. *Why not now?*

Pulling his hand back, he nodded. "All right. If you say so. I'll wait until we're underway before grabbing the Scotch. Malcolm has a ton of it and won't miss one bottle, as you say — or frankly ten. Not that we should drink that much," he quickly added.

"Of course not," Dafydd agreed before standing. "I should unpack and retrieve Idris. Mackie is that kind to watch him, but he's my responsibility." He smiled, a genuine look of happiness. "It will be nice having a beach to play on. I've never done such a thing before. I bet Idris will love it. Don't you think?" Dafydd opened a bag and started pulling things out.

Brenin did the same, glad for the change of subject and for the distraction a mundane task brought. "I'm sure of it. It's been ages since I've been to one. It's ever so much fun."

That's right. He should focus on the healthy choice of playing under the sun and not on the lure of that little bottle of pills.

* * * *

Ric jumped out of his Lyft ride, dragging his bags with him. Although he knew MacLerie wasn't going to take off without him, he felt guilty holding everyone up. He was in such a rush that it took him a moment to realize he was about to board something right out of a reality TV show about the rich and famous. It was nothing like the old fishing trawler that they'd taken to Wales. It was the kind of ship where one had cocktails on the lido deck, whatever the hell that was.

He craned his neck as he hurried down the dock and saw endless rows of shiny windows, brass and highly polished wood trim gleaming in the bright sun. Music was playing somewhere inside, the sort one heard in the club. He figured the boys had already gotten the party started with their men taking in the scene with equal parts indulgence and desire.

His theory was confirmed in the next instant when Mackie, wearing only his collar and a pink speedo that was modest by his standards, leaned over the railing and waved.

"Hey, Dr. Ric! Come aboard. This party boat is ready to set sail."

Waving back, he shouted, "Thanks for waiting."

He picked up his speed and plowed his way up the gangplank. Val was there to greet him, sunglasses and ball cap pulled down low to obscure his face. He repeated his thanks to the man.

"No worries, Doc. Happy to have you along."

"I got lucky. One of my colleagues was willing to switch schedules with me. I have four days off." He placed his duffle and the gift bag he carried onto the deck. "Can I help in any way?"

"Nope. MacLerie is a one-man operation with me to play swabbie. Go on into the saloon and get your bearings. Dafydd's in there," he added almost casually. Almost.

"Thanks."

Picking up his bags again, he sucked in a few deep breaths to calm himself. His half-formed plans made him nervous, but the first test of them would come from Dafydd seeing him. If the guy balked too much at his presence, then the rest of the scheme would go to shit immediately, and he'd have to fall back on simply ratting Dafydd out to Harry. He really didn't want to have to do that, but he also wasn't going to simply watch to see if Dafydd overdosed.

I wasn't willing to let him die in Wales, and I'm for damn sure not going to allow it now.

He walked out of the heat of the day into the cool of the air-conditioned saloon that could have easily accommodated the old nineteenth century ruling families of New York. MacLerie had spared no expense, and the sheer luxury of the setting made even Club Lux look like a tacky bar. And as he'd imagined, the boys had already created a party atmosphere with music and dancing. Each one of them was in various states of provocative clothing, except for Brenin, whose kilt seemed quite sedate in comparison to the thongs dotting the room. Alex and Emil sat next to each other, tracking their boys' movements with hungry expressions, while Harry and Lucien cuddled nearby. They all seemed perfectly at ease with the open displays of sexuality. Ric envied their lack of inhibition.

Dafydd, of course, was his main focus, and he was another outlier, dressed in a T-shirt and jeans, sitting on the floor in a far corner with Idris. He was watching his son play with alphabet blocks. But his gaze shot up and over to Ric within a few seconds of his entering the room. It was rather gratifying the way his presence was noted so quickly. It gave Ric some hope that Dafydd was more interested in him than he let on.

Maybe he's simply leery of me.

Regardless, there was no way Dafydd would be pleased to see him once he understood the reason why he had moved mountains to be able to take off with the rest of them. Vincente hadn't hidden his displeasure, notwithstanding that Ric's shifts were covered and wouldn't inconvenience the head pathologist in any way. He got the impression that his boss didn't think he was dedicated to his job. That wasn't true. It was very simply that Dafydd's safety took precedence over all other considerations. Ric was prepared to lose his job if it came to that, so long as he kept Dafydd safe.

He offered up a smile as he weaved through the tangle of dancing boys. Dafydd narrowed his eyes, then he broke contact with Ric and returned his attention to the baby. Idris took that moment to smack down what he'd built.

"That's not what they're for, Idris." Dafydd patiently picked up the blocks and put them in a neat row.

"Here, he might like this instead." Ric set his duffle aside and, kneeling in front of the two, pulled a box out of the gift bag. "I bought this a couple of days ago on impulse. I was going to bring it to Maine when I visited. Luckily, I was able to free my schedule and join you now." He smiled brightly while holding his breath.

Dafydd rolled his eyes. "You've come to keep tabs on me, then?"

"That's one way of looking at it," Ric replied cheerily, determined that his presence not cause alarm in the others. "Shall we open this?"

Dafydd shrugged. "As you like."

"Oh, I hope it's Idris that does the liking. See here? It's a garage." He spoke to the child, who eyed him with a look of suspicion that eerily mimicked his father's.

Wisely, he'd opened it before so all he had to do was flip the two halves of the top and tug the plastic building out. He set it on the floor then proceeded to unwrap the little people and vehicles that went with it.

"See, Idris? You put the car here, crank this bit and watch." He sent the car rolling down the ramp.

The baby shrieked with laughter and smacked his chubby hands together. "'Gain!"

"You got it, boss." Ric repeated the play then showed the boy other features of the toy. "You try it," he said, pushing it closer to where Idris sat.

The first thing the kid did was pick up the car and slobber all over it. After that, he got serious and went about playing with the thing exactly as Ric had showed him. It was both satisfying and disquieting. The alien intelligence of the child was obvious when one watched him like this. He didn't have much of the clumsiness of a human toddler, nor the need to try repeatedly to master a task. Still, he was well-occupied and amused and that was the whole point of the purchase.

Ric leaned back on his hands. "I hope you don't mind my taking the liberty."

Dafydd looked at him from under his lashes, expressing a coyness that went straight to Ric's dick. "Certainly not. Anything that keeps the boy busy is fine by me. What I do mind is having a jailer again."

"That's not what I am meant to be." Ric hated the idea of Dafydd feeling caged, yet what choice did Ric have? "I'm here to help."

"Is that what you tell yourself?"

Ric nearly flinched at the bitter tone. Understanding how both trauma and possible addiction worked, he kept his emotions under control. "Let me ask you a question in return. Did you ask Harry to give you a new round of pills?"

He could see in the way Dafydd's eyes darted away what the answer was. Before he could say more, the boat got underway with a lurch. The boys whooped or shrieked in various ways, but Dafydd swayed to one side at the sudden movement. Ric put his hand out without thinking to catch him. Dafydd jerked away from the oncoming touch and leaned against the wall.

Ric snatched his hand back. "Sorry." He turned his attention to Idris while Dafydd caught his breath and composed himself. The baby sat playing, unaffected by the sounds and movements around him.

"Nothing bothers him," Dafydd said in a slightly breathless voice. "And Harry did give me more pills. What of it? It's my choice to take them." He hesitated before adding, "I didn't bring any liquor, if that's your worry."

Ric switched his gaze back to him. "It is, and please don't insult my intelligence by assuming I have forgotten MacLerie's most excellent Scotch." He looked pointedly at the bar in the opposite corner. "I expect there's plenty to be found there."

Dafydd shrugged then stared at him in silence. His eyes held defiance, but more than that, there was a hint of fear. It made Ric's heart ache and he didn't want to be the cause of it. He also couldn't live with just letting Dafydd go on doing what was so clearly dangerous for him.

Ric sat forward and dangled his hands between his splayed knees. "Look… I'm worried about you. That's all. No, I have to be honest here. I care about you." *Okay, so leaving out the word 'love' isn't exactly being totally honest.* "And I respect your autonomy to make your own decisions, to a point. That's why I'm going to give you a choice. Either you accept my presence or I'm going to have to tell Harry about your drinking habits. He'll take the pills away. You know he will.

"You can take the medicine or drink, but you can't do both. It's practically suicidal." He took in a deep breath and shoved it out again. "Maybe you see this as being high-handed, and I won't try to convince you otherwise. Still, that's the deal." He made himself look Dafydd in the eye.

To his credit, the boy did the same back to him, unflinching and with anger shining through. "You don't give me much choice. I don't want all these men who have been kind to me to worry or watch me any closer than they do. So, what exactly is your bargain?"

This was the tricky part. "I've given it some thought and it's the nights that are the hardest for you, right?"

When Dafydd gave a curt nod, he continued. "I simply propose that I spend those with you."

Dafydd barked out a laugh—a short, almost ugly sound. Idris stopped playing for a second and looked at his father before going on. "And sure you do. A nice excuse to get yourself into my bed."

Ric tamped down his immediate anger at the accusation, if only because it was partly true, much to his shame. "I'm going to sleep on the floor," he ground out. "I'm only going to make sure you take the prescribed amount of pills and don't drink. That's all."

"And how long do you think you can follow me around like a puppy, making sure I'm a good boy?"

Ric rubbed his eyes. "As long as I can, which isn't very. I do have to get back to Boston and work, even if you all stay up there for weeks. I can drive up every night, if necessary." *If I rent a car, that is, which will put a big dent in my bank account, but fuck that.* Money didn't matter when it came to Dafydd.

"You're daft, mun. You can't keep it up forever."

"Do I have to?" Ric leaned forward in an effort to convey the depth of his concern. "Dafydd, please let us help you. We're not the enemy. *I'm* not."

Closing his eyes, Dafydd rocked his head back and forth. "If you think I can tell the difference, you don't know me at all. Do as you like, then. I don't care."

Well, that was a permission of sorts. Ric only hoped that he could work some kind of miracle in the next couple of days. Dafydd's very life was on the line, and in a way, that meant his was too.

Chapter Seven

Stuffed from Emil's amazing and bountiful lunch, Ric was surprised to find himself part of what he thought of as the war council. He sat with the other men around a large table on which Val had spread maps and aerial photos of the coast north of Putnam's Cove. Dafydd was safely tucked in his stateroom, having a nap with Idris. Ric had searched the place, guiltily, for liquor, then had doled out a pill to Dafydd while taking the rest of the bottle with him. It sat snug in his front pocket, a constant reminder of how he'd dared to barge into Dafydd's life and take control over it.

Only in this one way and only to keep him safe.

He figured Dafydd would never forgive him for it, but that hardly mattered. A living, healthy Dafydd who forever scorned Ric's love was far preferable to a dead one. Ric could survive the former, whereas the latter would be a tragedy that he couldn't recover from, not to mention the toll it would take on Idris when he got old enough to understand it all.

"Are you sure Brenin can drive this thing?" Val asked, taking Ric out of his own head, thank God.

"Aye, he's a quick study and took the helm for much of our voyage over. Stick to your lane, Val, and tell us what we're looking at."

The bouncer huffed before walking them through it. Ric leaned in to study what the others could more easily see with their alien eyesight.

"This is the spot that Dracul used over a hundred years ago to run arms." Val pointed to a spot by the shore that was a series of jagged lines. "There's a narrow path through the water for a shallow-draft boat to navigate. It leads into what appears to be a squat opening at the base of the cliff, but if you keep going, it opens up to a wide pool with a cave system beyond, although I don't know the extent of it.

"It was never good for much except the kind of arms that anarchists and the beginnings of organized crime were interested in obtaining. As far as I know, he abandoned it for more lucrative efforts abroad. In the last few decades he certainly ramped up the smuggling of higher-grade weapons to places like the Middle East. Little Putnam Cove had evolved into a tourist destination in the mid-twentieth century anyway. It's not so quiet anymore."

"It's very popular with my friends," Ric offered. "It's easy and quick to get to and very gay-friendly, as I mentioned before. I know it quite well, actually."

Alex turned his gaze on him. "We have considered that fact, Doctor, and are delighted you could join us today. Obviously, if any of us parade into town asking questions, we'll get noticed quickly. If one of Dracul's minions has reopened this channel for gunrunning, word of our arrival would possibly spread quickly."

"While no one will notice one more gay human, hanging out at bars and dishing on the local gossip," Ric finished for him.

"Exactly. I hope you don't mind," Alex added with a pointed look that nicely conveyed that they expected only one answer.

"Not in the least. As I've done twice before now, I'm all in on this. It's for my people, after all. I can't allow aliens to wreak havoc."

"Maybe not," Harry interjected. "This could be purely a human problem, and we don't expect you to take risks."

"We'll have you wired," Val confirmed.

"Glad to hear it." Ric swallowed back his natural nerves. He was a doctor, not a spy, as Bones might have said on his beloved *Star Trek*. "What exactly am I supposed to be asking about?"

Val moved his finger over to a print-out of Google Maps that showed a rambling house along the coast. "This, for starters. As I suspected, the vacant coast where the caves are has been built up in the last hundred years. This house in particular is right above where we want to explore. We need to find out who lives there and whether they are currently occupying it."

"Do you think they'd notice if you rowed in at night?" Ric asked, somewhat skeptical his alien friends could stay under the radar.

Malcolm nodded. "Possibly. That's our worry. My yacht has a good-sized tender onboard that we can use to approach the caves from the sea. But it would be powerfully awkward to explain ourselves if we're seen."

"It could also be that if this cave system is currently being used as a way-station for gunrunning, it's because the owner of the land is one of Dracul's men," Val added. "Or, a human coopted by them. That was Dracul's MO and there's no reason to doubt the others would use it now that he's been eliminated."

Ric tapped one finger on the table. "If there's a guy hanging around Putnam's Cove that looks like you, as you said, it would be noticed. I can ferret out that kind of information in five minutes. You guys are a gay man's wet dream." He blinked at his own boldness. "Sorry, I hope that wasn't weird or insulting."

Emil patted him on the back. "Not to worry, Doctor. If it weren't for gay men, we'd be very lonely on this planet."

Ric had asked many questions of Harry about their way of life, not the least of which had been why they never pursued women. He supposed that even with women gaining in size and strength and the ready availability of birth control, they'd fallen into the habit of forming relationships with only men, not that it mattered now.

"There's a club by the beach that's the perfect place for gossip. I'll go there as soon as we arrive, if that makes sense."

"It does," Alex agreed.

"And I'll wire you up once we're in range of docking so you'll be good to go quickly," Val supplied.

There was more discussion about the how and the when of their exploring the caves after dark. Ric tuned it out as it had no impact on his job and he had nothing of use to add. Instead, he spent the time worrying about Dafydd and wondering how he might finesse a discussion with Harry about keeping an eye on the boy in his absence. It was silly, in a way. Dafydd and the others had been managing just fine without him on a daily basis. Something about his newfound knowledge concerning the pills had left him feeling it was up to him to solve all Dafydd's problems.

His worry must have shown, because the moment the group broke up, Harry approached. "Are you troubled, Ric? Is it Dafydd?"

Ric snorted. "I guess I'm not good at hiding my feelings."

"No, and that's all to the good. How can I help?" *How. Not 'can I?'* Harry wasn't one to shy away from a problem and his confidence was inspiring.

And yet, Ric had made a deal of sorts with Dafydd. He couldn't go back on it. Perhaps he could use partial truths to get his way.

"I'm going to be spending the night in Dafydd's stateroom." He waited for recriminations. When none came, he blundered on. "It's to help him with Idris, as well as…you know, keeping him company. He was cooped up for so long that any change in location is bound to be disturbing to him."

Harry continued to say nothing. He merely stood staring at Ric almost unblinkingly.

Ric resisted the urge to squirm. "And it will make me feel better, to be honest."

"You love him." Harry's quiet statement sent Ric's heart into tachycardia.

"U-umm," was all he could stammer out.

Harry put a gentle hand on Ric's arm. "It's all right. I understand what it's like to love a brutalized boy. It's part guilt, part euphoria and a great deal of desperate hope that someday he could rise above his experience and love you back."

"Yes," Ric whispered, relieved to have his feelings laid out so elegantly.

Harry leaned in, making their quiet discussion even more intimate. "I trust you to do right by the boy, and please rest easy that we will watch over him when you aren't around."

It was on the tip of Ric's tongue to tell Harry how wrong he was in his diligence. He swallowed it back and said rather, "Thank you."

Harry patted his arm and pulled away. "We have a few hours before we arrive. How about we sit outside and enjoy the view?"

"Doesn't the sun bother you?"

"That's what umbrellas are for. Besides, Lucien is already out there. After all these years together, I still love being with him — and worry too, frankly. That is a feeling that never goes away, I'm afraid."

"Something to look forward to," Ric lamented, although in truth, he hoped he had a chance to do it. If so, it would mean Dafydd had let him into his life.

* * * *

No one seemed to mind that Dafydd hung around the pilot house as the men listened in on Ric's evening out. He'd expected to be shooed away at first sight, but Alex had merely nodded before turning his attention back to the speaker. Dafydd had slunk over to one corner, grateful for the chance to be a party to the monitoring, while also being irritated at himself for even caring.

Ric had taken over, after all — quietly, insistently and somewhat apologetically. Dafydd should have been furious at the man. Part of him was. The other, however, was just relieved. Someone else was in charge of his life again, and there was a strange kind of liberty that came with it. One pill only had been allotted to him that afternoon, which had pissed him off at the time. But he'd slept well and had woken without the usual heavy head. Idris seemed calmer, as well, as if sensing that Ric's even-tempered command was to be respected. He was playing in the saloon with his new toy under Mackie's watchful eye. Dafydd was free to do what he liked, and that had somehow ended with him coming there.

"Hey, Ric, first visit for the season?"

"Hi, Danny. You know it. One-Eyed Jacks is always stop number one. Looks like things are off to great start."

"Can't complain, although a lot of the regulars are family men now, bringing their kids. That means no clubbing. Your usual?"

"Sounds good, thanks."

There were sounds of music and multiple voices, raucous laughter, the clinking of glasses. Dafydd could only imagine what the scene looked like, and that was based on what he'd caught on TV or the Internet. The thought of being crushed into a small space with lots of men made his stomach clench. Ric seemed relaxed, though. Just one more way in which they were different.

He's not for me even if I were looking for a lover, which I'm not!

"Here you are, one Cape-Codder."

"Hmm, thanks. Just what I need after the trip up. So, what's the latest?"

"Nothing in particular. Like I said, lots more families. Lots more building, too."

"Houses, you mean? I was kind of thinking of buying up here myself."

"Oh, yeah. The doctor gig must be lucrative, huh?"

Ric chuckled. "Well, I'm no brain surgeon, but I do okay. I figure the prices in town are sky-high. Maybe I can find something farther north, just outside of town."

"Those are more affordable. Bigger lots, too, although anything on the coast is going to cost you bank."

There was an interlude while the bartender helped other customers, probably. The noise level picked up, and there were long minutes of nothing more than Ric occasionally shouting out a greeting.

"Another round?"

"Why not? Say, do you know of any property for sale? Or do you know any owners that are likely to sell out? Some of the older men must be thinking about it, although I expect developers have already swooped in like vultures. I bet they stand out among the usual crowd."

"You got that right, except they do their best to fit in. There are lots of *GQ* types trying to dress down. Some of them are even decent lays." There was a shared chuckle. "I don't know anything in particular, but I'll keep my ears open."

"Thanks."

With his hands jammed into his front pockets, Alex paced away from the group, heading in Dafydd's direction. He stiffened in reflexive fear. Alex must have detected something of his reaction, because he abruptly changed course and peered out of the window at the harbor instead.

"That answers one question," he said to the room at large. "If any of our kind were traipsing about town, surely Ric's loquacious bartender would have mentioned it."

"They're good at hiding." Dafydd blurted out the observation then shrank back when everyone in the room turned their gazes on him.

"How do you mean?" Alex's question was asked in a very gentle tone and his face showed no aggression.

Dafydd licked his lips. "I don't know. I shouldn't have spoken out of turn."

"No, it's fine, really." Alex pulled out his hands and put them behind his back. "Please tell us what you know. Your observations from your time with Dracul could be invaluable to us."

Dafydd dropped his gaze and tucked strands of hair behind his ear to gain some time while gathering his courage. He didn't like being the center of attention. That had always been a bad thing. He had to work at reminding himself that things were different now.

"Dracul and Petru created protocols long ago of how to go about their nasty business without drawing attention to themselves on a personal level. Once television then the Internet became available, it made it both more important to hide in the shadows and all the easier for them to operate remotely. You saw it already with…"

His voice caught and he nearly staggered as the vision of Cadoc crumbling into dust overwhelmed him.

Harry was by his side in a split second, hovering without touching. "It's all right. Take your time. We understand what you mean. Would you like some water?"

Dafydd shook his head. "No, I'm fine." He straightened and swallowed down his misery and shoved away a sudden longing for Ric. He didn't need the man's comfort. He could take care of himself…mostly.

"They use human surrogates. You know this, surely. If…if Bran is here, say, he's smart enough to have coopted a local boy or two to do his bidding. No one in town would likely have ever seen him. And don't look for recent activity, either. They started planning decades in advance. If they acquired property for smuggling, it would have happened long ago."

Val snapped his fingers, the sound sufficiently loud to startle Dafydd. "Right. That house I pointed out was built shortly after World War II. It's only ever had one owner."

The man that Dafydd thought of as Alex's version of Petru crossed the room in a blur and started tapping on his laptop. For a few minutes, everyone's attention was split between him and Ric's voice coming over the surveillance equipment. Dafydd was simply happy not to be noticed anymore.

"Yeah, I see it now," Val called out. "It's owned by Scotty Moran, who bought it when he was a twenty-year-old veteran from the Midwest, according to what I can find in the public record. He's a farm boy who never married and whose paper-trail is thin to say the least."

"That fits." Once again, Dafydd's mouth ran faster than his good judgment. "Someone would have seduced him, set him up for life then threatened him if he showed any signs of wanting out."

"He must be in his nineties," Harry observed.

Val nodded. "There's no record of a transfer of ownership, so that indicates he's alive and nearly ninety-two."

"That's a long time to be loyal," Emil interjected.

"They know how to ensure it," Dafydd replied with his stomach tying into knots at the memory of how brutally a boy could be encouraged to be faithful to the end. Feeling hemmed in, he pushed away from the wall. "If you'll excuse me, I need some fresh air." He didn't wait for permission. He just bolted.

* * * *

"Are you sure you're okay with this, Dafydd?" Brenin kept his voice low, although it was impossible to have any real privacy with so many aliens wandering about with their exceptional hearing.

"Sure, it's fine. Ric is sleeping on the floor, so he's the worse for the bargain. It means I can't share any of my pills and I'm that sorry."

"Don't be." When Dafydd had spilled what had happened with Paz, Brenin's first reaction had been one of relief. His intention of trading Dafydd's pills with booze had weighed on his mind all day. Now that there was no chance of it, he felt better. It wasn't his call anymore.

"It's the right thing he's doing. And doesn't it feel good to have the responsibility taken from you? That's my sense, anyway."

Dafydd frowned. "I don't want it to, but yes, it does. I'm a grown man, ancient by human standards. I should make my own decisions."

Brenin wanted to wrap his friend in a comforting hug. Knowing how that might be received, he refrained. "You'll get there. Give yourself time."

Wise words. I should take my own advice.

The doctor arrived at that moment and zeroed in on Dafydd like a laser.

"Did you enjoy your evening out, Dr. Paz?"

"Yes, although I think I've grown out of club-hopping already. I'm happy to be back." He turned his attention to Dafydd. "Where's Idris?"

"Playing with that stupid toy garage you got him, isn't he? Good luck tearing him away from it for the night."

Paz didn't appear fazed in the least. "Let's go put that to the test, shall we? Good night, Brenin."

"Good night."

With his own problems preying on his mind, Brenin put aside any worry for his friend. He went topside to the pilot house. Secure as the yacht was now that they had docked, he knew Malcolm would be running one more check of everything before turning in. He found his man, surprisingly, just standing and staring out at the town.

"It's bonnie, isn't it, laddie?"

Long past wondering how Malcolm could see out of the back of his head, Brenin went to join him. "It is, yes. Like a box of Easter chocolates, all pastel colors with scrumptious things inside."

Malcolm waited for Brenin to initiate physical contact before loosely wrapping his arm around Brenin's shoulders. "You and the other boys will be wanting to dander about tomorrow, I don't suppose."

"Unless Alex thinks we shouldn't."

"We've talked, and with the other lads not familiar for the most part to Dracul's men and with their laying low if they are in town, we figure it's fine. Stick to the streets closest to the docks and the beach. And much as it pains me, you should lose the kilt and dress like a typical American."

Brenin hated that idea. He'd become very fond of his Scottish form of dress. The mission, if they were even on one, came first, however. "All right." He pressed his head against Malcolm's arm. "Are you ready for bed?"

"Aye. Everything's secure, and it's been a long day."

"Not too long, though?" It would be easy to fall into a pattern of avoiding sex, and he didn't want that.

Malcolm grunted. "Never, laddie. I'm yours for the taking."

"Good."

They walked hand-in-hand down to their spacious stateroom. Most everyone else had already retired, although Emil and Jase were slow-dancing sweetly in the saloon. Once inside, Brenin pulled away and first undid his kilt then tugged off the T-shirt he'd put on against the chill of the evening. He let both pieces of clothing drop to the floor and stood in a relaxed pose while staring at Malcolm.

"Show me how much you want me," he commanded in a soft voice.

Malcolm's lips turned up and, in a blur of movement, he too was naked. With only the moonlight shining in from the large portholes, Brenin watched as Malcolm's cock rose from half-hard to fully erect. His large balls tucked up tightly to his body and his broad chest heaved with rapid breaths.

"You command my body, laddie. Never doubt that."

"I know. It's not you that I doubt. It's myself."

"Och, Brenin."

"Later. Please, let's fuck now and talk after. I have, um, things to say."

He made up his mind that very moment that he needed to come clean with Malcolm about what he'd contemplated. Seeing Dafydd struggle on his own had led him to understand it was the wrong way. Together, he and Malcolm could tackle anything. They'd brought down Dracul, hadn't they?

"Whatever you say."

"On the bed, then, face up. I'm going to ride your cock and you're going to drink my blood."

They both shivered at his words. Malcolm did as he'd ordered. That strong male was under his control, and what did that say about who was ultimately powerful?

While Malcolm pulled back the bedding to get into position, Brenin grabbed the lube from the nightstand. He squirted a dollop and reached around to coat his hole with it. A bit more eased his finger past the ring and into his channel. He didn't like to over-grease himself. There was some pleasure to be had in the bite of pain that came from Malcolm's dick stretching him wide.

His own shaft had risen and he gave it a few tugs as he approached the bed. "This is all the evidence either of us needs of how willing I am to be fucked by you."

Malcolm eyed him from where he lay in the middle of the bed. "You don't have to prove anything to me. All I want is for you to not fear me. Let me love you, Brenin."

"I don't and I will." He crawled up and over to him. Running his fingers down the ridges of his man's abs, he added, "However it needs to be done, I want to move closer to you, not farther away."

Brenin clasped the head of Malcolm's cock and rubbed his thumb across the slit. Pre-cum slicked the way. "I like this. It feels good when it's inside me." He slung a leg over Malcolm's hips to straddle him. "It's only that I need to be the one to decide when and how to put it there."

"A-aye." Malcolm's breathless reply was accompanied by a twitching of his hips. The man clenched his fingers in the sheet beneath him, testament to how hard he was working to keep himself under control.

Brenin teased the dick some more with his hand before tugging it toward him and lifting up. He'd become good at this, positioning the tip right outside his puckered hole, rubbing it back and forth, making both him and Malcolm a little crazy before sticking it in. His wince morphed into a smile as he slowly impaled himself on the shaft.

The girth of the thing stretched his channel all the way up. His dick jerked, spurting a bit of pre-cum, as the silky length of Malcolm's cock caressed Brenin's prostate. *Oh, such delicious pleasure.* To find it after all that he'd experienced was a wonder, and he was determined not to lose it. He sat flush on Malcolm's pelvis and stayed there. His only movement was to clench his hole in a pulsing rhythm designed to make Malcolm's eyes cross.

He succeeded.

"Och, laddie, if you're trying to test the limits of my control, you're doing a grand job of it. Please, for God's sake, move!"

Brenin laughed but wasn't so much of a sadist that he didn't heed the plea. He began to rock, then buck, up and down, riding the shaft with a proud skill he'd mastered. True to his promise, as always, Malcolm made no move. He let Brenin set the pace and did nothing more than arch his back and groan in pleasure. Brenin knew the man wanted more, needed more, and he wanted to give everything to him.

Lurching forward, he slammed his palms on either side of his lover's arms. "Take my vein, Malcolm." He twisted his head to one side to expose his neck.

The strike came fast, yet almost tenderly, as much as possible considering that Malcolm's fangs sank deep into Brenin's flesh. It made them both climax. Warm cum splashed into his ass while his own cock sent sticky fluid onto his stomach. There was no way to milk it dry with his hand without collapsing, but that was okay. He felt the orgasm with no less intensity, curling his fingers and toes and opening his mouth wide on a silent scream.

The tugging at his vein reverberated through every nerve-ending. It sent him into a languid state that turned his muscles to jelly. He collapsed into Malcolm with the surety that the man would hold him without binding him. In this state of coital bliss, there were no worries, only peace. He let go of…everything.

He came back to himself in the familiar position of being sprawled on top of Malcolm, his ass empty and his cock and balls depleted. Malcolm traced lazy circles across his back. He did the same on Malcolm's chest for a few seconds before pushing up to rest his head on his palm.

"Did I sleep long?"

"An hour or so. Do you want to freshen up in the loo before retiring?"

"Not yet." He eyed his lover. "Perhaps I'm not done having my way with you."

Malcolm chuckled. "Och, well then, we'll just lie here until you've made up your mind."

It would have been easy to either go to sleep for the night or numb himself with Malcolm's dick again.

Instead, he screwed up his courage to have the talk he'd mentioned earlier.

"I think I need some help, Malcolm. You know…professional, like Doc MacPhee has offered. Even though she's not a psychologist, she's a good listener and she can prescribe medicine."

"I thought you didnae want to take pills." Malcolm hesitated a second before carding his fingers through Brenin's hair.

"I didn't, but I hate how I feel, and I really hate how you have to be so careful with me, like just now. You shouldn't have to worry that something as simple as your brushing back my hair will freak me out."

"Brenin, it's—"

He put a finger to his lover's lips. "No, hear me out. This thing I'm grappling with—PTSD or whatever—is not going away by wishing it so, and I'm not sure time alone will help. Plus, I don't want to be passive about it."

He changed position to look at Malcolm more squarely. "Harry gave Dafydd something to ease his anxiety. I think they're short-acting, and maybe that's not what Doc MacPhee was talking about. It got me thinking, though."

He didn't add in any details about his deal with his friend or how Dafydd was unwisely mixing alcohol with it. That was something Paz was hopefully dealing with.

"If I want a life with you, Malcolm, I have to be willing to work for it." Flopping down onto his back, he added, "That includes drinking your blood more regularly."

Malcolm rolled to his side and peered down at him. "You dinnae have to, laddie. We have lots of time."

"I want to, and the time starts now. Give me your vein, Malcolm. Please."

With only a brief hesitation, Malcolm scored his own wrist and held it to Brenin's lips. "Drink as much as you'd like, my love."

Brenin flicked his tongue out to lick at first, then, wrapping his lips around the torn skin, he sucked as if his life depended on it. Because it did.

Chapter Eight

"It's ridiculous, mun, for you to sleep on the floor," Dafydd whispered into the room at large. "Idris' crib takes up so much space that you're like a pretzel down there."

"I'm fine," came the equally quiet reply. "And you should be asleep. Plus, you'll wake the baby."

Dafydd hung his head over the side and peered into the gloom. "It's not enough to control my pills. You think to tell me when I have to sleep? And Idris is like a log once he's down for the night."

With a sigh, the doctor rolled onto his side and looked up. "I am not trying to rule your life, Dafydd. I simply meant it's like one in the morning and I'm exhausted. Stay up all night, if you want, but please don't disturb me."

Dafydd made a face that he knew couldn't be seen. "I was only concerned about your comfort." He huffed and flopped back.

"That's sweet of you, but really, I'm fine."

Dafydd stared up at the ceiling. "Sweetness has nothing to do with. It's a matter of knowing how hard my life can be when a man who is chopsy from lack of sleep controls it."

There was a long sigh. "Oh, Dafydd, you know I would never hurt you, don't you?"

He wanted to say he knew no such thing. It was hard, though. The earnestness of this man was too obvious to deny. Dafydd didn't have it in him to be quite that mean. "Not intentionally, no, but not allowing me my nightly ritual isn't exactly a kindness. I can't sleep after all. I need another pill and some Scotch to wash it down."

"No, you don't. Tell me, how do you feel?"

"What do you care?" he shot back. When no answer came, he relented. "Calm, I suppose. Not sleepy, though, and that's the point."

"Those pills are meant to do just as you describe — reduce anxiety, not put you to sleep. It was the booze, frankly, that was causing you to pass out. I bet you've been waking with a wicked hangover. Plus mixing the two can actually bring on the symptoms of PTSD that Harry is trying to help you cope with."

"So you say." He resisted the urge to pound the bed in frustration. *Know-it-all!*

"I'm going to stand."

"Why bother to tell me?"

"In order not to startle you."

Damn the man for his consideration. He glowered at the figure that rose on the side of the bed. Bare-chested as he was, the doctor's trim yet toned physique was easy to see. Dafydd's eyesight was keener than a human's, plus the moonlight shone in through the small windows of the cabin. Try as he might, he couldn't work up too much anger. Quite the contrary, and the bit of pull he felt toward his new jailer irritated him.

"May I teach you a technique that's very effective for getting to sleep? It works with daily anxiety, too."

"Suit yourself. You don't have to wear those silly pants, either. I'm used to seeing men's naked bodies whether I want to or not."

"They're called sleep pants, and I'm being courteous to you. I'm not going to dangle my dick in your face without invitation."

"You'll have to wait a bloody long time, then. Eternity," he bit out, hating his waspish behavior yet unable to rein it in.

"I understand, and that's fine. May I help, please?"

"Like I said, suit yourself."

"I'll take that as a yes. The idea is to isolate small parts of your body from your head to your toes, tensing each one before relaxing it. Do you understand?"

"I suppose. Will you help?"

"Of course. I'll walk you through it."

"Are you going to do it standing there?"

"Where else? Do you want me farther away?"

Dafydd wrestled with the ridiculous notion rattling around his demented head before blurting out, "No, closer. Come lie down next to me."

"Dafydd, I don't think—"

"Well, neither do I, mun, but there it is. Being in this floating bedroom is giving me the shivers. I think, maybe, your being here helps. It's stupid, I know."

It was, too. The last thing he should want was a man lying beside him, crowding him against the wall, blocking his escape. And if he thought of it in terms of Dracul or any of his vicious men—or even some theoretical man—panic threatened to overwhelm him.

It wasn't so with this particular man, however, and the why of it mystified him.

"Not stupid. You've been dragged around a few times since Wales. I'm partly responsible for that. I can well understand your unease. I'm surprised my presence helps, yet also pleased to be of service. If you're sure?"

By way of answer, Dafydd scooted over to make room on the bed. But he stared at the ceiling as Ric climbed up and lay down beside him. "How does this work, then?"

"We start with the head. Tighten up all of your facial muscles as hard as you can. Really scrunch them up. Now relax them again. Do the same with your neck, except be careful to keep your head and face relaxed while you do so. It's hard. Do your best."

Dafydd followed the instructions, although what he really concentrated on was the tone of Ric's voice, low and soothing. Quietly encouraging. A balm to his nerves. Calm washed over him. By the time he'd finished scrunching up his toes, he'd drifted into the waiting darkness that for the first time didn't seem so scary.

* * * *

"Good morning, Dafydd. Ric, if you're finished eating, Alex would like for you to join us for a meeting in the pilot house." Harry's invitation was delivered with a relaxed air.

Dafydd's stomach tightened regardless. He didn't much like the idea of again being among all those aliens in a small space. What could they want with Ric anyway?

"I am," Ric replied. "Dafydd?"

As his breakfast plate was scraped clean, the only possible answer was, "Yes." His appetite had been keen after the most restful night he'd had since he could remember. Ric's silly technique had helped. As had his presence, although Dafydd didn't much like analyzing the whys and wherefores of that revelation.

He started to gesture toward Idris, who sat happily in his highchair, gorging on pieces of scrambled eggs and pancakes, but Harry had anticipated that possible delay.

"Demi, you're on Idris duty for the next hour or so."

"Yes, Papa." The hybrid bopped over and took the seat next to the baby. "Hey, Idris, how's breakfast going?"

The baby held up a fistful of food. "Yum!"

There was nothing for it, then. Dafydd stood and followed in Harry's wake up the saloon steps and on to the airy room where the yacht was controlled. He could feel the steady presence of Ric behind him. That did help, which in turn soured his mood. There seemed to be no end to his conflicting feelings for the man. Now was not the time to dwell on any of that, however. He needed to stay alert for whatever this meeting was about.

All eyes turned to them the moment they entered. Dafydd shrunk back on instinct, bumping right into Ric. The man said nothing, nor did he move out of the way. Instead, he placed his palm lightly at the small of Dafydd's back. It had the surprising effect of anchoring him. These scary men who echoed Dracul's worst characteristics weren't hard to face with Ric guiding him forward, staying at his back. Dafydd straightened his shoulders and didn't avert his gaze as he usually would.

Alex waited until they had joined the group around the table before speaking. "Thank you for coming. This meeting is mostly about prevailing on Dr. Paz for more help, but we also hope Dafydd has information that will prove useful."

"I'm game," Ric replied, "so long as it doesn't involve putting Dafydd at risk."

The hard edge to the pleasantly stated words made Dafydd smile. *He's protecting me.* He shouldn't have been surprised, and he wasn't. It just made him happy to experience this new sensation of someone having his interests at heart. It didn't even matter if it was all part of some scheme to get into his bed. He understood those dynamics. They didn't frighten him. More, deep down, he didn't believe that was the case.

"Not at all, dear Doctor. We merely realize that Dafydd was made privy to Dracul's modus operandi and that extra knowledge could prove useful in bringing down what's left of his organization." Alex stared at Dafydd with kindness. "He underestimated you, didn't he?"

Dafydd lifted his chin, proud to be able to answer. "He did, yes."

"His hubris got the better of him." Alex tapped a print-out on the table in front of him. "What we need to do before exploring these smuggling caves is confirm whether this Mr. Moran, elderly as he may be, was and continues to be coopted by Dracul. So, the question is, can we do that without making him suspicious? Is there an easy way to make him think that someone such as Dr. Paz is in on the game in order to get him to spill his secrets?"

Ric leaned forward, keeping his palm in place. "You want me to pay dear old Scotty a visit?"

"If you don't mind," Alex replied.

"Not in the least. If nothing else, these older men who were out and proud even before being gay was no longer illegal are often interesting guys to talk to. I don't mind dropping in on him for a chat."

Alarm shot through Dafydd. "What if the caves are being used now? Won't that mean whoever it is you seek is staying with this man? Ric would be in danger if he goes nosing around."

Ric slid his hand up to gently cup the back of Dafydd's neck. "It's okay. I won't be entirely alone, right?"

Val shook his head. "Nope. Duncan is arriving this afternoon and he'll be your back-up. Plus, the rest of us will be here — listening, as always. If it looks dicey, we'll be there pronto."

Dafydd gasped. "How fast is that, exactly? You can't fly, mun. And what use is a human compared to your alien strength? You think even that cop could be of help? Ric's neck could be torn open in a blink of an eye. I've seen it done plenty, I assure you." His breath started coming in great, heaving lungfuls. He blinked against his tunneling vision.

Ric's thumb around his neck moved in slow circles. "Easy. It's all right. There's nothing to panic about. I'm here and safe. Nothing's going to change that."

The soothing words barely registered. A whimper passed his lips and he found himself turning to Ric and pressing against his body. He laid his forehead on the man's shoulder and grabbed fistfuls of his shirt. His heart raced and thudded against his chest, hard enough to burst.

Ric held him loosely in an embrace, running circles again across Dafydd's back. "Shh, it's okay. Honestly, guys, didn't it occur to you to speak with me first?"

"My apologies, Doctor," Alex said. "We misread the...'situation' between you."

"Yeah, well..."

"Perhaps you would like to escort Dafydd down to the saloon and we can continue our discussion with only you."

"No!" Dafydd pulled away and glared at the others. "You'll not make plans without me."

Ric cupped his face. "Of course we won't. Would you like to sit down?" When Dafydd shook his head, he continued, "Then we need to know that dear Scotty is alone in the house when I approach him."

Dafydd didn't question his impulse to turn in Ric's arms so that he faced the others and could lean against him. The doctor's touch was proving to be more effective on his nerves than any amount of pills and liquor.

Val raised his eyebrows before saying. "We can do that. When he arrives, I'll show Duncan how to work the heat-seeking equipment. I've modified it in particular to pick up traces of our physiology. He can do a recon before you approach the house." The man's gaze homed in on Dafydd. "Does that work for you?"

Being asked his opinion, to have it be counted as relevant, was a new experience. He almost believed he was imagining it.

"Yes," he replied in a shaky voice that made him wince. "That will do," he added more firmly.

Alex clasped his hands together. "Excellent. Now, to the issue of how the doctor gains entrance. Any suggestions?"

Dafydd gnawed at his lower lip as he considered what might help. "Usually, they used force and threats, nothing subtle or collegial." Ric patted Dafydd's hip where his fingers had landed, a subtle gesture of sympathy. "But Petru had always advocated a softer approach when they were setting up plans that were more long-term and uncertain. He used a combination of bribery and flattery—sex, too, of course, except it was the kind one would want to experience again."

He made a face, couldn't help it, then moved on to the part they were really interested in. "He called these boys 'brown dwarfs'. I had no idea what it meant, at first, and frankly didn't care. Eventually I looked it up and got the celestial reference, although I don't know why he thought it was so clever. Anyway, I expect if Ric can somehow work the words into his greeting, this man would think of him as being an ally. Assuming he's one of them to begin with."

Ric's warm breath tickled his ear. "If he isn't, I'll merely sound a bit odd. Either way, I hope he's in the mood for company."

"It's settled, then," Alex said with a nod. "Nothing much can be done before Duncan arrives. Thank you both for your time."

Dafydd knew a dismissal when he heard one and was glad of it. Ric must have as well. He turned Dafydd and guided him out of the pilot house and back to the saloon. Every touch, every move, was free of any kind of demand or high-handedness. Ric's behavior demonstrated caretaking, which wasn't surprising. No, the amazing thing was that Dafydd instinctively perceived it in that benign way. He would have thought no amount of familiarity could change his view of the world in general—and men in particular.

What's wrong with me? I should resent this.

He didn't, though, and the peaceful feeling that went along with it was soothing. When he entered the saloon and caught sight of his son playing happily with his garage on the floor, it brought a smile to his lips.

"He's going to wear that thing out before this journey is over."

"If he does, I'll buy him another one."

The easy way in which Ric assumed they would continue to see something of each other was yet one more thing that he didn't mind. "How has he been?" he asked Demi, who was down on the floor, as well.

"He's been a very good boy, haven't you, Idris?" By way of answer, the baby waved a car at Demi.

Mackie sat on the other side. "We're all going to go to the beach soon. Want to come with?"

"Oh, um…" His instinctive reaction was to refuse. Then he remembered how he'd thought both he and Idris would enjoy it. "Why not? I've never been myself and I hear it's quite fun."

"It is," Mackie confirmed. "We can make sandcastles and chase gulls and sandpipers, eat lobster rolls and fried clams. And there's ice cream! Lots and lots of it," he added, poking his finger into Idris' belly.

His son giggled with delight, something Dafydd rarely saw or heard. *Everyone is better with him than I am.* Putting that useless thought aside, he resolved to throw himself full tilt into the day's plans.

He turned to Ric. "Are you coming, too?"

"No." He made an aborted movement to touch Dafydd's face. "I want to discuss this surveillance in more detail with Val and Alex while we wait for Duncan to arrive. With any luck, I'll have been in and out of Moran's house before you return from your outing."

Dafydd didn't like the idea that he wasn't going to be part of the monitoring done up in the pilot house. It was on the tip of his tongue to say he would stay onboard when Ric overrode his thoughts.

"Please do go without me. Playing on the beach is one of the happiest memories I have as a boy. Knowing you're spending your day like that will make it easier for me to do what I have to. I don't want you staying here and fretting over me."

Dafydd huffed. "And what makes you think I would be?" He softened his words with a quick grin. Really, it was ridiculous how one night of good sleep was coloring his attitude.

Ric shook his head. "Dafydd, you aren't nearly as mysterious or standoffish as you think you are. Have fun and have care. I'll see you later for dinner."

With that, the man turned and left. Dafydd watched his back for as long as he could, not very concerned that the others saw his interest.

* * * *

Duncan slipped back into the driver's seat and placed the surveillance device on his lap. "Okay, the coast is clear, Doc. I can confirm that there aren't any aliens inside the house. Only one seriously old man is shuffling about."

Ric glanced down. "Does that thing actually tell you his age?"

"Naw, but he's moving slowly so I did the math." He shook his head once. "Hard to believe Dracul thought this far ahead or that an elderly human would still be loyal after decades of disuse."

"If Dafydd says that's what they did, then that's what they did."

Ric was surprised, and also not, that his first impulse was to defend the boy. After a torturous night of lying beside his heart's desire, he was also a little cranky. Dafydd may have slept well — and thank God for it — but Ric had only catnapped, afraid he might roll too close in his sleep. His overtures toward Dafydd were going remarkably well. He didn't want to fuck it all up by doing something stupid — like pressing his unavoidably hard dick against the poor guy.

Duncan held up his hand. "I'm not arguing the point. I'm just saying it wouldn't have occurred to me. Are you ready to rock and roll?"

"I suppose. Do I look all right?" he asked, giving himself the once-over. He felt a little douchey in his Tommy Bahama Shadows in Paradise camp shirt and linen shorts. But paired with his Sperry Baitfish flip-flops, they would lend credence to his claim that he'd been walking along the beach and thought he'd drop in for a visit to this lovely cliffside home.

"Sure." Duncan grinned. "I'd want to fuck you — if I were a ninety-year-old man. I'm certain you'll have no trouble sweet-talking your way into the guy's home."

There was a snort from the speaker phone mounted on the car's dashboard.

Ric glared at it. "No comment from the audience, if you please. I'm nervous enough as it is. The boys are safe, right?" He couldn't help adding in that question, even though he knew the answer already.

"I can see them from here," Val assured him. "Everyone's taking a little lie-down under the beach umbrellas. Lucien is playing mother-hen and he has strict orders to keep them right there until I give the word. No worries, Doc. Your boy is safe. Both of them are."

He almost denied that Dafydd and Idris were his, then realized that would be a ridiculous lie. Without saying anything, all the aliens had managed to convey to him their support and approval of his budding relationship with Dafydd. He only hoped their confidence in him was well-placed.

He flipped his Ray-Bans open and shoved them onto his face and opened the car door. Duncan had parked away from the house, so it meant a bit of a walk. He didn't mind. In the waning heat of the day, it was glorious to be outside. He hoped he could come back to Putnam's Cove sometime later in the summer for a real vacation. He could picture walking around town with Dafydd's hand in his and pushing Idris in a stroller.

You're getting ahead of yourself. That way leads to disappointment.

Moran's house was a lovely two-story, rambling, shingle-style affair, accented with sea-foam green shutters and doors. It seemed too big for one person, although perhaps Moran had built it with plans of having a family one day. *Yeah, of aliens.*

The front boasted a small, manicured lawn surrounded by riotous flowers. Someone was keeping it up, and given the age of the owner, it must mean that he paid for the help. If Val's information was accurate, Moran had no history of employment after the military and yet no discernable trust or other family money. Ric didn't need to be a strategist or a super-smart alien to recognize the obvious. Moran had to be a kept man, and at his age, who could possibly continue to do that other than someone who lived far longer?

As he walked up to the front door, his palms began to sweat. He rubbed them on his shorts before ringing the bell. The sound of it was clearly audible, although after a few seconds of waiting, he heard nothing else. He tried it again, and still there was no response. Peering through the window beside the door proved to be no help. All he could see was a nicely-decorated entryway and, beyond that, an equally lovely living room. Everything looked expensive and neat, serving to bolster his suspicions about Moran—who wasn't showing up to answer the door. Ric decided he needed to take a ballsier approach. No way Moran had tottered off in the few minutes it had taken Duncan to get back to the car.

So, Ric followed the slate walkway around the house, opened the gate leading to the backyard and ventured forth. He found Scotty Moran sitting at a wrought-iron table under an awning. He held a glass of some cloudy iced beverage in one hand, while the other stroked a fat tabby in his lap. His expression as he stared out at the ocean was serene until he heard Ric's approach. Then there was nothing complacent or doddering about him.

"Who are you?" Old, yet sharp, eyes gave him an assessing look.

Ric smiled broadly and slowly took off his glasses in order for the man to see him better, and hopefully see nothing threatening. "I'm sorry, sir. I rang the bell."

"And when I didn't answer the front door, you decided to trespass around back? Didn't your mother teach you any manners, or are you so pretty that you're used to ignoring the rules?" The man's look morphed to predatory.

Okay, Ric could work with that—had wished for it, actually. Notwithstanding the umbrage he'd taken at Duncan's teasing, he understood his appeal and wasn't above using the lure of sex to advance his agenda. "Can't blame a boy for using what God gave him, can you?"

Scotty's eyes lit up. "Do I detect a hint of the exotic Latin in you?"

"Yes, sir." Ric enhanced his normally muted accent, given that it was working in his favor. He assumed an invitation, as well, closing the distance between them.

Scotty removed his hand from the cat and lifted it in greeting. Ric took the limp fingers and pressed his lips lightly to the knuckles. He tried to channel a bit of Antonio Banderas.

"My name is Ric, although some have referred to me as a brown dwarf."

His host stiffened slightly and his nostrils flared. "You don't say? I'm Scotty."

"I've heard. You have a beautiful house. I was wandering along the beach and couldn't resist dropping by for a visit."

"A purely social call?"

"Yes. I hope that's all right?"

"Oh, dearie, company is always welcome. Have a seat." He waved to the chair on the other side of the table. "Would you like a nice, cold glass of Arnold Palmer? It's my own special recipe with home-made iced tea and lemonade, spiked with vodka, don't you know."

"Thank you, that would be lovely. Shall I fetch a glass myself from the kitchen?" Val had said to try to scope out the house if possible.

"No, no. Sit. I'm not that old." Shoving the cat off his lap, he stood with a steadiness and grace that belied his age.

Perhaps he'd been fed alien blood sufficiently to give him a longer, healthier life without fully changing him. There was such a lot for Ric to learn about this alien physiology. He waited patiently while Scotty rummaged around inside, returned and poured him his drink.

Ric took a sip and genuinely was able to appreciate it. "Delicious and refreshing. You're very kind." He shifted his gaze. "Your view is spectacular."

"Isn't it, though? I was lucky to snag this piece of land right after the war. The big one, you know. It was pretty wild along here at the time. Now, it's all built out. There's not as much elbow room and my neighbors have turned into the most frightful bores. It's all families these days, can you imagine? I mean, was leading dreary bourgeois lives what Stonewall was all about?" He gave Ric the side-eye. "You don't have children, do you?"

He thought of Idris then squashed it. "No. It doesn't fit with the, um, *program*, does it?"

Scotty's expression turned sly. "It does sometimes, I've heard. Not with me, though. Thank God." He shuddered with exaggeration. "I saw once what too much of a good thing can lead to. You know, *blood*," he mouthed. "A drop here or there can do wonders for a boy, of course." He waved his hand down his body.

Okay, there was confirmation that Moran's long life and relative robustness was from alien intervention. It was nothing like what had transpired with Dafydd, though.

"That was plenty for me. The rest of it struck me as *disgusting*. Who wants to be a girl?"

Ric drank some more before answering and tamped down his natural inclination to argue the point. Dafydd and the other changelings remained men by their own definition, even when they chose to undergo the transformation. Besides, Scotty's catty remark was insulting to any and all genders. *Dick.*

But his mission was to coax information out of the guy, not get into a socio-political argument, so he went along with the sentiment. "It's more of a commitment than I'm willing to make." He forced himself to make a face.

"We're of like minds there. Fortunately, I was given a choice. Such a relief. Or, possibly I was a little disappointed," he allowed. "I confess I would have done anything for my man and it would have meant spending more time with him." He moaned breathily. "To capture all that raw, masculine attention on a daily basis and to be filled with the biggest, most powerful cock in the world…" He moaned again. "What more could a boy want?"

Ric nearly choked on his drink. He turned it into a chuckle. "I couldn't have put it better. We're very lucky. A little loyalty and devotion is a fair price to pay, no matter how long it takes for the bill to come due."

"Sister, you've got that right." Scotty sighed. "It's hard, though. I must confess to have lost my own allure." He ran a hand along his slightly wrinkled neck. "I'm not the ingénue I used to be, although I had a good run. Longer than most, so mustn't grumble. At least my replacement, whoever that might be, isn't being waved in my face."

Ric considered his next question carefully. "No visits?"

Scotty rolled his eyes. "Not after the recent initial one and brief reunion. He barely stayed five minutes and there was no fun to be had." He fluttered his hand. "Well, I can't say I'm surprised. There's no reason to, given that my ass isn't worth reaming and there are younger, prettier mouths to choke his cock with."

There was a small sniffle, and Ric found that he felt sorry for the man. Scotty had once been seduced by the baddest of bad boys but might never have understood that he was being used by aliens to wreak havoc on the world – or, not to the degree that had been going on. He might have convinced himself that he was playing out some sci-fi fantasy, especially when there'd been no public acknowledgment that some kind of invasion was occurring.

"Say, you're not my replacement, are you?" Scotty's eyes narrowed and it made Ric reassess how innocent the man really was.

Holding up his hand, Ric said, "No. I swear. I'm with someone else." That was certainly true. "I'm simply at loose ends here in Putnam's Cove and thought getting acquainted with you would be fun. I mean, I'm not on duty much until nightfall," he added with a smirk.

That seemed to do the trick. Scotty's suspicious expression disappeared.

"Hmm. One thing I have to admit is that no work and all play has made my life very agreeable. I've never been lonely up here. I have, to this day, plenty of scrumptious young things more than happy to let me suck their cock or willing to fuck my ass, for that matter. It's not the same, but it's hardly nothing." He gave Ric the side-eye. "I don't suppose – "

"Sorry." Once again, Ric both sputtered on his mouthful of spiked Arnold Palmer and held up his hand. "I am not at liberty to play with anyone other than *the* one." That was the truth of it. Since meeting Dafydd, he had no interest in other men.

"Pity. You'll stay and keep an old soul company for a while, though, won't you?"

Although he figured he'd gathered the information needed, it didn't hurt to indulge the man. Duncan was monitoring the place. If any of Dracul's men showed up, Val could warn him. The wire he wore included an earpiece for them to talk to him. There was a risk, of course, and he had promised Dafydd that he'd be careful. And yet, he sensed in Scotty a loneliness, for all his bravado, that would never be satisfied with mere human company — and platonic at that. In some sense, the man was as much a victim of Dracul's ambition as any other human who'd gotten in the way. Ric would try, nevertheless. Compassion was an important distinction between him and the aliens he helped to fight. He couldn't lose sight of that.

"I can't think of a better way to spend my afternoon," he said, lifting his glass in the man's direction.

Chapter Nine

Brenin sat up and stretched his arms over his head. "This has been an awesome day." He patted his bare stomach. "If I keep eating like this, I'm going to develop a pot, though."

"You can work off the calories with sex," Mackie said from where he remained lying on his towel. He was the only one not taking shelter under one of the two big umbrellas they'd stuck in the sand.

"It doesn't burn that many," Lucien countered without looking up from the book he'd been reading. Demi's father was nominally their chaperone, with the job of making sure they didn't wander off. It would have been insulting if the man weren't so utterly chill.

"Ugh, Dad, please don't remind me that you and Papa still do it."

"Forgive me, Demi. I had thought you and your friends were all mature." Lucien's dry put-down surprised Brenin. The man appeared docile and conservative, and yet he was no pushover and far more fun than expected.

"I'll never be that grown-up."

Lucien sighed. "See what you have to look forward to, Dafydd?"

There was a subtle shift in the atmosphere around them, as if everyone worried about how the former slave would react to something that should have been mundane for the average father.

From where he lay on his side, watching his son sleep off his ice cream coma, Dafydd appeared relaxed. "I've got lots of time for that, don't I?"

There was another silent shimmer in the air around them as everyone else accepted that there'd been no faux-pas. While it was hard to identify exactly how, Dafydd was different that day. It had started at breakfast when he'd entered the saloon with Idris on his hip and Ric trailing behind him. Dafydd had appeared well-rested and almost cheery. Then there'd been the way he'd returned from the pilot house, again with Ric close behind. If Brenin hadn't known better, he would have pegged them as a couple. Add to that how Dafydd had readily joined them in their beach excursion and there was a definite sense of optimism.

His friend was improving, and it wasn't because he was popping pills indiscriminately with booze chasers. Brenin was certain of that for two reasons. One was that Ric obviously had taken on the task of monitoring Dafydd. The other was that no one as clear-eyed and energetic as Dafydd seemed could have been loaded to the gills.

Brenin wanted to ask Dafydd about it, but he feared if he did, it might break the cycle of good cheer. Since the previous night and his frank talk with Malcolm, he'd become more determined to get help from whatever source. To that end, he glanced at Jase. Seeing the boy had also sat up, he decided to get better acquainted with him and pick his brains for solutions. Of the three of them who'd suffered horrible abuse, Jase seemed the best adjusted. It could be a good front, yet he didn't think so.

Standing, he stretched once more and sauntered to the far side of Jase. He plopped his ass on the fine sand and ran some through his fingers. "Hi."

"Hi." Jase's face was wide-open and completely guileless.

"Did you enjoy the day?"

"Absolutely. I haven't had many chances to hang out on the beach. It was fun. Plus, my being entertained and occupied eases Emil's mind. It's a win-win."

"Yeah, I can see that. He's sweet, your mun."

"He sure is. I can't believe how lucky I am."

Brenin clawed at the sand, working up the courage to say what was truly on his mind. "I bet this time last year you didn't have any hope of a life like this." He felt bad being so blunt, yet he was too desperate to help himself to muster much tact. "I know I didn't."

Jase relaxed position didn't change. He simply stared out at the ocean. "True. You reach a point where you accept that it's your life and you're stuck with it, that nothing will change for the better. Emil showed me differently."

"Malcolm did the same...except how do you get past it, or over it—or whatever?"

Jase swiveled his head in Brenin's direction and furrowed his brow. "You don't. It's crazy to even try. What you do is find ways to *deal* with it. You can't change what happened or the way it impacted you. All you can do is control how it affects you now, and to not allow it to ruin your life. You cope," he added with a firm nod.

Brenin pulled up his legs and rested his chin on his knees. "Okay, I get that. What do you do to cope, then?"

Jase sighed. "Emil. It's him, plain and simple. I've put my trust in him. He's like a balm to my soul. I know he'll never hurt me. And when I have my bad moments or days—and I do—he's there to help me through them."

"I believe that about Malcolm, too, and I know he'll do whatever I need him to in order to help, but somehow it's not enough."

Jase twisted around to face him. "In what way?"

"I don't know. Well, yes, I do." He proceeded to explain his recent interactions with his man and the anxiety he was feeling. "I've decided to accept Doc MacPhee's offer for a prescription."

"Nothing wrong with meds, when prescribed and used correctly. I've considered it myself and might do it at some point."

"I don't think that's the only or final answer, though."

"You're probably right. For what it's worth, Emil and I took a page out of the BDSM playbook. The real one, not the fake stuff the men who possessed me used. It works like this. If Emil is doing something that makes me a little anxious, I say 'yellow'. That's his cue to slow down. If I'm getting really freaked out, I say 'red'. He stops whatever he's doing instantly."

"And that works?" Brenin was skeptical.

"Yup. It's quick, easy and effective. There's no room for misunderstandings or hard feelings, either. You should try it."

He gave the idea about a second's worth of thought. "I think I might." Anything that could possibly help deserved exploration. He loved Malcolm and wanted to help preserve and grow their relationship. Not communicating effectively wasn't going to accomplish that.

"You should give progressive relaxation a go, too." This came from Dafydd. When Brenin and Jase looked over at him, he explained the process further. "Ric taught it to me last night. It worked. No one was more surprised than I was," he added with a one-shoulder shrug.

"Huh." Brenin sent his gaze across the sea. He suddenly couldn't wait to see his man again or for night to fall, so that he could put his newfound knowledge to the test.

* * * *

"You did fine work this afternoon, Doc."

Ric turned from where he'd been staring at the harbor through one of the long windows that flanked the saloon. Malcolm stood next to him, his imposing figure not intimidating the way it had been.

"Thanks. It was exciting, to be honest, and not nearly as frightening as what we did in Wales."

"Aye, we got lucky. Whoever Scotty Moran's contact is within Dracul's circle, he obviously doesn't feel the need to keep the old man happy. Can't say I'm surprised."

"Nor I. He is an interesting guy, though. He's lived a colorful life, and I'm not certain he truly understands what he got himself into."

"Hard to say. He must know he's involved in something illegal and otherworldly. As to whether he's kenned to his friend's true evil nature and despicable plans?" He grunted. "Well, that's another matter, not that it impacts our next step."

"Which is what, exactly? Not that you need to keep me in the loop," he added, suddenly hearing how his question might sound impertinent.

Malcolm held up his hand. "You never have to worry about your place here, Doc. You made yourself our ally, and that means you're one of us, in our culture. Plus, you've put your life on the line more than once. Going to that house counts because there was always the possibility of it going pear-shaped. Never hesitate to ask questions, and I can promise that with few exceptions, if any, we'll always answer them."

Ric was slightly taken aback—not by the words but by the almost-vehemence with which Malcolm had said them. It had sounded more like a solemn vow than a mere point of information.

"Th-thank you. I appreciate that. I guess I came into this thinking I was conducting an experiment. Now, it's become…personal." Thoughts of Dafydd crowded his mind. *Very personal.*

Malcolm tugged at one ear. "I ken well what you mean. Something's—someone's—hit you right between the eyes and there's nowt you can do about it. You take your best shot and hang on for the ride."

Ric leaned back with his elbows on the sill. "It's hard, though, isn't it? What I want and what's good for him won't necessarily jibe, no matter hard I wish it to be true."

"Aye, I ken that, as well. But in answer to your question, we're going to do a wee bit of recon with the full expectation that we'll find at least one of our enemies holed up in those caves."

Ric straightened. "You'll have to approach by the sea, as Val mentioned earlier. The path leading down to the beach won't get you close enough. I've seen for myself that the bar of sand ends with huge boulders built right into the cliffside. I don't think you can even see the cave opening from land."

"Aye, you've got the right of it."

"You'll be sitting ducks. Anyone inside could shoot you before you get anywhere near the mouth."

"True, if we were boating all the way in, which we're not. We'll get in position sufficiently far out to sea that we can't be easily seen from land. Then, we're going to swim to the shore underwater. Silent and invisible, we hope to take them by surprise."

As he ran his hand down his face, Ric shook his head. "I don't envy you, and I'll be of no help, I'm afraid. I can snorkel, but I can't scuba dive. The Atlantic is freezing, besides, summer be damned."

"We wouldn't ask that of you, anyway. The cold won't bother us. It's heat that does. Summers in this part of the world suck. We can also hold our breaths for a very long time compared to a human. Plus, a firefight in close quarters is too risky for anyone other than us. Alex, Val, Emil and I will go. Harry will stay with the tender offshore, while Duncan will stand guard back here, just in case. It helps knowing you're here, as well. Our lads are fierce for sure, but we'll fare better at our task if we know they're safely guarded."

Ric raised his eyebrows. "I fear you're showering me with more confidence than I deserve."

Malcolm shook his head. "No, I'm not." He studied his feet for a moment. "In fact, I came over here to ask you something personal, if you dinnae mind."

"Of course not."

"See, the lads were gabbing in the beach about" — he blew out a breath — "ways to cope with their experiences. And Dafydd mentioned you'd taught him some technique for relaxing at night. Brenin relayed it to me, and I was wondering if you could walk me through it. I want to help my dear, wee lad anyway possible. It fairly breaks my heart how he suffers from what Dracul did to him."

"It's called progressive relaxation. It's easy, although it takes practice." He walked Malcolm through the process, the big Scotsman staring at him with a look of concentration, as if he were hanging on to every word and committing them to memory — which, of course, he was.

"That's all there is to it, really," Ric said with a shrug. "Everything is worth a try, including drugs that are prescribed and closely monitored."

"Aye, Doc MacPhee can help there. Brenin is open to the idea."

"Good." Ric thought of the bottle tucked in his pocket and how he'd guiltily hid it while he'd been out on his recon mission. "Be careful, though. They can be abused."

"Aye, I'm aware. Brenin is a sensible lad, but the demons that plague him are powerful and they pop up at unexpected times."

"And mixing them with alcohol is a bad idea with lots of these kinds of meds."

"I understand."

"Hey, what are you two doing squirreled away over here?" Brenin came up and wrapped his arms around Malcolm's waist. "The dishes are done and we're going to have a dance party." He grinned at Ric. "Where's Dafydd? Surely he hasn't gone to bed already."

"No, but he is putting Idris down. I'm pretty sure he's coming back with a baby monitor in tow."

The words had no sooner left his mouth when Dafydd appeared at the saloon's entrance. Ric did a double take when he realized that the boy had changed from his jeans into — sleep pants? Yup, Ric's, with the bottoms rolled up so that they didn't drag. The sight of Dafydd wearing something of his caused a funny feeling low in his belly. And the guy knew exactly what he was doing. He looked at Ric from across the room with a 'what?' expression before going to curl up on one of the sofas. He put the monitor on a nearby table and sat back to watch the others start to dance.

"That's a new look for Dafydd, I think," Brenin commented slyly. "Come on, Malcolm. Let's get our groove on, as Mackie would say."

"Och, now you ken I'm not one for dancing. I'd rather watch you."

Ric lost track of them, his attention taken completely by the fetching sight of Dafydd. Music filled the room, the kind of thing they played at the club. Normally Ric loved to dance himself. With Dafydd to watch and study, he felt entertained sufficiently, however. There was nothing overtly coy about the guy, other than his unexpected decision to borrow Ric's pajama bottoms. As Dafydd sat, he tucked his bare feet under his small bottom and tapped his fingers on his thighs to the beat of the song. Every so often, he would glance in Ric's direction, although it was hard to tell if there was an invitation being issued.

"Fuck it." Ric decided to assume there was. He crossed the room and sat beside him without asking. "Did Idris go down all right?" He could have smacked himself. Talking about the baby hardly was conducive to forging a romantic evening.

"Yes, he did. A day on the beach tired him something fierce, even though he got a nap earlier." He flicked his gaze in Ric's direction. "I take it your venture went well?"

"Yes, it did. There was only the old man there, and I was able to confirm that he is both a recruit of one of Dracul's men and that he's been visited recently by the guy. Alex and the others are pretty convinced the 3-D printed guns are being smuggled in by way of Putnam's Cove." He shrugged. "The evidence is circumstantial, but even if it's not those guns, someone's doing something here and they intend to stop it."

Dafydd eyes narrowed. "With your help? I saw you gabbing with Malcolm just now."

Touched that Dafydd continued to be worried about him, Ric nevertheless wanted to reassure him on that point. "No, my part is done. I promise that my spying days are over."

Dafydd appeared mollified by that. "Fine, then. Not that it's any of my business what you do."

"Oh, Dafydd, it is, you know?" Ric dared to lay his hand gently on Dafydd's thigh. "I think I've done a poor job of hiding how I feel, and it matters to me what you do. I don't want you to be worried about me, for your sake. For my own, it makes me rather happy. I hope you don't mind my saying so."

By way of answer, Dafydd merely shrugged and kept his attention on the other boys bopping around the room. "They all do a good job at having fun, don't they?"

"Yes. The music, the movement, it's good therapy. Why don't you try?"

Dafydd shook his head. "No. There wasn't much of it when I was a lad, and it was a girl thing mostly anyway. There's been no chance since then, needless to say."

"There is now," Ric prodded gently.

"No. I…no." Dafydd stood abruptly and, snatching the monitor, raced to the door.

Ric was up like a shot, following him. He hadn't gone far. Ric almost ran into him leaning against the wall outside the saloon, staring past the stern at the ocean. The music was still audible, although at a more muted level. *Youngblood* started playing and Ric couldn't help moving his body to it.

"This is a great song," he said in Dafydd's direction. He swayed to the rhythm as if he were dancing in a club. He didn't have a specific agenda. It was nice to cut loose for a few minutes and enjoy himself. If it inspired Dafydd to do the same, that would be a bonus.

He sang along with the chorus, too, not really heeding the words or their meaning. Suddenly, Dafydd was flying toward him, colliding with enough force that Ric staggered back and had to grab on to Dafydd's waist to keep them both from falling.

"Is that how you feel and is that what you think?" Dafydd demanded in a voice laced with tears.

"What? No, it's only a song. I like the melody, that's all."

"Is it? You don't think I keep pushing you away? Do you think I should welcome you with open arms and…what? Cast aside how my life's been like for nearly four hundred fucking years!"

Alarmed, Ric cupped Dafydd's face with his hands. "Shh, baby, it's okay. I didn't mean anything by it. I'm not rebuking you and don't expect anything. I know you're not ready to trust anyone to love you, let alone a man. You may never be. It makes me unbearably sad, but I understand it. Christ, I don't even know if you're gay."

The realization hit him like a two-by-four right between his eyes. He'd been acting as if Dafydd's trauma might be all that stood between them. And he'd been so inured to seeing the aliens with their voluntary male partners that he'd lost sight of the fact that Dafydd had been conscripted to that way of life. There was nothing to say that had he been given a choice, even by medieval standards, he would have wanted to pair up with other men.

I'm such a fucking idiot! An abject apology was on the tip of his tongue when Dafydd's response shut it down.

Dafydd closed his eyes. Tears leaked out, which would have been alarming if not for his next words. "I am, you know. *That*. It was forbidden in my time, then Dracul punished me for my sin in ways no priest had ever thought of."

"It's not a sin," Ric was quick to reassure him, pathetically grateful for the boy's confession. "I was raised to believe that, as well. I know it to be a lie now. I'm proud of who I am. That town behind us is full of people who feel the same way. I hope that one day, you will too."

Dafydd opened his eyes, which were shining wet. "Maybe I will, but that's as far as it may ever go. To act on it, to let a man touch me like that?" He shook his head. "I don't want to be broken, but I think I am. I can never be fixed."

"Don't say that!" Ric had to swallow back his rage. "No matter what, you aren't to think less of yourself.

Dafydd, you're beautiful and courageous and brave. You're also smart, smarter than that fucker Dracul ever was. I admire how strong you stayed after all those brutal years. You should be proud of yourself, Dafydd. Can't you see the amazing man that I do?"

"No."

"Yes." And that was when Ric lost control. The next thing he knew, he was kissing Dafydd, not aggressively, merely a soft coupling of their lips.

Dafydd's were sweet and silky. Ric savored every taste. He slanted his mouth to cover every inch and used the light hold he had on the boy's face to guide his movements. Even in his insatiable state, he made sure to make Dafydd feel cherished, not dominated. He could break Ric's hold and the kiss at any time. Ric was careful, as well, not to allow his hard dick to get anywhere near Dafydd. He leaned into the kiss from the waist up and kept his lower half angled away. While he reveled in the joy of it all, a voice screamed inside his head, *Don't freak him out!*

Every second the kiss lasted, Ric expected Dafydd to pull away. Yet, he didn't. Instead, he remained placid in the face of Ric's gentle assault, a faint quiver vibrating his lips. He didn't simply accept the touch, either, though. No, he melted into the kiss with a tentative, yet undeniable, interest. In the end, it was Ric who pulled away, determined not to be greedy. A little discipline and self-denial now would hopefully lead to a better future, one in which he could kiss Dafydd every day and more besides.

With a flutter of his lashes, Dafydd opened his eyes. Ric peered into them, looking for signs of distress. He found none, only slightly dilated pupils and a bit of wonder.

"No one has ever done that to me before. Kissed me, I mean."

"Oh, Dafydd." Ric pressed another one against the boy's forehead. "You break my heart."

"I didn't tell you in order for you to feel sorry for me." There was bitterness in those words.

"It's not pity," Ric was quick to reassure him. "More, it's—"

"What?"

Ric shook his head. "No, I'm not going to burden you with my own issues."

"Not even if I want you to?" Dafydd stiffened.

Not wanting to cause discord or dispel the good feelings lingering between them, Ric rubbed his hands lightly down Dafydd's arms before letting go entirely. "I'm not going to be one more person in your life that makes demands or puts pressure on you to meet expectations beyond those that are purely for your own good."

"Don't be patronizing."

The stern rebuke caught Ric by surprise. "I'm not. I'm trying to be—"

"Noble?"

"No. I was going to say 'considerate'."

"Don't be."

This assertiveness was new in Ric's experience. He liked how Dafydd was standing up for himself, standing up to him. He appreciated what it meant about the man's growth. The best way to show Dafydd he was wrong about Ric's attitude toward him was to be as honest about his feelings as Dafydd was demanding.

To put temptation out of reach, Ric took a step back. "I'm falling in love with you." He shook his head a moment later. "No, I *am* in love with you. That's the unvarnished truth, Dafydd."

When the guy stood blinking at him without saying anything, Ric decided to lay it all out.

"Part of me is thrilled to be your first. The other is furious about what that monster put you through. I mean it when I say I admire how you survived and ultimately became the instrument of your own rescue. But I also want to wrap you in my arms and protect you from anything bad for the rest of your life. My biggest fear is that I'll do something that hurts you, that no matter how careful I am, it will never be right. That I'll remind you of that horror."

Dafydd scoffed, almost chuckled. "Seriously, mun? You think that could ever happen? You're all the good and gentleness that I always dreamed was waiting in the world for me, yet never experienced. Not before you came into my life, that is." Dafydd plucked at the sleep pants with his free hand. "I'm not worried that you'll hurt me. I'm worried that *I* will hurt *you*, that I can never give you what I know you want."

"Anything will be enough." Ric meant it.

"You say that, but how can it be true? I understand what drives men and it's not lying untouching in bed or playing with a baby on the floor."

"Those are both very good starts."

"What about the end?" Dafydd challenged and, hugging the baby monitor to his chest, dropped his head.

Ric bent to try to catch his eye. "Do we need to worry about that now? Like the beginning of any relationship, can't we simply see how it goes? I'm a very patient man, you'll find, and you are certainly worth the wait." When Dafydd scoffed again and started to argue, Ric put his finger to the boy's mouth. "Don't. The one thing I can't stand is your not valuing yourself."

Saying nothing, Dafydd nodded once.

"Can I ask you something? Why did you change into my sleep pants?"

Dafydd shrugged. "Don't know, exactly. It was an impulse, like."

"It makes me really happy."

"Oh? You best have another pair because I'm not sure I'm going to give them back. They're very comfortable."

Ric grinned. "That's fine. I have others, although not with me. Is it okay if I sleep in my underwear?"

Dafydd nodded then lifted his gaze. "I'm not scared of you, Ric."

His heart did a slow roll. "I think that's the first time you've called me by my first name."

"Oh yes? I suppose I should do that more. It's rude to simply call you 'you'."

"I don't mind. Whatever is easier."

"No. I think maybe it's time for me to do things that aren't easy but are better, like caring for Idris full-time and not depending on Lucien to swoop in when it gets hard. Taking your advice about using my medication properly and not counting on alcohol to numb the pain. You can't monitor me every night, after all."

"I wouldn't mind, if you like it, too. But you make good points about taking control yourself. It's all to the good."

"Not tonight, though, heh? You'll stay with me and help me with the relaxation?"

"Of course."

"And when we get back to Boston, perhaps we can see more of each other. Deliberate, like, not just because you happen to come to the club."

Ric barked out a laugh. "I'd love that, although I have to confess I've never 'accidentally' seen you. Every visit was planned on my part. I'm sorry about that."

"No, it's okay." Dafydd took Ric's hand. "I'm that glad you did, and I kind of knew anyway."

"No surprise. You're a very smart man, Dafydd."

"I might be. Let's go to bed. I'm not much one for partying, even if I did enjoy watching you wiggle about."

They started walking toward the steps leading to the staterooms. "Is that what I was doing? I've always fancied myself a good dancer."

"You are, mun. If you ask, Alex would definitely give you a job as a go-go boy."

Dafydd was teasing him! The knowledge lifted his heart. "I'll keep that in mind if this whole doctor thing doesn't work out."

They walked hand-in-hand into the room and stopped to check on Idris. The baby was sleeping face down with his bum in the air. So sweet, his two boys, and while it was premature to think it, he couldn't help doing so.

My family.

Chapter Ten

Brenin's expression went all mulish. "I don't like the idea of staying behind while you go haring off into danger."

Malcolm suppressed his impatience. Things between them had being going well and he didn't want to say anything to interfere with that. Nevertheless... "You do try a man's resolve, laddie, but I'm not changing my mind on this. You're safer staying here and we've enough manpower to get the job done without you."

That didn't help matters. Brenin crossed his arms. "You couldn't have succeeded back in Wales without me. You know how strong a swimmer I am."

"Aye, and it nearly tore my heart in two letting you go into that cistern and the castle alone. This time around, we don't need someone small. The cave entrance can accommodate a dingy, let alone a man, even one as big as we are. We'll make it through fine. By our nature, we can also hold our breaths a long time. We don't need your help for any of it. Besides, once we get inside, there won't be the kind of room you'd find in a castle. The fewer bodies crammed in, the better we can launch an attack without worrying about friendly fire."

Clasping his boy's shoulder, Malcolm leaned in closer. "If you're not there, I can concentrate on taking out whoever I need to without distraction. I know what you're going to say," he added when Brenin opened his mouth. "It matters little how well you can take care of yourself. I'll nowt be able to let go of my fear for you. Call it a failing of mine," he added with what he hoped was a disarming smile.

He saw the moment he'd won the argument. Brenin's face fell and he dropped his forehead onto Malcolm's chest. "Okay. I'm sorry to fuss. I worry, too, you know?"

"Aye." Malcolm kissed the top of his lad's head before setting him back again and letting go. "I'll return before dawn. Please stay here and help Duncan keep watch. Whoever is lurking down there may have been scoping us out as much as we've been doing to him. It will ease my mind to know that you're being vigilant."

Brenin nodded firmly once. "We'll be fine. The only helpless person on this ship is Idris. You just concentrate on coming back whole and healthy. We'll do the rest."

"I will, I promise." He gave his lad one more quick kiss for luck and left to find the others.

He passed a lot of unhappy faces when he joined Alex, Val, Emil and Harry by the stern of the ship. No one liked the idea of being left behind. Duncan was the only one who appeared relaxed. Despite the warmth of the night, the cop wore a windbreaker. Malcolm knew that was to hide an arsenal of weapons around the man's waist and under his arm. If he stooped down to lift the man's pant leg, he knew he'd find a clutch piece or two for good measure. Knowing that the cop was locked and loaded in defense of Malcolm's family eased his mind further.

"I don't envy your job, Duncan. Keeping this lot on lockdown isn't going to be easy. You know we'll cut you up into fish bait if any of these boys leave to come help?"

The human lifted his palm. "Understood, MacLerie. I swear to you that this time, they'll stay put. I'll tie them all to the mizzen mast, if I have to."

Malcolm rolled his eyes. "This is a motor yacht, not a sailing ship, but I take your point and appreciate it." He hesitated to leave. "You know if this goes south, you're going to have to run. If we're not back by mid-morning, take off. Brenin knows how to pilot this thing. Making for Scotland will be your safest bet. Don't even stop in Boston. My man, Darling, can get in touch with Willem, plus there are others scattered here and there who are loyal to Alex and will come when called. You'll need all the help you can get, regardless of Dracul being out of the picture. Petru, if he's about, is just as dangerous."

Duncan held up his hand again. "I understand all this. I've already received these instructions from Alex…and Val…and Emil" — he sighed — "and Harry." He tapped the side of his head. "It's all planned. Now, please go take down whatever fuckers you find without the distraction of worrying about the rest of us."

"Aye. Will do."

Malcolm stripped off his shirt and tossed it on a nearby deck chair then paused to yank off his boots. The large rubber dingy that served as the ship's tender had been dropped into the water already. It wasn't all that big and there was no sense clogging it up with stuff that could easily be left behind. He would have taken off the kilt except that it wasn't so late that there weren't a few other boaters around. Humans were ridiculously squeamish when it came to nudity. There was no sense attracting unwanted attention when their activity demanded stealth.

He found his compatriots ready to go, each in various stages of undress and sitting in the dingy. He climbed down to join them. It was a tight fit with the five of them, but they'd decided that they had to go in with full strength. There was no telling how many of their kind they'd find lurking about. Most of Dracul's men had been eliminated at one point or another, ending in Wales. Assuming the bastard himself was indeed dead, that still left Petru, Bran and three possible others to contend with. If they were all together now, it would be foolhardy to go in without close-to-even numbers. Someone needed to stay with the craft, however, Harry being the logical choice. Of all of them, he'd had the least amount of battle experience, having chosen to heal instead.

He braced himself as his presence caused the boat to rock, then took his place by the motor. He couldn't help glancing at the yacht. Only Duncan was visible, and Malcolm was both relieved and disappointed that he couldn't see Brenin. "What odds are we placing that the boys stay put?"

"A hundred percent," Val answered. "Harry and I both laid down the law, and this time, we covered every conceivable loophole. Plus, I promised Mackie that if he disobeys me, I'll punish him in all the ways he really hates."

Starting the motor, Malcolm eyed the man. "I'm not sure I can rely on that, Val. Your boy is devilish when he sets his mind to it."

"And Lucien can be surprisingly stubborn," Harry chimed in, "except I've tasked him with protecting Dafydd and Idris. He takes his role as protector seriously. Plus, Dr. Paz will do his bit to keep them in place."

"Duncan has wisely included Demi in guard duty," Alex added. "Emil and I have blessed Quinn and Jase in joining him in his endeavors. It's an important job and one which will keep the boys distracted."

"I did the same with Brenin." Malcolm steered his craft deftly away from the yacht and headed farther out. The plan was to approach the cave from a distance then swim the rest of the way in. "I hope to God it works."

That was the end of the conversation. Not knowing who or what they faced, they had to be prepared for a close-quarters fight to the death. While Malcolm ferried them, Val rechecked their arsenal. Each of them would carry an array of small arms and knives strapped to their waists, arms and legs. It had been rare for Malcolm to fight with anything other than his claymore. The impracticality of swimming with a large sword across his back was obvious. He'd have to make do.

Once they arrived about a half mile from their destination, Malcolm cut the engine and waited with the others while Val used his surveillance gear to study the coast.

"There's no movement along the shore and the mouth of the cave is completely filled with water, as we anticipated."

"High tide will give us cover," Alex observed unnecessarily, as that had been the plan all along. "We can only hope that the cave system is extensive enough that when we rise up, we aren't right in front of their eyes."

Val put his equipment away. "I wish I had more intel on it. There has to be at least one more cavern farther in that sits above sea level. Otherwise, it would be useless to them. They have to have somewhere dry to stash their deliveries."

Emil lifted his ass off his seat to pull down his jeans. "We won't know until we get there."

The obvious having been spoken, the rest of them followed suit. Malcolm whipped off his kilt and started strapping weaponry to various places on his body. His guns were secured in dry bags that he tied to a diving belt, and each of his knives — one around a calf and the other on his left biceps — were snapped into their sheaths. The weight of it all gave him some comfort. He wouldn't be going in unarmed, while at the same time, it wouldn't slow him down on his swim to shore. Luckily for his kind, human armaments had always been manufactured with the weaker species in mind.

When they were all ready, Alex dove into the water without another word. Val, then Emil, followed him. Malcolm stood to do the same. He shot Harry a glance.

"See you in a bit. Mind the store, heh?"

Harry patted the automatic rifle lying across his lap. "Not to worry. Good luck."

"Aye, we can always use a bit of that."

Malcolm sliced through the surface of the ocean, finding his friends waiting for him beneath like mermen. Scary ones. Alex signaled and Val shot off on point with Alex, then Emil, in his wake. Malcolm covered their six. Given the distance, they did have to come up for air once during their journey before plunging down again. The coastal Maine waters were quite frigid, but Malcolm barely noticed it. He was only grateful that Brenin wasn't needed this time around.

As they approached the shore, the bottom of the sea came closer and rockier. Waves helped to bring them in, but it also took more effort to swim in order to keep from dashing against the rocks looming on either side of the mouth of the cave. Malcolm trusted Val to navigate them safely. He concentrated on making sure nothing and no one crept up behind or beside them and followed Emil through the opening.

The moment they entered the cave, the sound of the sea around them changed. Everything was more muted, and although the temperature of the water didn't increase noticeably, it felt different. If his eyes hadn't been open, he still would have known that they were in a very different place than they had been. The sandy bottom beneath him became reachable with his feet within seconds. He remained submerged, however, until Val popped his head through the surface and signaled the others to do the same.

The cavern was wide, a good twenty feet across, and with high tide starting to recede, it wasn't entirely under water anymore. In the back of it, the ground sloped upward to a narrower entrance somewhere deeper inside the cliff. They sloshed through it and found themselves in a spot with a higher ceiling. There was also a tunnel leading farther into the cliffside. Even with his acute vision, Malcolm couldn't see beyond the pitch blackness. He could barely make out his friends in the faint moonlight that penetrated over the water. He strained to hear if there was anyone rummaging about back there, but all he could detect was the pounding of the waves. He waited like the good soldier that he was, gripping the sandy edge of the entrance and riding out the ebb and flow of the water. This was Alex and Val's operation. He was there to lend muscle.

Val unstrapped night-vision goggles from his waist, freed them from their protective covering and slid them onto his face. Everyone waited as quietly as possible while he peered beyond the opening. Then the man hoisted himself onto the small spit of dry sand and got closer. Whatever he saw must have given him comfort because he waved at the others to join him. Silently, Malcolm and the others rose from the water and joined Val on what bit of ground they could balance on with their big feet. Their weapons were drawn. Malcolm gripped a semi-automatic pistol in each hand. He could and would use them with equal skill and accuracy. Although they had no idea who they faced, the plan was simple. Whoever it was would never leave the caves alive and whatever they stored there would be destroyed.

They lined up single file. There was unfortunately no other way to proceed. Val lifted the goggles onto the top of his head, confirmation that he'd spotted light farther on. Then, he stepped into the darkness. Alex followed with Emil on his heels, and Malcolm brought up the rear. He kept one eye on the progress in front of him and the other on what was behind him. His job was to make sure no one came out of the sea to trap them. Despite the darkness and the stealth, there was always the possibility of someone having seen them. With Moran still coopted by Dracul's plans, his house remained a source of danger. Alex had decided against any effort to secure it, preferring to trust in a quick strike rather than risk showing their hand too soon.

Val led them beyond the opening, down an ever-drier natural stone path and Malcolm spotted the faint glow of a light beyond a bend they'd crept to. The others pressed against one wall within a few feet of the source of the illumination. Malcolm did the same, although he kept his sight on where they'd come from, trusting Val and Alex to launch an attack when they deemed it the right time. They waited a few minutes. No sound reached him. Either there was no one about or they were asleep. It didn't seem likely that the vicious men they knew would be stupid and not set watch. *Who knew?* With the head of the snake cut off, perhaps the others were proving to be weak and dumb as rocks. Malcolm had never been impressed with any of them except Dracul himself and Petru.

Emil tapped him on his arm. By the time Malcolm had turned his head, Val had sprung forward. There was a loud pop. Malcolm knew it for what it was — the sound of a gun going off with a silencer attached, the name of the device way overselling its actual functionality. No one outside would ever hear the bang, but it wasn't undetectable this close. With his guns up, Malcolm hurried to join his compatriots while continuing to cover their six. He kept waiting for more gunfire. None came, and when he finally entered the lit cavern, he saw why.

"Fuck me."

Petru knelt at the far end near a basic bedroll. He was naked, as if having been asleep when the assault had happened. None of those facts were notable. No, the utterly surprising part was that the man had his hands up — and he was smiling.

A quick glance confirmed that a pile of ash lay beside a large cache of 3-D printed guns. They were stuffed into wooden crates that stood open. There wasn't much else inside the small area except for some personal items and food rations. Malcolm wrinkled his nose at the salty and sour smell that told him Petru and his companion had been occupying the area for a while. Something wasn't right. There had to be more than these two, and there was no way Petru would leave himself so easily trapped. For damn sure, he wouldn't surrender. While Alex had required that they always be ready to take prisoners, that was not a thing that had proved true among Dracul's men.

With his sight still on the way they'd come, he asked no one in particular. "Who was it with him?"

Alex grunted. "That idiot maintenance drone who followed Dracul like a whipped dog."

Malcolm pictured the low-level crew member and dismissed him with his next thought. "Who else is there?"

"An excellent question," Alex drawled. "Care to answer it, Petru, before we turn you to ash?"

"There's only me and the 'idiot'. Thank you for taking care of him for me. His moronic patter was driving me crazy."

Malcolm had forgotten how much he hated the sound of the man's unctuous tone of voice. "Don't play the fool with us, Petru." He inched more into the room.

"I wouldn't dream of it. I've been waiting for you. You made good time, I must say. I wasn't sure you'd put the pieces together so quickly and I'd be forced to languish in this hellhole for weeks, if not months."

Keeping his gun ready, Alex stepped closer to the man. "Explain yourself."

"Gladly, *sir*. I wanted to speak with you but assumed I wouldn't get much of a chance to if I approached in a more conventional way." His gaze flicked to Val. "He would have killed me before I'd opened my mouth."

Val bared his teeth. "You've got that right, asshole."

"I would have done the same, once upon a time, for Dracul." His expression turned feral. "Not anymore. In any event, I thought my chances better if you came to me. My scheme was simple. I gave away these defective, new-fangled guns to foolish humans who I knew operated in your city with the hope of gaining your attention. Then, I assumed Val would have learned about Dracul's old gunrunning operation here and you'd check it out. It worked, obviously."

Malcolm huffed. "You made and gave away defective 3-D printed guns to humans so that they'd explode on them?"

Petru shrugged. "They're not all defective. And it caught your attention, didn't it?"

"Aye. Fucker that you are. We did the math."

"Exactly. And who cares about a few humans? *Vermin*. And stupid besides. So self-destructive. Even after a couple of guns exploded, I still had orders to purchase them. If nothing else, I would have made a pretty penny off the sales. That wasn't Plan A, however." Petru regarded Alex. "You've always been fair-minded. I counted on your not killing me outright in these circumstances. I'm helpless and capitulating. Are you really going to execute me?"

"Give me a reason not to."

Petru smiled, a truly nauseating vision. "I can help you find and stop Dracul once and for all."

The bottom of Malcolm's stomach dropped. "He's already dead," he spat out before anyone else could.

"You think that, do you?" Petru shook his head. "None of you are so naïve. You didn't actually see him crumble into ash, did you?" When they said nothing, he smirked. "Thought as much. He lived."

"You lie." Malcolm's fury rose, taking control of him. He stepped forward with his gun raised. All he could think of was his darling lad being at risk again.

Petru didn't so much as blink. "There's no reason for me to. After you left with the castle smoldering, I waited in the woods for someone in particular. He never showed. My only explanation is that he left with Dracul."

"Meaning that you never saw Dracul after our raid," Alex interjected. "Your belief that he lives is purely supposition, just as much as ours that he died."

"An educated one, though. Who better than I to know him and how he operates? And I believe with every fiber of my being that he did survive. I want to bring him down myself. I figure if I join forces with you, it increases my odds of finding and truly ending him."

Malcolm actually had no trouble believing the man when he said he wanted to kill Dracul. He remembered the point in the battle when Petru had had the chance to intervene and try to save his master. His failure to do so had puzzled Malcolm at the time. Trusting him to be an ally was another matter, however.

"Why?" Alex asked the obvious question. "After centuries of being his right-hand man, why would you turn on him now?"

"Because he stole something from me. *Someone*," he amended. "And I want him back, or at least, I don't want Dracul to have him."

"A boy," Emil said.

"Yes."

And Malcolm remembered that, as well—the almost-feral lad with the strangely striped hair and mismatched eyes who'd flown to Dracul's defense with suicidal rage. *So, he was once Petru's slave? It must have stung to have his toy snatched away by a bigger bully.*

Val grunted. "We don't trade in humans. You know that."

"I'm not asking you to. I simply want to end Dracul out of spite. You can understand that, surely."

"We can," Alex allowed. "At least we can understand why you'd be motivated by such. It doesn't convince me that we need you."

"There is no one who knows Dracul—the way he thinks, the contingency plans he's made, the property he owns—like I do. You need me, Alex. Keep me locked up, if that makes you feel better. But I will help you, make no mistake. And when it's finished, all I want is your promise to let me go. I will never again do anything that impacts you or your unfathomable desire to protect humans. I have my own money, enough to live happily for the rest of my life. I won't give you a moment of trouble ever again."

"That's for certain," Alex agreed.

Malcolm huffed. "You cannae be considering this. You know he cannae be trusted."

Alex eyed him. "Of course he can't and I don't." Without another word or any warning, Alex lashed out with a roundhouse kick that hit Petru square in the face. The guy crumpled silently to the ground. "Secure him, Val, for the trip back."

"Alex"—Malcolm approached his old friend and captain—"it's not safe, man, to bring him back and keep him prisoner. Think of Quinn and the other lads. I'll be heading back to Scotland soon, but you'll be stuck with him where? At the club? He's a danger to the ones we love."

Alex's eyes were troubled. "He is that. But if he's right and Dracul still lives, Petru is also, as he says, the best suited to find him and know his weaknesses."

"And if it's part of a trap set by Dracul?"

"Then we have to finish it—again." He watched Val truss Petru with zip-ties. "As you well know, we've always been prepared to take prisoners. It has just never come up. There's a room in the basement of the club that is intended for this very purpose. Even if he's lying, we chose long ago to play by our own rules of engagement. The moment he put his hands up, he stopped us from firing because we don't kill prisoners. Not without provocation," he amended. "I know it's a lot to ask, Malcolm, but we need to bring him back to Boston on your ship."

Malcolm sighed. "There's no asking, Alex. You're the boss, and if you say we haul his sorry ass with us, then that's what we'll do."

There was no question of the way this night was going to end. Malcolm followed Alex's orders because he trusted the man. He simply wasn't sure how Brenin would react to seeing one of his torturers again. He'd do anything to shield his lad from the pain. And Dafydd… Och, what a fucking misery it was going to be for that poor man, as well. There was no hope for it. They needed to make sure, however, that this threat-turned-unexpected-ally remained well and truly under their control.

Chapter Eleven

"It's almost dawn." Ric knew he was stating the obvious as he stood propped against the railing staring in the direction the raiding party had gone.

"Yeah, it's making me squirrely, too," Duncan admitted.

The cop had been patrolling the deck all night, armed and vigilant, despite having help from the rest of them. Only Demi, however, had carried a gun. Everyone else had declined to do so, including Ric. He'd discovered back in Scotland that despite years of playing video games, actually holding a weapon with the expectation that he might have to use it against a living creature was not in his comfort zone.

Apparently he wasn't alone in that sentiment in this particular company. Even Lucien, who'd spent over a century in the aliens' orbit, had refused. Dafydd had fled with Idris back to his stateroom with Ric's blessing. If something nasty went down, he wanted those two as far away from the action as possible.

There was only a hint of pink hanging low in the far horizon across the water, and yet he expected that within the hour, people in the Putnam Cove harbor would begin to stir. The last thing anyone needed to see was a boatload of mostly naked giants looking like bandoleros skipping along the waves. That would be an awkward conversation if the Marine Patrol spotted and stopped them.

"Come on," Duncan muttered into the air in general. "The raid on Dracul's castle took less time than this. Where the fuck are you?"

Ric didn't say anything to the obviously rhetorical question, but the cop's nerves only served to increase his anxiety.

Demi came racing up. "They're coming."

"They are?" Leaning over the railing, Ric strained both his eyesight and his hearing and detected nothing. Of course, he didn't have Demi's alien physiology. It took a couple more minutes before the sound of an outboard motor reached his ears. Not long thereafter, the small boat carrying their comrades came into view.

Without saying a word, the three of them headed toward the stern to help the others get back on board and secure the tender. He let Duncan and Demi get ahead of him, knowing that he wasn't much use compared to the skill, experience and plain muscle mass of most everyone else. He stayed on the top level while Duncan and Demi climbed down to the platform. The relatively small space would be crowded enough, and even those two weren't necessary, given that Malcolm jumped the gap between the two vessels with ease, lines in hand, securing them with a flash of movement that made Ric dizzy.

He stood gawking at the proceedings like a tourist, feeling superfluous, while determined to be available should he be needed. That seemed unlikely. He didn't have much to offer. With Harry around, even his skills as a doctor were redundant if someone had been hurt, which didn't appear to be the case anyway. Gathering intel had been his one big contribution to this venture and that had come to an end. Nevertheless, he wasn't going to lounge about if there was work to be done. It was just not in his nature to be idle.

He stood gripping the rails, watching as the aliens boarded just in time to benefit from the remaining cover the night afforded them. The gloom couldn't hide the fact, however, that while five men had left, six were returning. He blinked rapidly to make sure it wasn't a trick of the light or his tired eyes seeing double. But no, there was definitely a manly form wrapped up in a tarp and slung awkwardly over Val's shoulders. Ric's mind worked at making sense of what he was seeing. He knew what happened to the aliens when they died, so either this was a human ally that they'd chosen not to kill or—

"Who the hell is that?" Duncan demanded as he grabbed a bag from the dinghy.

It was Malcolm who answered, curtly. "Petru. Where's Brenin?" He practically jumped up the stairs and sped past Ric.

"In the saloon, I think," Ric answered, "with Quinn and Jase, resting," he added to Malcolm's retreating back.

Emil came next. "He wants to break the news to his boy himself and make sure he doesn't have to see the fucker while we secure him."

Ric eyed the limp, wrapped form that Val carried with ease now that he had more room. "I don't think anyone can survive in that tarp. Can the guy even breathe with that plastic around him?"

"Who the fuck cares?" Val growled. He took off for the stairs leading below deck with Harry trailing behind him.

Alex came next and flashed Ric a smile. "It's a bit of a strange tale."

Duncan, with Demi in tow, joined them. "What the hell took you so long? I was beginning to worry."

"Very sorry, Sergeant. The takedown of Petru and his one cohort went quickly, but destroying the cache of weapons they'd stored in the cave system took longer. We couldn't simply rig an explosion without risking bringing the cliff down and calling attention to it all. We ended up smashing thousands of guns by hand."

Alex flexed his fingers. "Tedious work, to be sure."

"I'll bet," Duncan said, gathering Demi to his side. "That doesn't explain why we have your sworn enemy tucked up here."

Alex sighed. "Yes, well, he surrendered instead of trying to kill us immediately like the other one did. And he insists that Dracul is alive. He's offered to switch sides, as it were, for personal reasons."

Duncan let out a string of curses, but Ric was focusing on one thing.

"Dracul lives? Seriously? That has to be a lie. This guy's messing with you, surely, to save his own life."

Alex shook his head. "I don't believe so."

"Dafydd." Ric felt as if he'd been punched in the gut as understanding dawned. What would this mean to the man he loved? "If Dracul's still out there, he'll come after Dafydd."

"Perhaps," Alex allowed. He put his hand lightly on Ric's shoulder. "We won't let him get anywhere near him or Idris. I promise you."

"No, not good enough." Ric's mind raced with fear. "I have to go warn him, like Malcolm is with Brenin. Then I have to protect him. I don't want him out of my sight until this thing is settled — for real this time."

He knew he was babbling and his insistence on taking care of Dafydd was almost laughable, given his acknowledged lack of skill in the area of combat. He couldn't help it, however. The instinct to guard Dafydd and the baby from harm overrode all rational thought.

Alex peered down at him intently. "I understand your feelings on this matter, Doctor, and I honor your claim over Dafydd and his child. So long as Dafydd is in agreement, you are more than welcome to move into the club. Although," he added with a frown, "quarters are getting a bit tight. It's time to expand into the adjacent building that I purchased a few months ago."

"Whatever," Ric replied. He didn't care if he had to sleep in a shoebox. So long as Dafydd was safe, nothing else mattered. "Excuse me."

Not bothering to wait for a response, he took off for the stateroom he by default shared with Dafydd. When he entered it, he was relieved to find both of his boys asleep. Idris was in his usual tortured bottom-up position. Dafydd lay on his side with his back to the wall and a fist tucked under his chin. A bit of the last of the moonlight shown in through the porthole, casting a glow over his beautiful, pale face. At rest, he looked young, essentially how he must have looked when Dracul had found him long ago. The alien blood had arrested his development to a large extent. It was a heartbreaking sight, and Ric had to remind himself that centuries had passed in Dafydd's life. He'd ceased being an adolescent through experience and a maturity of his mind that wasn't reflected in his outward appearance.

He had only a moment to gawk, however, before Dafydd's eyes flew open. The obvious evidence of how alert Dafydd had been forced to become broke Ric's heart all over again. He really didn't want to have to give the news he had, yet there was no waiting on it.

Dafydd propped himself up on one elbow. "What is it, then? Bad news," he concluded when Ric didn't answer immediately. "Who did we lose?" Dafydd's tone was so bleak, so resigned to misery.

"No one," Ric quickly assured him. He went to the bed and sat gingerly on the side. He tried to be careful not to crowd the boy. "The mission was successful and one more of Dracul's goons has been eliminated."

How odd that how quickly I've changed the way I think and speak. His vocabulary had become martial instead of medical. Someone had died that night, been killed. That it was an alien and an enemy shouldn't matter. He should feel worse about it, as his training had molded him. Every life was worth saving if at all possible. That was the way an ED doctor should think. It was what he would have said only a few months ago. Everything was different now. He was. That unnamed asshole in the cave had gotten what he deserved and could no longer threaten his beloved.

Dafydd pushed up to a sitting position, his legs crossed under the covers. "It's not the whole of it, though. I can see there's more in your expression."

Ric shifted his gaze away before forcing himself to look Dafydd in the eye. "The other guy, Petru, surrendered. He's being held onboard."

Dafydd scoffed. "Go on and pull the other one. Petru would never give up."

Ric angled his body in order to face the boy more directly. "He had a good reason, assuming he isn't lying."

"He lies like another would breathe."

"I'm sure you're right." Ric was desperate to latch on to anything other than the idea that Dracul lived.

Dafydd studied his face intently. "You don't believe that. Tell me, then. What bad news do you bring?"

Ric took a deep breath and spilled it all out. "He says Dracul is alive and he wants to join forces with Alex to bring him down."

Dafydd didn't say anything for so many long seconds that he could see it worried Ric. There was no hope for it, because he truly couldn't manage a single rational thought or response to the news.

The monster lives.

He wasn't surprised. Not really. Part of him had always been skeptical of the tale that he'd been killed. Without seeing it himself, he couldn't trust the assertion. Yes, Petru lied, but Dafydd didn't think he was this time.

"It's because of Andri," he said, to himself as much as Ric.

"What is? And who?"

"Petru's defection is because when Dracul banished me to the tower room for Idris' birth, he took Petru's slut from him as a replacement for my hole."

Ric winced. "Please, baby, don't talk about yourself or any unfortunate slave in that castle like that."

He shrugged. "It was the way of things for hundreds of years. I can't see them differently yet. Maybe not ever."

Ric reached out and clasped Dafydd's knee over the covers. Although his first instinct at the unexpected movement was to flinch, he made himself stay still. Ric's touch was nice, not menacing. Dafydd didn't want to make him feel bad. Besides, the warmth from Ric's hand crept through the blanket and into Dafydd's naked skin. It was comforting.

"You will. I know it. You'll soon come to truly believe your worth. And it sounds like this Andri is someone in need of rescuing if Dracul is alive and holding the boy. Petru's motives notwithstanding, if he can lead us to the right place, it will be worth the risk of keeping him around."

"If Andri is with Dracul, I don't think he'll thank you for your help. In fact, he should be treated as a source of danger."

"I'm sure Alex and the others will know how to handle it." Ric squeezed lightly. "I'm so sorry to have to tell you all this. I know how frightening it must be."

"I suppose." Dafydd searched to identify his feelings and realized he was merely numb. Until, that is, he thought of his son. He grabbed at Ric's hand. "Idris! We can't let him get the boy."

Ric grasped both his hands. "We won't. I promise you that he won't get anywhere near the baby…or you."

They sat quietly holding on to each other while Dafydd struggled to get his burgeoning panic under control. He was acutely aware of every place where his body touched Ric's. It was the warmth of the human body, so unlike the coldness of the aliens, that caught his attention the most. It didn't make him want to pull away. He didn't have to fight the instinct to do so.

Finally, Ric said, "I want to protect you, Dafydd. I know I'm nothing like the others in that regard, but please let me do what I can."

"I don't know what you're asking me, mun. I have no power over anything, including my own life right now."

"That's just the thing, Dafydd. You do. I'm asking your permission."

"For what, exactly?" This type of discussion confused him. What did Ric want him to say? "We already agreed you'd come visit me at the club the way you've been."

Ric's tongue flicked over his lower lip. Dafydd couldn't help tracking the movement. The man really was strikingly handsome, with full pink lips and straight, white teeth. His brown skin was an interesting contrast to Dafydd's pasty coloring.

Ric stared intently at him with his deep, dark eyes. "I want to move in with you—at least spend every night and my days off there—in the club, I mean, not in your bed." He dropped his gaze. "Although we're sharing one now because of the…you know, I don't want you to think that I'm making any assumptions about us."

Oh, yes, the good doctor was a noble man. He wanted Dafydd. Centuries of catering to a male creature's wants had made Dafydd an excellent reader on such matters. That kiss the previous night and Ric's own words left no doubt, either. He wasn't going to force the issue. He would be patient, waiting for Dafydd to approve each new step their relationship took. Dafydd had the feeling he'd wait until his dying breath for

Dafydd to give permission for him to do anything more than what they were doing right at the moment.

In the face of everything that was transpiring, it seemed suddenly ridiculous to keep the man at arms' length. What if Dracul was alive and came for him and Idris? There was certainly no chance now to forge a new, independent life, not when danger lurked outside of the relative safety of the club and the orbit of Dracul's enemies.

Dafydd needed the protection of a strong man. It was almost a relief to have the issue thrust upon him. He really wasn't suited to making his own decisions, perhaps never had been. His only problem was getting Ric to put aside his noble intentions and take charge. He was scared to death of failing.

"What if I don't mind your doing so?" He shrugged, trying not to show the tumultuous thoughts whirling inside him. "It makes sense, after all. I'm not able to take care of myself, let alone Idris. This world is too much for me. I don't know how to live in it. I can't keep on like I am, raising Idris in that club, always the poor relative surviving on charity."

Ric's grip tightened again. "That's not how the others see it."

"I do, though. And I want Idris to have something more like a normal family life—a proper home, not a room above a place where men play sexual games."

"Alex told me that he bought the building next door. He's going to expand the living quarters."

"Truly? That's good, then." He blew out a breath and took a moment to collect his thoughts before giving Ric the kind of demure look he knew men liked. "Idris and I need caring for, regardless. You could do that for us, couldn't you?"

"Of course." Ric's tone was fierce. "Nothing would please me more. But—"

"I can make it work," Dafydd hurried to assure him. "I know how to please a man, and I know things would be different with you—gentler, pleasurable even, if that kiss was anything to go by."

"Oh, Dafydd." His name passed Ric's lips on something like a sigh. "You don't have to use your body as currency. I'll gladly take care of you and Idris even if our relationship is nothing more than what it is right now. I meant it when I said it last night. I don't expect you to simply get over centuries of abuse. I also really don't want you to have to fall back into the habits of your previous life with that fucker Dracul. I understand it's all you know, but we can establish a new and better one between us."

Dafydd lifted his gaze. Ric was so totally earnest in what he said, yet Dafydd knew that it couldn't last. No man wanted the burden of a family without the benefit of someone warming his bed. Before his enslavement, he'd heard men talking when they didn't know he was around about how being able to sink into a warm pussy at the end of a hard day was what made life worth living. Dafydd might have changed over the centuries, but other men hadn't. "I believe you. Truly. Except you're a man with all the needs that go with it. Eventually, you'll want more."

"And eventually you may be able to give me more."

Dafydd shook his head. "I don't want that possibility, not promise, hanging between us. It will be like a weight bearing down on us both. What kind of life would that be, and how would it affect Idris? You'd come to resent me."

"Never."

Dafydd couldn't help smiling. "You're stubbornly sure, aren't you?"

"When I have to be, yes. You're worth the wait, Dafydd."

"And what if I don't want that, the waiting, I mean? I get to say when I want us to do more than lie next to each other, right?"

"Absolutely."

"Well, then," Dafydd sighed, his mind rapidly forming a plan.

He was being honest in his desire to set a future for himself and Idris that involved a man taking care of them both. There was no need to look for that solution when Ric was there, a decent man who wanted to give Dafydd everything. And Dafydd really liked him. After hundreds of years of enduring the monster's attention, it would be easy enough to give Ric what he needed and put up a good front about it into the bargain. Ric didn't ever have to know how Dafydd truly felt about their physical relationship.

Besides, there was a small measure of hope that he would come to like it. Anything was possible, and if there was any chance of such a thing, Ric being the man he was increased the odds to the greatest degree. It was hard to imagine there was any other man out there who would serve Dafydd's needs better. Plus, Ric knew all their secrets, so really, there was only one logical answer to Dafydd's problems.

It was merely a matter of convincing Ric of it.

Wiggling a little closer to the man, he said, "I don't want a lot of fuss over what my life's been like. I'm not much different than I was as a lad back in the seventeenth century, truth be told. All this talking about feelings and trauma and whatnot is beyond me.

I just want to do what makes me happy and being with you does that."

"Does it, really, Dafydd? I don't frighten you?"

Dafydd snorted, happy to be completely honest in this regard. "Not in the least, mun. You make me feel safe but oddly restless at the same time." This was also the truth. "Do you think you could...kiss me again?"

Although his experience with the act was limited, he'd seen others do it often enough and knew what it typically led to. That was why, after all, the crones in the village used to harangue young couples they saw doing it. While he felt a little bad at playing the man, he was also excited at the idea. That made whatever he did all right, didn't it?

After tugging his hands free, he scooted back toward the wall. "This time, maybe you could take off your clothes and we can do it lying down."

Ric stared back at him skeptically. "I don't think that's a good idea. I'm happy to kiss you, of course, but you know it's going to arouse me."

Dafydd rolled his eyes. "Of course. You think a stiff cock bothers me?"

"Yes," came the frank reply.

"Okay, then, keep your underclothes on, like I have."

Ric cocked his head. "Aren't you wearing my sleep pants?"

Dafydd's cheeks heated. It embarrassed him that he'd given in to the strange impulse, although it was working to his advantage now, perhaps. "It was too hot during the night."

"Ah." He stood, grimacing for a few seconds. "All right. If this is what you want."

"It is."

Dafydd slid down onto his back and at the same time pushed the covers away in order to make it easier for Ric to get under them. He made himself watch as the man peeled away his tight-fitting clothing. It was no surprise that he dressed that way. His body was something to be proud of. It wasn't bulky like the aliens. It was leaner, yet well-toned. It wasn't unlike his own, when he thought about it.

Years of confinement hadn't made him soft, undoubtedly another by-product of the alien blood. Running around after Idris gave him some exercise these days. He supposed he would have to stop taking fitness for granted and start learning how to use that fancy gym stuff at the club. A man such as Ric would want his partner to stay attractive, surely. Beauty was the only thing he had to offer.

He was so inside his head that he missed Ric climbing in beside him until he suddenly felt that warmth again. The automatic stiffening from anyone getting close gave way to both a sense of peace and anticipation. As Ric wiggled under the sheet, Dafydd rolled onto his side and dared to reach out. Ric stilled instantly when Dafydd slid his palm across the back of the man's hand, then over to his hip until finally resting on his slightly ridged abdomen. The muscles rippled under his fingertips and Ric's breath hitched. The outline of the man's hard cock was easy to see. It pressed against the thin material encasing it. All Dafydd would have to do was lower his hand a few inches… But no, that would be pushing it. Besides, Idris was in the room. Best to take matters slowly, as agreed.

"How does this work, then? The kissing while lying down."

Ric turned to face him, dislodging Dafydd's hand, but also giving him the chance to lightly clasp the man's hip. Dafydd's little finger brushed up against the swell of the man's tight ass. Ric's breath wafted over to him, smelling faintly of coffee. That didn't bother Dafydd. It was pleasant, actually, not the fetid odor of blood that Dracul had assaulted him with. And once again, it was the warmth of it that caught and held Dafydd's attention. That one critical difference between the two men, in particular, was what would make this new beginning easier.

Without saying a word, Ric leaned slowly toward him with his eyes open. He gave Dafydd every chance to pull back or tell him to stop. He didn't do either. Closing his eyes, he met the man halfway. Like before, their lips barely touched at first. Everything was soft and lazy, Ric skimming his mouth across his. Then the contact became firmer and more constant to the point where their connection didn't break. Dafydd curled his fingers to tighten his grip on Ric's hip. A moment later, Ric's tongue joined in. He flicked it against Dafydd's lips a few times before using the tip like a silky battering ram. Dafydd took the hint and opened for it to slide in.

Here was a different kind of experience altogether. Ric plundered his mouth in the sweetest possible way, making a languid sweep to every corner before teasing Dafydd's tongue into a sensuous dance. Dafydd had come across knowledge of this way of kissing at some point, but he'd always dismissed it as some vulgar form of dominance—a thing men did because shoving their dicks in one hole at a time wasn't enough. Oh, how wrong he'd been. This held its own form of pleasure. He felt it all the way down to his cock. It stirred with a weak effort to harden. At the same time, he used his hold on Ric to try to tug him closer.

Ric resisted, holding his body away from Dafydd's, then he broke the kiss. Dafydd made a noise that was disturbingly like a whimper. That led to Ric giving him a quick peck before pulling away.

"I think that's as much as we should do right now." The man's voice was breathless and Dafydd felt a certain pride an knowing he'd done that to him. "It's been a long night, and Idris is only a few feet away."

"He's always going to be that, isn't he?" Now Dafydd sounded petulant. *Have you lost your mind, mun? He's pleased with what little you gave him. Shut up, already!*

"Onboard, yes. Back home, we'll eventually have our own room, if you decide you still want me to move in with you."

"I won't change my mind about that."

Ric graced him with another quick kiss. "Good. For now, though, let's go to sleep — or, at least I need some." He yawned loudly, making Dafydd feel guilty. Ric had stayed up all night guarding them. He deserved some rest.

Dafydd reluctantly let go and rolled onto his back. "Of course. I'm sorry. I'll try to do the same but I'll be quiet, regardless of whether I succeed. Idris will be awake in a couple of hours, though. I'll get him out of here as quick as I can."

Ric yawned again, flopped on his back, and said, "I know, and it's fine. Don't worry about disturbing me. I think at this point, I'll sleep through anything. Oh." He flipped to face Dafydd once more. "If we don't leave Putnam's Cove first thing, how about we go out for lunch?"

Dafydd frowned "Go out? To eat at a restaurant, you mean?"

"Yes. A date, Dafydd. I guess you've never been on one." There was sadness in his tone.

"No." Dafydd tried to sound indifferent. "We don't have to go through all of that nonsense."

"I want to." Now Ric's voice held a hint of steel. "You deserve to be wooed."

Dafydd scoffed. "I'm not some silly girl."

Ric blew out a breath. "Dating is for everyone, Dafydd, including me. Please, I want to go out."

Feeling flummoxed at this unexpected turn of events, he said, "Idris—"

"Will join us."

"That's not very romantic, if that's what you're going for, mun."

Ric traced one finger down Dafydd's cheek. "Let me be the judge of that. You're a package deal, you and Idris. I understand that. It will be fun for the three of us. Please."

Dafydd huffed, surprisingly pleased by the man's words yet unable to admit it. "All right, then, if it makes you happy."

"Thank you." One more quick kiss and Ric settled down. Within minutes, his breath became deep and even.

Dafydd lay beside him, his mind in turmoil because he was not quite sure whose plan was actually being implemented—his or Ric's.

Chapter Twelve

"Oh, what a big boy you are! I bet you have an appetite to match." The server grinned down at Idris.

The baby pounded his chubby fists on the highchair tray and shouted. "'Ood!"

The man chuckled. "Right away, sir. You folks enjoy your drinks while I put in your order. Wave me down if you need anything else in the meantime."

Ric nodded. "Thanks."

Sitting back in his chair, he surveyed the restaurant before reminding himself that there was nothing for him to worry about. The bad guys around here were either dead or locked up. This was going to be a happy day of touristing and nothing else. Thank God Alex had already decided to leave Putnam's Cove later in the day so that they could dock in Boston under cover of darkness. No one wanted their prisoner to be noticed while being transported off the boat. It'd be hard to explain away the human-shaped bundle Val would be carrying.

He picked up his glass of chablis and took a sip. "Hmm, nice. I'm glad the server suggested it."

Dafydd, looking uncomfortable, did the same. He'd surprised Ric by ordering wine instead of something non-alcoholic. The server had carded him, of course, and had eyed the fake ID Val had produced for Dafydd with skepticism. No surprise there. The official word was that Dafydd was twenty-two, but he obviously appeared to be far younger. Ric wondered how long that would be the case. It was one more question to ask Harry. He'd started compiling a mental list and it was getting longer every day.

"Hmm, not bad, although my experience runs more to reds than whites." Dafydd glanced around the terrace area that Ric had chosen for them. It was roomier than inside, and a flight of stairs leading down to the street was right behind Dafydd. A form of escape hatch that Ric assumed would put Dafydd more at ease among a crowd. "It's pretty here, and I appreciate how you chose a spot with both a view and elbow room." He shot Ric a smile.

Gratified that he'd done well by the man he loved, Ric returned the look. "I'm glad you like it. I want you to enjoy the day, Dafydd." He gestured toward the harbor, which was on full display, given the location of the restaurant. "I love this view. I've never come to this place before. It was always too much of a family spot when I was a single guy on the prowl."

Dafydd opened his mouth then had his attention taken by the baby when the boy threw his sippy cup on the floor. "Idris! We don't do that. This is a nice place, so be a good boy."

In response to his father's rebuke, Idris only bounced his legs and clapped. Dafydd shook his head, picked up the cup then grabbed his napkin to clean up the milk that had dribbled out onto the deck's flooring.

The server came running up before Dafydd had a chance. "Oh, sweetie, don't worry about that." Crouching down, the man swiped at the liquid. "This is nothing compared to the spills we get. The treated wood can handle it." He beamed up at Dafydd.

"Oh well, you're that kind to help." Dafydd sat back and took an awkward sip of his wine.

The server tickled one of Idris' feet before standing. The baby giggled and bounced some more, proof that he was like any other human and not some strange alien. "Are you giving your dads a hard time, little man? Where are you from, by the way? I just love your accent." The guy was staring right at Dafydd and giving him a coquettish smile.

Ric's blood pressure rose a notch and he leaned on the table with his elbows.

Dafydd's gaze slid over to Ric before answering. "Wales."

"Oh." The server—what had the little fucker called himself? Parker? Yeah, *Parker*—placed his hand over his heart. "I've always wanted to go there. It sounds so romantic. Is it beautiful?"

Ric hadn't thought of himself as the jealous type, and yet here he was, tamping down the urge to shove back his chair then jump to his feet to toss Parker over the railing. He had to let go of his glass of wine, lest he break the stem.

Dafydd tilted his body closer to Ric's, the small gesture being the one thing that throttled back Ric's growing rage. "It is, yes, although you've got plenty of that here. I like it better than home."

"Hmm, I guess the grass is always greener." Parker was apparently a poet-philosopher, too. Ric wanted to dump Idris' sippy cup over the man's head. Something of his feelings must have showed in his face. "I'll go check on your order," Parker said before hurrying away.

"Here," Dafydd said to the baby, "be a good boy and eat this." He broke up a piece of bread and scattered it on the highchair's tray.

Ric forced himself to calm down. There was no need to ruin the day with pettiness before it got started. Picking up his glass, he sipped his wine while staring out at the harbor.

"Are you angry?" The question, asked with such obvious trepidation, forced Ric to refocus his attention on Dafydd.

He could see the worry in the boy's eyes. "No, of course not." He reached over to grabbed Dafydd's hand and immediately regretted his rash movement when Dafydd jerked, although he didn't pull away.

Too ingrained not to resist. He couldn't stop that ugly conclusion from popping into his head.

Dafydd dropped his gaze. "Please don't lie. I could see it in your face. Is it because of Idris acting up?"

"No," he was quick to reassure him. "Idris is a toddler, and that's what they do. They throw and knock things over and generally make you crazy. I won't be surprised if he has a major meltdown for no discernable reason before the day is out." He shrugged. "It's normal, and while it's irritating, I'm sure, it's part of the package." He gently lifted Dafydd's hand and kissed the inside of his wrist. "If I appear mad, I apologize. It's jealousy, plain and simple. Parker's attention to you irritated the crap out of me."

Dafydd stared back at him, wide-eyed and flicking his tongue over his lower lip. "Why is that, then? Shouldn't I have answered that man when he asked where I was from?"

"Of course, you should have." Closing his eyes briefly, he shook his head. "I'm making a hash of this." He huffed out a breath. "It's the server I'm mad at. He's flirting with my...you."

He edited his words at the last second, not wanting to appear overly proprietary when his instinct was to stand and pee his chablis in a circle around Dafydd.

Dafydd smiled. "Really? That's it? You're not worried that I want that, are you? I'd as soon he not speak to me at all. Men's attention unnerves me." Dafydd's cheeks pinked up. "Besides, he's not to my liking. I'm attracted to more masculine men."

"Oh." Ric's heart kind of sank at that admission. "That kind of lets me out of the running." He chuckled nervously.

"Don't be daft, mun. You're exactly my type. It doesn't matter if you're not so large like the...others. You're bigger than me and your muscles are impressive."

Ric stared at him, looking for signs of empty flattery. He saw only sincerity. No, more than that. There was a genuine interest in Dafydd's look.

"Thanks," he said with an uncharacteristic shyness.

"It's none of my doing. I only state what I see. That server-man's attention bothers me. You'll take care of it, won't you?"

Ric's chest all but puffed up at the request. Damn, he hadn't ever thought of himself as the macho type. And yet here he was, acting possessive and proud over Dafydd's compliments and his handing the reins of control to him. He vowed to himself that he would never take advantage of that trust.

When Parker returned with their food, Dafydd kept his head down and left it to Ric to answer the server's questions and order more milk for Idris. Both Ric and Dafydd tucked into their lunch, pausing for the occasional mundane back and forth that all couples had during a meal. The baby was given macaroni with butter and Parmesan to mess about with, and his sippy-cup privileges were returned to him. No one was surprised that it landed on the ground again. Ric merely laughed, picked it up and wiped it off before putting it back on the tray. It was all perfectly normal.

They passed on dessert with the promise of getting ice cream later. Then, after strapping Idris into his stroller, Ric took control of steering the thing through the crowded sidewalks of the tourist town. He worried about how Dafydd would handle the crush of people and was delighted when the boy slipped his arm through Ric's and walked tightly to his side. He couldn't keep the shit-eating grin off his face as they ambled around.

They spent the rest of the afternoon checking out the shops, something Dafydd had never done before, naturally. It was fun watching him react to all of the myriad kitsch available. They bought an 'I am crabby' T-shirt, along with a stuffed lobster, for Idris. The baby's expression adorably mimicked the one of the crab on his shirt, while he elected to chew on his toy's claw.

They bought ice cream cones from a small place that made their own. Ric quickly devoured his then parked the boys on a bench in the square to eat theirs. It was all part of a hasty plan to keep them occupied while he dashed back to a store where Dafydd had admired a green sea-glass bracelet. Dafydd had insisted it was too 'dear' to buy. Ric's credit card tended to agree with that assessment, but he was determined to buy his love something suitable to remember their time together. Upon his return, there was no more room on the bench, so he knelt beside the stroller instead.

"Here… I want you to have this." He took the bracelet out and clasped it around Dafydd's slender wrist. "Perfect," he said, then licked away the line of ice cream melting down the cone Dafydd held. It wasn't quite a proposal, but it would do for now.

Dafydd blinked rapidly at him. "You shouldn't have," he said in a low voice.

"I wanted to." He stood. "It made me happy. Do you like?"

Dafydd's cheeks pinked up fetchingly. "I love it. You know I do. Thanks…and all."

Before Ric could reply, Dafydd jumped to his feet and planted a sticky kiss on Ric's cheek. He surprised him further by returning for another, this time on the lips. And it was Dafydd's tongue that begged entrance, plundering Ric's mouth.

A quick learner.

He could have stayed there forever, tasting the sweetness that was both ice cream and pure Dafydd. He would have spent the next few minutes, certainly, doing so if someone calling his name hadn't caught his attention.

Reluctantly breaking the kiss, he turned to see a couple of old summer friends, Joey and Greg, strolling up in their Speedos and flip-flops. "Hey, good to see you." He didn't really appreciate the interruption and was aware that Dafydd stiffened by his side.

The guys stopped in front of them, hips cocked and wearing mirror expressions of obvious curiosity, if not cattiness. They went through the formality of hugging and air-kissing before Ric reached for Dafydd, only to find that he'd retreated to the bench and was trying to wipe Idris' face with a tiny napkin.

Greg eyed the scene. "Good heavens, Ric, I didn't know you were into twinks—and breeding ones at that."

For a split second, Ric thought his friends actually knew that Dafydd had given birth, then logic stepped in and he realized they were simply being snarky.

"Talk about robbing the cradle," Joey added. "Do they take turns in the stroller?"

There had been a time not long ago when he would have viewed the world the same way. All that had mattered to him besides practicing medicine was getting laid and having a good time. Things had changed dramatically for him. There was no denying that. And he found that he liked it—no, loved it. Spending the day lying in the sun then clubbing at night no longer held any appeal for him. This was what he wanted—a family. There was no reason to deny it, to himself or others, nor did he need to justify his plans by insisting it was based on what was best for Dafydd.

He made a point of turning his back on the two men and going to stand behind Dafydd. He placed his hand on his shoulder and said, "This is Dafydd, my partner, and Idris is our son."

A noticeable shiver ran through Dafydd yet he said nothing other than, "A pleasure."

Joey and Greg stood with mouths agape for a few seconds. "You've been domesticated?" Joey asked finally.

Ric grinned. "Yup. You should try it."

Greg pointed at Idris, who, despite his father's efforts, was painting his face with chocolate ice cream. "It looks *messy*."

"It is," Ric confirmed cheerily. "Wonderfully so."

"We'll take it under advisement. See you around, Ric." Looping his boyfriend's arm, Greg sauntered away with him in tandem, their twin pert asses swinging provocatively.

They held no allure for him whatsoever. "Sorry about that."

Dafydd twisted his head around to look at him. "No need to apologize on my account. It was you they were insulting, mun."

"Not from my perspective." He gnawed at his lower lip. "I hope you don't mind what I said, you know, about our being a family."

Dafydd's expression softened. "No, it was nice, like, wasn't it?"

Sometimes Dafydd's Welsh speech pattern left Ric unsure of how he truly felt. This time, though, he decided to take it on face value.

He leaned down to give Dafydd a quick kiss. This was becoming a habit that he could get used to. And honestly, he could survive on Dafydd's kisses for a very long time, even though he did hope for more at some point. "Yes, it was. Let's get Idris cleaned up and get back to the ship. I think we could all do with a nap."

"Good idea. This one could use a good scrubbing, as well."

There wasn't much they could do to clean Idris' face with napkins. Giving up, they headed back to the ship. Once again, Dafydd took Ric's arm while Ric pushed the stroller. They really did look like a family, and more importantly, felt like one. Ric knew a moment of inner panic at the notion that it could all change in an instant if Dafydd wanted it to. Then he told himself to settle the fuck down. There was no sense in getting ahead of everything. He needed to appreciate the here and now, focus on what he had and trust that the rest would follow.

With most everyone else on the upper deck hanging around Malcolm's small pool, they encountered only Val lurking about as usual as they made their way over to the back stairs. Through the tinted glass of the saloon, he could see Malcolm and Brenin in an intimate embrace. He hoped the Highlander and his boy were weathering the effect of Brenin's captivity on their relationship. His own experience told him it was not going to be anything easy or quick.

At the top of the stairs, Dafydd hauled Idris to his hip. Ric folded the stroller. Before continuing down the stairs, however, he had to ask the question burning in his mind.

"Did you enjoy yourself?"

Dafydd stared back at him with wide eyes. "Don't be daft, mun. It was the best day of my life." With that, he carried Idris away.

Ric watched them descend to the lower level before shaking off his surprised glee and following.

* * * *

Brenin melted against Malcolm's chest with the man's hard dick fully embedded. Thank God his lover was an alien with an inhuman amount of stamina. Brenin had been demanding sex every few hours since the early morning. Malcolm had accommodated him each and every time with boundless energy. Brenin's ass practically swam in the man's cum, like now, with the sticky fluid drying on their conjoined laps. He didn't care. He needed the contact, the reassurance and the distraction. It didn't matter that they were sitting in the saloon with the raucous sounds of the others enjoying themselves outside before they set off for Boston. With his kilt splayed out around them, they were sufficiently covered, not that anyone would care.

This time, Malcolm had fed from him, at Brenin's insistence. His man needed the energy boost, plus being drained of blood along with the cum made him more fuzzy-brained and he wanted that mental bliss. It kept him from dwelling on his fears arising from the fact that evil resided below. It didn't matter how much Malcolm or the others reassured him or his own logic told him that Petru couldn't escape—the terror lurking within threatened to erupt at any moment. A shudder ran through him, despite the effects of his most recent orgasm.

Malcolm's loose hold tightened a bit—not to constrain but to comfort. "Easy, laddie. Did I take too much?"

Brenin nuzzled his neck. "No. Not enough, maybe. The way I feel, it's tempting to have you drain me dry."

"Och, now." Malcolm rubbed his chin against Brenin's head. "Never say such a thing. I should have ended that arsehole back in the cave. I'll do it now to spare you this pain."

"No." Brenin forced his head up and he peered into Malcolm's troubled eyes. "I won't ask that of you. I don't want to make you into something you're not—a stone-cold killer."

"Nothing about my feelings for you are cold, my bonnie lad."

The fierceness in the man's gaze made Brenin shiver in an entirely different way. He clenched his hole and felt an answering pulse from the thick cock. It swelled, stretching his channel more with the promise of another vigorous fuck.

"I love that you're willing to kill for me," he said in a breathless voice. "I shouldn't, but I do." He stretched to kiss Malcolm with a hunger that started with his tongue and ended with his teeth. He tasted blood and went back for more, appreciating how it boosted his energy.

Malcolm allowed him the freedom to take what he wanted then lapped his own skin to close it when Brenin pulled away. "Does it make you feel better?"

Brenin nodded. "Stronger."

"Good." Malcolm tucked some of Brenin's hair behind his ears. "My offer stands. If it is to be done, then it best be soon because I need to prep the ship to get underway."

Leaning back, Brenin rocked, liking how the small movement pressed Malcolm's dick against his prostate. His poor cock was wrung dry, yet the pleasure was still there nonetheless. He cupped Malcolm's pecs and ran his thumbs across the nubs. "No. It's wrong, and besides, if he's right about Dracul, we need him."

"You understand, laddie, that if he helps us, Alex has promised him his life. I can't go back on that. It's one thing to go against Alex's promise now, but after Petru fulfills his end of the bargain…"

"Aye, I ken." He giggled when he realized what he'd said. "You're rubbing off on me. If I'm not careful, you'll make me forget I'm a Welshman, *mun*."

"Dinnae you worry, laddie, I'll remind you, *like*."

They shared a laugh over their crossed idiomatic expressions and accents. For a while, Brenin forgot his worries.

"Oops, sorry! We're not looking," Mackie said, as he backed out of the saloon with his eyes shielded. Quinn, Demi and Jase were behind him.

"Oh, come back," Brenin called out. "Malcolm has work to do anyway." He lifted off his lover's cock, missing it immediately, and un-straddled him. Wetness trickled down his thighs. He made a face. "Guess I need a shower."

"We both could do with a bit of a wash." Malcolm rose and scooped him into his arms. "The saloon's all yours, lads."

Malcolm carried him down to their stateroom and squeezed them both into the narrow stall in the bathroom. They took turns scrubbing each other's backs then hair, and there was one more quick, almost brutal, fuck before they got out.

"Go to the pilot house, why don't you? I'll be along shortly. We can stick together for the rest of the night."

Brenin wrapped his clean backup kilt around his waist. "Okay, but first I'm going to find Harry. I'm, ah, going to ask for something to calm my nerves. As much I'd like to try, I don't think we should have sex while you're steering." He flashed a cheeky grin.

"Aye, that does sound like both a wonderful and a terrible idea." Dressed in his own kilt, Malcolm came over. "Whatever you think is best, Brenin, I'm fine with."

"Good, and when we get back home, I'll ask Doc MacPhee for a longer-term prescription."

"All right, except…"

"What is it?" Alarm shot through him, testament to how on edge he was.

"Dinnae fash yourself. I'm going to speak to Alex, is all, about our returning to Boston. He's renovating a building to provide more living space for the family and I want a floor. You deserve some peace and quiet and the security that will come from knowing you have all of us, not just me, to protect you. Dracul will *never* touch you again."

"Oh." Brenin hadn't considered the implications of the monster being alive. He'd been too focused on the more immediate concern of his henchman being onboard. He clenched his hands together at the thought. "I see your point, although," he added, swallowing down his fear, "that's not fair to Darling and the others. We can't leave that mess with them indefinitely."

Malcolm grimaced. "I've given that some thought. The humans aren't much of a problem. Seems to me that Doc MacPhee knows how to handle them. It's the hybrid who's the issue. I propose we bring the lad and his father back with us and see what Harry and Lucien can do with them. They'll live separately from us," he quickly added.

"Okay." Brenin closed the gap between them and leaned against Malcolm, taking comfort from the solidity of the man. "I trust you, Malcolm, so long as I can stay with you."

Malcolm put his hands loosely on Brenin's hips. "Always, laddie. Always."

Chapter Thirteen

Ric plopped onto the front stairs of the building that housed the medical examiner's department. He couldn't make it to the sidewalk, he was shaking that badly. And because nausea was roiling his stomach, he put his head between his knees.

"Your first kid, huh?" Vincente sat down beside him.

Surprised at his boss's arrival, he lifted his head. "Yeah." This was just perfect. Not only was he having a hard time dealing with autopsying a child, he had given Vincente another reason to ride his performance.

"I could say it gets easier, but that would be a lie." Vincente sighed. "You get better at hiding it, that's all, even from yourself."

He angled himself to look at the man. "Really? That's kind of what I thought I'd accomplished working in the ED." He shook his head. "I've treated plenty of kids, lost a few, as well. This, though... How the hell can anyone deliberately do that to a child, let alone her own father?" He clutched his stomach as if he could hold the contents in. "It's sickening."

"Yeah, it is. But that's the job. If we'd wanted unicorns and rainbows, we'd become…shit, I don't know, professional clowns or something."

Ric actually managed to bark out a laugh. He wouldn't have pegged his boss in a million years as having either empathy or dry wit. "You're right, there. Thanks," he added, because somehow the interaction had eased the shakes, at least.

"No problem. That's what I'm here for, Paz, to help you learn and cope. You're good, you know. You'll develop the hide for the work."

"Thank you, sir."

They both stood. Vincente looked around. "Beautiful day and there's some of it left. You got a guy out there waiting for you?"

Ric pictured Dafydd and nodded. "Yes, and he comes with a little boy. I love them both."

"Excellent. Go hug them. It helps, trust me. I'll see you Monday."

With that, the man hustled down the stairs. After a few seconds, Ric did the same, although he headed for the subway, not the parking lot. Normally, he would go home first and change, but he knew Vincente was right. He needed the comfort of seeing Dafydd and Idris, confirming that they were safe. In the two weeks since they'd returned from Maine, he'd practically moved in. Despite intending to go slowly, he'd ended up leaving a bunch of personal items at the club, including clothing. He could shower and put on a T-shirt and jeans without going to his apartment. Dafydd wouldn't mind — or if he did, he wouldn't ever say.

That was what worried Ric. The burgeoning relationship between them was progressing, slowly and satisfactorily. Yet he couldn't quite shake the feeling that things weren't as they seemed. Dafydd appeared to welcome the kissing and other 'second base' kind of affection they'd shared. Ric wasn't worried that the physical responses weren't genuine. The stiffening at his first touch had disappeared. Dafydd rarely flinched, although Ric was also careful to make his every move visible before any actual touching occurred. Perhaps most tellingly was that Dafydd was becoming aroused by their interactions. His jeans, and certainly Ric's sleep pants that the boy had stolen, couldn't hide that fact.

As a doctor, Ric knew not to read much into the physiological change, however. The human body was hard-wired to do what it did. That said nothing about Dafydd's real view on matters. What worried him was that Dafydd merely did what he thought Ric wanted. If that were the case, they could be building a life together founded on a lie. A nice lie, but nevertheless one that bothered Ric. It was imperative that he keep taking things slow. Patience was its own reward, as his *abuela* had often said. In this case, it was the only way to be sure Dafydd wasn't falling into the familiar pattern of giving a powerful man what he wanted as a survival instinct.

The subway was crushed with people desperate to get both home and out again on a Friday night. He suffered through it, knowing that catching a Lyft in rush-hour traffic would be the same slow process, only with more elbow room and at a higher cost. With the hope of a family in the not-too-distant future, he was watching his pennies more closely than usual. Not long ago, he would have been like a lot of his fellow travelers, looking forward to having a good time and not worrying about dipping into their pockets. Life had changed, and he couldn't have been happier about it.

As he stood pressed against strangers, he amused himself with visions of what waited for him, including a fabulous dinner courtesy of Emil and his amazing kitchen. Ric felt rather guilty at all the free meals, although Alex had simply raised his eyebrows when Ric had offered compensation. If he'd asked to drink the alien's blood, he didn't think he would have received a more dismissive reaction. Oh well, he supposed he'd earned his keep to some degree by joining their forces, and the war wasn't over, apparently. The bigger issue was going to be whether Dafydd could switch to less luxury once the danger had truly passed. Ric wanted to make as normal a life for his family as possible, and that meant living off his salary, not Alex's charity.

Can Dafydd settle for a middle-class existence? Is it fair for me to ask it of him?

Those were questions that were harder than he could deal with at the moment. Plus, there was no way of knowing when or if they would become pressing. For now, it was about forging a real bond with his lover and making sure the monster-lite who dwelled in the basement of the club never came near Dafydd or Idris. While he trusted Alex and Val implicitly to do their jobs, he was never going to let up his vigilance.

The first word that came into his head when he approached the club was 'home'. It wasn't merely because he'd become used to being there. It was Dafydd and Idris that made it so. Being Friday, the place was already coming to life. Rich men could afford to knock off work early at the week's end, he supposed. He gave a brief nod to the boy at the door, then marched through the downstairs area over to the elevator. Kitty was polishing her bar, per usual, which Ric had come to appreciate was her way of working off energy. She appeared calm, but he sensed a strong undercurrent in her. He hoped Anderson was helping her find a different outlet. She flashed him a smile regardless, making him feel welcome.

After a quick look told him Dafydd wasn't in his room, he took the liberty of showering. Washing the grime off his body proved easy. The emotional dirt was ground in, though. Water was useless in dealing with it, but the anticipation of being with his boys worked wonders. By the time he'd dressed in clean, comfortable clothes, he was eager to see them and lose himself in the pleasure of a visit. He knew where to look and found Dafydd and the baby with Lucien in his and Harry's living room. Idris, to Ric's delight, was playing with his garage.

Dafydd's and Lucien's heads were close together as they peered at a laptop on the coffee table.

"There's too many choices, mun, and the cost is very dear for all of this. I don't need to spend that much."

Lucien sat back. "You said you wanted conservative and masculine. Stickley fits that bill very nicely. I intend to buy quite a few pieces myself when the rest of you have moved over to the new building. It's time to redecorate."

Ric paused in the doorway, unseen. His heart sank at the notion that Dafydd was looking at such expensive stuff. Ric's budget didn't run to high-end furniture. Then again, if Dafydd bought it now with Alex's money, it would mean he and Idris would have long-lasting and lovely stuff. Shit, he hadn't thought of these economic issues when he'd made his play for being

Dafydd's lover and maybe husband one day. He'd been so focused on the issue of healing Dafydd and helping him move past his trauma, emotionally and physically, that he hadn't considered whether he deserved him.

"That's it, then," Dafydd observed. "I'll take these used bits off your hands. They're plenty fine for me." Dafydd caught sight of Ric. The way his face lit up in the unguarded moment helped ease those pesky concerns that he was putting on an act. It did nothing for these new money worries, though.

"You're early. I thought you'd go home first." There was only welcome in the tone, not censure.

I am home. Ric stepped into the room and headed over. "I had the urge to come straight here," was all he said. He wouldn't bring with him the ugliness of his work.

He kissed Idris on the top of his head before doing the same with Dafydd on the lips. "What's up?" Although, he knew, he didn't want Dafydd to think he'd been spying.

"We're shopping," Lucien answered. "Alex is plowing through the renovations next door, so everyone has to be ready to move in in about six weeks. That means picking out everything from wall paint, to carpeting, tiling, drapes, appliances — "

Dafydd put his hands over his ears. "Please, mun, it's more than I can handle. Can't everything be white?"

"Linen white or eggshell white, or — "

Ric laughed at Dafydd's groan. The pains and tedium of decorating were nice, normal problems to have. "How about I help you? We can spend the weekend at it. I have a good eye for color, I've been told."

"Fine, then, you pick out everything."

"No, baby. We'll do it together. This is going to be your home for the foreseeable future. You should like the space."

Dafydd huffed and waved his hand at the living room at large. "Can I have all this, then, Lucien? At least that will solve the furniture part."

"Sorry. Demi has claimed what he calls 'first dibs'. He'll put it into storage until he and Trey make their home together. He's determined to live on his husband's salary and refuses to buy anything new."

It was on the tip of Ric's tongue to say something about wanting to do the same. He said nothing, however, because that would be his ego and insecurity speaking. Dafydd deserved the finest. Besides, they had nothing like the promise that Trey and Demi had exchanged. It would presumptuous to assume Dafydd would ever agree to marry him.

He stared at the computer screen. "What's our budget?"

"Budget?" Lucien echoed. "Alex hasn't set one. You simply pick out what you want from the sites I've bookmarked. Those are the ones that Alex's contractor has identified as his sources of materials, plus furniture stores that fit what Dafydd says he likes best. They all deliver. No need for you to go out physically."

Bless Lucien. He understood that being in crowds would bother Dafydd. "Surely Alex has a limit on what he wants to spend on…us," he finished lamely. How could he point out that Dafydd and Idris weren't Alex's family without it seeming cruel?

Dafydd must have understood and brought it up himself. "I'm not like the rest of you. Alex shouldn't be showing such generosity on my account."

Lucien's face softened. "Dafydd, I know it's hard to understand your own worth. Believe me, I do. But these are hive beings. They share everything." He chuckled. "Besides, you couldn't possibly spend all of Harry's money, let alone Alex's, even if you were the greediest boy in the world."

Dafydd went quiet. He slumped against the back of the couch, his body language screaming out his being overloaded. He looked at Ric with panic and a silent plea in his eyes. It was obvious that, Ric's intentions notwithstanding, Dafydd needed him to step in and take charge. With a lifetime of servitude in which no decisions had been his to make, something as simple and fun as decorating was beyond his ability to cope with at the moment. The fact was that Dafydd might never be able to stand on his own two feet. It was a heavy burden to take on, and yet Ric had no doubt about what he was willing to do.

Picking up the laptop, he closed the cover. "You know what? It's dinner time. Let's put this away for now and go to the kitchen to eat. I bet Emil has something fantastic on the menu tonight."

Dafydd visibly relaxed in an instant. He smiled. "That's not much of a bet, given that it's true every day."

"Excellent point," Lucien agreed. He stood, but not before shooting an understanding look at Ric over Dafydd's head. "I think I'll go see for myself."

Lucien started to leave then paused. "Oh, Dafydd, I wonder if you would do me a favor? Demi is going to spend the night over at Trey's and Harry will be holed up in his lab doing God knows what. Could I please have Idris for the night to keep me company?" The man's expression was utterly guileless, although even Idris would have seen through the ploy.

Dafydd twisted his fingers together. "I don't know, mun."

"Please? You've been hogging him ever since we got back from Maine." Lucien shot a wistful look at Idris. "I'm going through baby withdrawal."

Okay, now it's getting really convincing.

Seeing that Dafydd was still torn, Ric intervened. It was partly a selfish act because he wanted more alone time with his lover. There was also a concern, however, that Dafydd was pushing himself too much out of a sense of guilt. Having rejected his son for a couple of months, he judged himself harshly.

"That's actually a great idea. It will give us time to shop online tonight, then tomorrow we can take Idris to the aquarium. What do you think of that plan, Dafydd?"

"It's a proper one," he agreed with a nod and obvious relief.

Ric gave him an encouraging smile. "Thanks, Lucien."

The three of them left the apartment together. Ric grabbed Idris, who insisted on taking one of the little plastic people with him. The boy settled on Ric's hip without further resistance and happily gnawed on his toy the whole way down to the kitchen.

The place was hopping with the growing Friday night crowd. The family table already contained Alex, Quinn, Val and Mackie. Ric knew they liked to eat early in order to work the evening away. Lucien headed for the buffet table. From what Ric could see, Emil had given them a choice of shrimp, beef and chicken kebobs with rice pilaf and a mixed green salad. Ric's mouth watered at the sight of it. He couldn't wait to pile his plate. First, though, he dragged Idris' high chair over to one end of the table and settled the kid in.

"I'll get his food." Dafydd brushed his fingers across Ric's arm as he spoke. The casual touch was both encouraging and electrifying. "You should go on and fix your own. You've been working all day and must be that hungry."

Ric almost balked at the idea, wanting to wait on them both. He held his tongue, however. It was a good thing for Dafydd to be proactive in his care for Idris, and his concern for Ric's needs wasn't a sign of subservience. Any stay-at-home partner might make the same observation and offer.

"Thanks." He made quick work of heaping his plate and going back to sit on Idris' left. The baby offered him a chance to suck on the plastic person. "Thanks, but I'm happy with what I have."

The boy's eyes went flinty right before he threw the thing at Ric's face. He caught it handily, astonished at the aggressive move. He held the wet toy in his hand, unsure of how to react.

Dafydd had no such problem. Holding a plate of rice and cut chicken, he raced back to the table and let out a torrent of what Ric could only assume was Welsh. He'd never heard the language before in any appreciable amount and was surprised at how unusual it sounded. Everyone else at the table went silent as Dafydd scolded his child with unfathomable words and a wagging finger.

Idris, however, had no trouble understanding his father—or so it seemed to Ric. The baby froze with wide eyes at the dressing-down. When it stopped and

Dafydd's finger pointed at Ric, the baby shifted his gaze to him.

"'Orry." He stuck his thumb in his mouth and stared at Ric with his beautiful violet eyes.

"Oh." Ric looked at Dafydd. "How do I say 'forgiven' in Welsh?"

Dafydd seemed surprised at the question. He answered anyway. "*Maddau.*" Then he repeated it.

Ric said the word to the baby, certain he was mangling it and unsure if the child would know the word. It did the trick, though. Idris pulled his thumb out and gave him a toothy grin. "Here." Ric gave the toy back.

He realized everyone else at the table remained quiet. They were all staring at them. He shrugged. "I guess that settles who's the boss."

"Indeed," Alex agreed before resuming his conversation with Val.

Dafydd sat opposite Ric in order to feed Idris. They shared a smile. Nothing needed saying. Dafydd was acting like a real father, and more importantly, Idris was accepting his authority. The small interaction proved that with the right upbringing, Idris could overcome his evil paternal heritage.

As dinner progressed, Ric felt the weight of the day lift. He was able to enjoy his meal and look forward to having a night with Dafydd to himself. The possibilities were intriguing and nerve-racking. Without Idris to cock-block them both, was tonight the time to take their relationship to another level?

No, don't be greedy. You're taking it slow, remember?

"Dr. Paz?"

"Sorry?" He looked down the table at Alex.

"Has anyone informed you of the accelerated renovation schedule?"

"Ah, yes, Lucien mentioned it. I'm going to spend this weekend helping Dafydd pick out what he needs for his apartment."

"Excellent, thank you." He leaned over the table and dropped his voice. "Malcolm and Brenin are keen to return."

"I think I heard him mention that on the voyage back from Maine." He wasn't sure where exactly this conversation was going. Dafydd played with his food, though, obviously listening and trying not to show concern. Ric wasn't fooled.

"Is there a problem?"

Alex glanced at Val. "Not as such, no. It's only that they intend to bring a couple of their newly-acquired charges from Wales with them, along with Willem and his daughter. With matters unfolding as they are, I want everyone under one roof, as it were, better to be contained in a defensible position. And Annika may prove particularly useful with our guest, if in no other way."

Ric figured he understood what the guy meant. The hybrid was a problem. If he were brought here, he could be controlled better with so many alien men to lend a hand. As for the girl…he remembered how strange she was. How that fit in with anything wasn't obvious.

She's not human.

The truth hit him like the proverbial thunderbolt. While in Scotland, he hadn't had much time or opportunity to dwell on it. The mission, then caring for Dafydd, had consumed him. He'd brushed off noting that an alien had adopted the child of a dead lover.

Now, he could see the obvious. The girl had been preternaturally intelligent and her knowledge of the alien language was impossible for a human. Ric might never do a good job of twisting his tongue around to pronounce Welsh correctly, but at least it wasn't sounds that required a different physiology. But how had it happened? He'd thought these aliens could only produce sons.

He shook his head. "Wait…what?"

Alex held up his hand and glanced around the kitchen. Emil's human staff hustled about. "I apologize. This isn't the place and, really, there is nothing to tell until they arrive. I am as mystified as you are, Doctor."

Ric reached across the table without thinking and took hold of Dafydd's hand, who didn't resist when he clasped it. "This doesn't present any greater danger to Dafydd or Idris, does it?"

"No. If anything, it will make them safer."

"All right, then. Just tell me what you need me to do and I'm there."

Alex nodded. "I'm counting on it."

Chapter Fourteen

Dafydd let Ric hold his hand all the way from Lucien's apartment to the bedroom. It wasn't far and it obviously made Ric happy to have the contact. It felt nice, as well, truth be told. Like kissing, it wasn't something that anyone had done with him, at least not once he'd passed early childhood. There were no bad memories to associate it with, so falling into the habit was easy.

"Lucien seemed genuinely happy to have Idris for the night, don't you think?" he asked, trying not to worry that he'd given in too quickly.

"I think he really is. But, I also think he's being nice and giving us time alone."

"Oh." Dafydd worried his lower lip. "Perhaps I should go get the boy, then."

"No." Ric shook his head. "I'm only telling you that because I want you to trust that I'll be honest with you. It's okay to take a helping hand now and again. You're doing remarkably well with the baby."

The praise warmed him. "You think?"

"Absolutely. You tamed the beast like a pro during dinner."

"Oh, that." While pleased with himself, he didn't want to make much of a fuss about doing the ordinary. "I channeled my gran, that's all. She would have added in a boxed ear, but I don't want him to grow up thinking it's okay to handle problems with violence."

"I agree wholeheartedly."

When they entered the room, Ric dropped his hand in order to go put the laptop he carried onto the dresser. Dafydd missed the contact immediately. Still surprised at his reactions to touch, he stared at his hand and flexed his fingers a few times.

"Is something wrong? Did I hurt you?"

Dafydd waved the concern away. "No. I like holding hands."

Ric was pleased by the admission. "Good. We'll do it more, then. All day tomorrow on our outing, if you like." He sighed. "Tonight, though, we have to look at paint swatches."

Dafydd took a tentative step forward. "Do we?" He threw his arms out. "We've a night to ourselves. I bet there's all kinds of things we could do instead."

He swallowed hard against his boldness. Matters between them hadn't progressed very far, not much more than what they'd done in Maine. And while he liked the kissing and the cuddling and could feel how he and Ric were getting closer from it, it wasn't going to be sufficient for much longer. Not only did he know for a certainty that the man wanted more, but he also felt a growing restlessness within himself. Seducing Ric was part of the grand plan for sure, but Dafydd was beginning to believe that his own happiness depended on a deeper, more physical relationship. If he didn't move forward soon, he worried that he'd be forever stunted by his experience.

The very thought of it made him want to weep.

Without thinking, he plowed into Ric and wrapped his arms around his waist. "Please, won't you fuck me?"

There was a horrible second where Ric froze, not saying or doing anything. Then he brought his arms around Dafydd and kissed the top of his head. "Sweet Jesus, you surprise me — and scare the crap out of me, frankly."

Dafydd buried his face in the man's chest. "I don't know what that means. Is it a yes or a no?"

"It's a maybe."

Dafydd wanted to wail in frustration. He did thump his hand against Ric's back. "Why?"

"Come on. Let's sit." Ric steered them over to the bed and forced Dafydd onto it, because he gave him no help whatsoever.

Once they were both down, however, Dafydd flopped backward, taking Ric with him until they lay sprawled across it. The weight of the man's body caused an initial jolt of panic. He wrestled it back, as this was his idea. If he couldn't stand this much, there was no hope for it.

Taking Dafydd's face in his hands, Ric got him to pull away so that they could look at each other. "Dafydd, please take it easy. If you want to do more than we have, there's the whole night in front of us. There's no need to rush anything. And if you don't mind, I prefer to call anything we do 'making love'. There's nothing wrong in my book with using the word 'fucking', except that to me that's a quick, purely physical act. I want it to be more with us."

"All right, then. I want you to make love to me." The words tumbled out of his mouth almost of their own volition. He ignored the frisson that racked him.

Ric raised his eyebrows. "If you could see your own expression, baby, it's not very encouraging. And you're *trembling*."

"With anticipation." The words were lame and entirely unconvincing, yet now that he'd considered it, he wasn't willing to let go of the idea of giving himself fully to Ric.

"*Dafydd*." Ric's tone was laced with the kind of patient tolerance that he might use with Idris. "That honesty thing is a two-way street. I want you to tell me how you really feel, not what you think I want to hear."

"I know." Duly chastised in the nicest possible way, he dipped his head and plucked at his shirt. "It's the truth that I want to fu—make love. I'm afraid that if I wait too long, I'll never have the courage to do it." He stared at Ric. "Can't we please try, and if I get overwhelmed, we can always stop. Right?"

"Of course. You have the right to withdraw your permission at any time."

They lay quietly for a few minutes, Ric staring at a spot on the ceiling, running his hand along Dafydd's shoulder. He could all but see the man's mind racing over what to do. Having made his wishes clear, Dafydd knew he was at Ric's mercy. While it was nothing new, it was the first time that Dafydd hoped a man would put his own desires above noble intentions. He dared to try to move things in the right direction by reaching for Ric's dick. It pressed against the zipper of his jeans, apparently not conflicted about what it hoped the night entailed. If Dafydd could urge it along…

"Uh-uh." Ric grabbed his hand before it made contact. "My cock doesn't get a vote in this. It can't be trusted to be enfranchised. But I think I have a good idea," he added with a quick peck on Dafydd's nose.

Next thing, Ric was rolling off the bed and headed for the bathroom. "I'll be right back. I want to get some stuff from my toiletry kit. You make yourself comfortable, baby. Sit up against the headboard and settle in for a show." He winked as he disappeared around the doorway.

For a few seconds, Dafydd merely stared after him, then did as he'd been told and propped himself up with the mound of pillows Lucien had given him. He crossed his legs and placed his hands on his lap, unsure of whether he should take off his clothes. Except no, if Ric had wanted him to, he would have said. The good thing about giving oneself over to another was that it cut down on the thinking. Maybe someday he'd want to be the boss of their relationship, but he doubted it. Dafydd hadn't been raised to be anything other than servile, and in truth, he didn't mind so long as his master was a good one.

He didn't have long to wait. Ric reappeared with something in his hand that he placed by the laptop. It looked like a small tube. The man had shucked off his trainers and socks, leaving his nice, bare feet on display. Dafydd leaned forward to get a better view, and Ric laughed.

"Seriously, my feet?"

Dafydd shrugged. "And why not, then? It's a thing, isn't it, for some people? A fetish, like? Back in my day, a man with such clean and pretty toes, no bunions or calluses, would have been a god in the eyes of most."

Ric cocked his hip. "Well, feel free to gaze upon them as much as you'd like. I hope the rest of me is as pleasing."

That got Dafydd's attention. Pulling his knees up, he rested his arms on top of them. "Are you going to take off your clothes?" When Ric nodded, Dafydd reached for his own shirt hem. "Shall I join you?"

Ric held out his hand. "Wait. Not yet, okay? I want this night to be all about you. To that end, I figured I'd make my stripping enjoyable."

Dafydd didn't have time to pose a follow-up question. After pulling his phone out of his back pocket, Ric added it to the pile on the dresser and pushed a button. The room filled with the sounds of a familiar song.

"Is this the one from the ship?"

"Yup. It's 5 Seconds of Summer's *Youngblood*. Forget the lyrics and just watch, baby."

With that, Ric started to move his body in time to the music. His hips and, yes, those pretty feet, swayed and twisted in sensual ways. It was nothing elaborate, not like the complicated routines the boys practiced downstairs, yet it was sexy and entertaining. It lured in Dafydd's avid attention with an irresistible invitation. As the beat picked up, Ric bucked his hips, a different kind of solicitation that Dafydd had no trouble understanding. Ric twirled around the room with the same grace and enviable ease as the go-go boys. The lack of polish was adorable. He had been right about Ric being qualified to work at the club.

When Ric turned sideways and wiggled his way toward the bed, gnawing at his lower lip and eyeing Dafydd with an unspoken promise, Dafydd's body flushed with a strange warmth. He fisted his hands on top of his knees and his breathing sped up. A tingling sensation infused his lower parts. His cock was swelling and straining. Saliva pooled in his mouth, and he felt an urge to reach out and grab Ric as he twirled closer.

The man dipped away just in time, putting himself out of reach, then tugged the hem of his shirt up his smooth, cocoa-colored chest and over his head. He whirled it around his head before tossing it aside. Dafydd giggled at the over-the-top display. His breath caught on a gasp, however, when Ric unsnapped his jeans. Dafydd hugged his knees to his chest in anticipation. But the song ended and Ric froze. Disappointed, Dafydd opened his mouth to urge his lover to keep going, music be damned.

Another tune filled the room, something about counting stars. He knew this one, too, sort of. What mattered to him, though, was that this time, the lyrics seemed to mean something. He heard a promise in them and saw it in Ric's expression. He danced around with his zipper part-way down, the swell of his ass tantalizingly visible, yet not nearly enough. Dafydd couldn't keep his gaze off the man's every move, waiting for more. He bounced and rocked along, feeling a part of the show — and not only as an observer. The appeal of the club to its members became clear to him.

Finally, the pants and the underclothes, as well, came slithering down and off. Ric kept his eyes on Dafydd as he exposed his hard dick. With such intense concentration, it was obvious the man was looking for signs of distress, notwithstanding the sexy little smile he was shooting Dafydd's way. It didn't present a problem, however. Dafydd wasn't disturbed in the least—or rather, it was a good kind of disquiet. The sight of how much Ric wanted him was enticing, not frightening.

Dafydd licked his lips, unsure of how to convey his interest. Playing the coquette was beyond his experience. He for sure didn't want Ric to think his obvious arousal put him off. Unfurling his fingers, he dared to raise his hand and beckon his lover. Ric's eyes blazed for a few seconds before he went to shut off the music and sauntered over. Normally the sight of a hard man coming his way would have scared Dafydd or disgusted him. Not so now, although he did have to tamp down a bit of nerves. While he knew that Ric would be gentle with him, he also didn't think he'd ever get used to being invaded by a man's cock. Thank God, being human meant Ric wasn't as large as the monster had been.

Don't think of him! You'll lose your bottle and hurt Ric's feelings.

When Ric was only inches away from the edge of the bed, Dafydd's heightened senses permitted him to *smell* the man's arousal. His stomach clenched just for a moment before he forced it to relax again. He couldn't be surprised that his body had these automatic responses. It was merely a matter of his intellect and desire overriding the visceral memories threatening to derail the night's plans. It helped that Ric smelled delightfully of cologne, as usual.

Ric palmed himself. "I don't want you to be afraid of this…of me."

Dafydd lowered his legs so that his own erection was visible. "I'm not. Not really, like." He swallowed his nerves back down. "It's only my past trying to interfere with my present. I won't let it." He tugged at his shirt with a sudden fury, determined to get as naked as Ric.

"Wait. Let me do that. Please?" Ric didn't give Dafydd any time to respond. Instead, he knelt on one knee at the edge of the bed. "I want tonight to be all about your pleasure. And peeling those clothes off you would make me very happy, if you don't mind?"

Dafydd shook his head and, letting go, lay back against the pillow. "All right, then. I don't mind a bit of pampering."

Ric's face lit up, as if he'd been given a wonderful treat. "Thanks, baby. I'm going to show you all of my best moves. I hope you like them."

"I will." He grabbed Ric's hand before he could do anything. "But promise me you'll show me how to please you, too?"

"Believe me, what I'm about to do makes me very happy."

There was no more talk, only touching, as Ric slowly pulled first Dafydd's shirt then his trainers and socks off. Dafydd couldn't help wondering what the man saw. Dafydd didn't have nearly the physique that his lover had. Lying there bare-chested, he felt too thin and pasty. He put his hands across his chest and looked up at Ric from under his lashes.

"Don't be shy, baby. You're beautiful."

"I'm skinny, like, and pale as milk."

"Oh, Dafydd, have you no idea how utterly perfect you are?"

He rolled his eyes. "Don't be daft, mun. I'm a dirty village boy for all that I've been through." It was the way he saw himself—a serf grubbing around in the muddy fields and dusty roads at a time when bathing once a week was considered high living. When he looked in the mirror, that was mostly what he saw. He was almost frozen in time since he'd been abducted, both growing into someone different and not.

Ric cupped his face and placed a short, sweet kiss on his lips. "You're more than that. I'm going to show you how much."

Slowly, Ric reached for the snap on Dafydd's jeans. The sound of the parts uncoupling was loud to Dafydd's ears, as was the rasp of the zipper going down, down. His unimpressive dick happily peeked out from its confines before standing fully erect when the cloth was pulled away. Next to Ric's, it looked puny, but there was no denying that it was hard, with a tiny pearl of milky white clinging to the slit. He stuttered out a breath at its sight.

"I thought this part of me might be dead for good." He flicked his gaze up. "You've done this to me."

"I'll do more, if you'll allow it."

"Whatever you want, Ric." He didn't use the man's name very often. It was hard to get past the ingrained fear of being overly familiar. It felt right and proper at the moment, however, and it seemed to please his man. Yes, *his* man. "I trust you."

"That's good, because I'm mad for a taste."

"A taste? Oh," Dafydd nearly jumped out of his skin as Ric bent down to lap at the head of his cock.

This was new, to be on the receiving end of a blow job. Knowing that it could be used as a way to punish and dominate, he forced himself to lie still. He would take whatever Ric was willing to give...and gladly. Ric twisted around, tugging the pants down Dafydd's legs while stealing licks along the exposed shaft. Ric only let go to wrestle the jeans entirely off, then he returned to straddle Dafydd's legs. With his arms and legs loosely caging Dafydd, Ric feasted on the dick in earnest. He licked a stripe from root to tip and swirled his tongue around before retracing his steps.

Dafydd sank farther into his pillows and the bedding, his muscles going lax while his brain struggled to accept all the amazing sensations. Ric assaulted every bit of Dafydd's dick then balls, briefly sucking the tight sac into his mouth before releasing it again. That would have been a crying shame if the man hadn't made up for it by taking in Dafydd's cock instead. He gasped as his shaft got swallowed down, then sighed on a silent 'oh'. There was no mystery why men liked this kind of thing, none at all. Dafydd could easily imagine leaving his dick encased in the velvety warmth for hours on end.

Ric didn't merely hold it. Using his throat muscles and tongue, he lavished it with attention. Soon, he had Dafydd moaning and writhing. The sensations were intense. He felt the old and almost forgotten awareness of an orgasm building. Like in his youth, it was a quick and determined event. He clenched the covers and bucked his hips in anticipation of coming, then Ric thwarted him. Pulling back so that only half of Dafydd's dick remained in his mouth, Ric grabbed the base of the shaft and squeezed, not hard enough to hurt, but sufficient to stop the climax.

"No!" Frustrated, Dafydd pounded his fists on the bed like Idris having a temper-tantrum.

Ric merely chuckled, the vibration shooting up Dafydd's dick. He let go entirely, lightly grazing his front teeth across the head. The sting was surprisingly erotic. There was no time to ponder that new information, however. Ric recaptured his attention by lapping up Dafydd's abdomen, then stomach, until finally reaching his pecs. Now it was Dafydd's nipples getting all the attention with flicks of Ric's tongue. While he did that, the man stroked Dafydd's cock slowly, keeping him on edge, yet any time Dafydd's movements became too animated, Ric would strangle the orgasm once again.

"Is this your idea of torture, mun?"

"Hmm," was all Ric said.

He sucked in a nipple and proved that there were more ways to please a man than Dafydd had ever realized. He worked on both for long minutes until Dafydd was incoherent with need.

"Please," he begged, no longer caring that he was demanding to be breached, a thing he'd thought he dreaded.

"Anticipation is wonderful, isn't it, baby?" Ric didn't give him a chance to answer. Instead, he moved to take Dafydd's lips in a long, deep kiss that robbed him of what breath he had left.

He tried to lift his knees to expose his ass in a wordless invitation for Ric to plunder it, but the man had him hemmed in. There was no way to get past the larger body straddling him. He raised his hands and, slithering them between their bodies, shoved against Ric's chest.

Ric broke the kiss immediately and sat back on his haunches. "Are you all right? Is it too much?"

Dafydd wanted to erase the concern from his man's face. "No. It's not enough. Come on. Give me what we both want."

"You're sure?"

By way of answer, Dafydd groaned out his frustration.

"Okay. I get the message," Ric said with a grin. "Wait here."

He sprang from the bed and went to the dresser. Dafydd took the opportunity to get into position — on his hands and knees. He knew they could do it face-to-face, yet this first time, it might be easier this way. It gave him greater freedom and would be less intense, he thought, because he wouldn't be staring at Ric and seeing his need written across his features.

"Wrong way, Dafydd."

"Oh." All right, then. If Ric wanted him on his back, he could handle that. He had to or their life wouldn't move forward.

But when he turned around to lie down again, Ric shook his head. "That's my spot."

"I don't understand."

"I want to feel your cock in my ass, Dafydd." He held up the tube he'd retrieved. "This will prep me. I have condoms, too, although Harry insists we can't spread disease between us. If it will make you feel better, of course, I'll get one."

Dafydd shook his head, still trying to make sense of what he was hearing. "No, it's fine. He's right. I don't understand. You want me to top you?"

"Sure." Ric joined him on the bed and kissed him again. "I love doing it both ways, and I figured this first time, you'd enjoy topping more…unless it really bothers you?"

Dafydd frowned. "No, I don't think so. I've never thought about it, to be honest." In all the times during adolescence when he'd dared to dream of being with a man, he'd always been on the receiving end. The idea of taking the lead and claiming one of those big, strong warriors had seemed ludicrous.

"What if I hurt you?" He knew what it felt like to be forced, stretched and ripped. He would rather die than do that to Ric.

"You won't. I promise. Because you'll help me get ready to take you, and we won't progress until I say so. That's how it's supposed to work, baby."

Dafydd took the lube from him. "With this, then?"

"Yes."

"And you'll teach me how?" Sadly, he had no personal experience in the matter. No one had ever bothered to prepare him.

"Absolutely." Ric nudged him over so that he had room to lie down. Then he spread his legs and raised his knees until his feet were flat on the bed. "I'm going to play with myself while you prep my hole."

So saying, Ric palmed his dick and stroked it with slow, even movements. He nodded at the lube. "Put a dollop of that on two fingers. I'm pretty experienced and we don't have to do too much. When and if you feel up to being on the receiving end, believe me, we'll take a lot more time."

Dafydd grimaced. "I'm more experienced than you are." He squeezed some of the slick onto his fore and middle fingers.

"No, baby, you're not in the way that counts. I won't ever forget that." He lifted his hips, exposing his hole.

Dafydd was fascinated to see it. This wasn't like the times he'd tended to the hurts of Brenin or others, where he'd tried to avoid looking too closely at their ravaged flesh. Ric's puckered ring was slightly darker than the rest of his skin, but it was otherwise unmarred. He swore it winked in invitation.

"Come on, Dafydd. Don't make me wait."

Determined to get this right, he pushed against the underside of one thigh to raise Ric more. Then he swirled his lubed fingers around the man's hole. Ric moaned immediately and closed his eyes. Encouraged, Dafydd kept circling it until the ring felt softer and more pliable. Despite what Ric had said, he dared to only slip one finger past the muscles. Satiny tightness greeted him. He thrust gently at first, then faster and deeper.

"Yes, like that. Harder. Put the other one in. Please." Ric groaned and flexed his hips.

Emboldened with his obvious success, Dafydd did as his lover demanded. He hadn't expected to play this role, but he delighted in the way he made Ric squirm and moan. The man had promised to show him how to give pleasure, yet nothing could have prepared Dafydd for the immense satisfaction and feeling of power that came from it.

"Crook your fingers," Ric gasped, rolling up his hips to expose himself even more.

When Dafydd did, he felt the rough walnut-sized spot and understood what it was. He still wasn't expecting Ric to yell. He stopped immediately, not sure if it was from pain or pleasure.

"Don't. Stop. Shit, *do* stop. Take out your fingers and shove your cock in. Now, Dafydd!"

He's desperate for it.

He couldn't keep the wide grin off his face as he did as he'd been told. Knee-walking between those spread thighs, he grabbed his cock and tugged it a little before lining it up against Ric's hole.

Be bold, mun.

He took a deep breath and slid the shaft in balls-deep with one long thrust. His climax burst out of him before he could stop it. Ric yelled once more, and clamped down on Dafydd's shaft with a quick, hard clench that jolted them both. Now they both cried out and shuddered into each other where their bodies joined. Dafydd slammed his eyes closed, relying on his other senses to retain the connection with Ric, although they had dimmed with the intensity of his orgasm.

He tried to hold himself in place, failed and pitched forward right into Ric's waiting arms.

Chapter Fifteen

It didn't bother Ric that he'd come immediately like an untried seventeen-year-old. Dafydd lay sprawled on top of him, cuddling and murmuring with contentment. That was all that mattered. His lover had found his pleasure and that act alone had sent an already-crazed Ric over the edge. He was grateful, even, that Dafydd had caused the abrupt climax, because up until that moment, Ric had feared he'd lose control first and spoil what amounted to Dafydd's first sexual experience. Simultaneous orgasm, no matter how quick, was surely a good omen of their compatibility.

I did this. Is it possible to be too happy?

Now, he was looking for trouble. He needed to stay in the moment, appreciate how far Dafydd had come. And it wasn't only Ric who could claim success. If not for Dafydd's determination to overcome his brutal past, they wouldn't be there. They wouldn't be anywhere. The Welshman had shown tremendous courage. It was awe-inspiring.

He ran his hand down Dafydd's head, feathering the silky strands through his fingers. "You're the most beautiful man I've ever seen and I love you more than I can say. You don't have to say anything back," he added quickly. "I just needed to reiterate my feelings after what we've shared."

Dafydd snuggled closer, even though there wasn't an inch of space between them. "I like hearing those words, especially after what we did tonight." He paused. "I can't tell you how I feel beyond happy and appreciated and...hopeful. You've given them all to me, Ric."

"Those are excellent starts, as far as I'm concerned."

Dafydd pushed away a little to look at him. "I can't imagine my life without you, and for sure, I want you here with me and Idris — not only as a visitor, but as my partner." He put his head down again. "I'm not sure I know what love feels like, so I'm loathe to say the words. But if that's not the right way to describe my feelings right now, well, then I don't know how I could want you more."

"It's okay," Ric was quick to reassure. "So long as you want me in your life, there's no need to put a label on it."

"That's good, then. You're very patient...and tight. God, mun, I couldn't stop from coming to end my life!"

Ric laughed. "That's okay. We were both really primed."

"And whose fault was that?" Dafydd rose once more to frown at him. "Can we do it again?"

Ric's dick and hole both twitched at the idea. "Absolutely. Give me about twenty minutes. I'm not as young as I used to be."

"You're an infant compared to me," Dafydd reminded him, which only led to an awkward silence because of why that was so. "It's not all bad, you know, what his blood did to me," he offered. "Only, now that I'm not drinking any, Harry thinks I'll age naturally."

Ric had supposed that, yet felt lighter hearing Dafydd confirm it. "Does that bother you? I only ask because it's nice to know we'll grow old together. It would be very human of us."

Dafydd smiled. "It would, wouldn't it?" His expression turned a bit coquettish. "Is it all right for me to top or do you want to switch?"

Ric noted the uncertainty in his lover's eyes. "Whatever you want, baby. I'm yours any way you'll have me. There's no hurry or pressure to do anything else."

"Good, except I don't want you to think I'm a selfish boy."

Ric didn't understand what he meant until Dafydd slithered down and latched on to a nipple. Then Ric didn't think at all.

* * * *

Ric woke the next morning, sore and groggy from sleeping little and late. The sliver of bright light through the seam in the curtains told him it was well into the morning. He sat, stretched and stumbled out of bed and into the bathroom. Dafydd was nowhere to be seen, although that didn't worry him. He assumed he was with Idris and that they were both either with Lucien or still in the kitchen to give Ric a chance to lie in.

A quick shower later, he went to find them, and when they weren't on the upper floor, he headed to the kitchen. The sight of the two of them hanging at the family table with Val and some of the boys made him stop in his tracks. He had to simply *look*. It was all perfectly ordinary, and yet for him, it was a minor miracle. A fierce protective feeling welled up inside him. He knew in that moment he would kill to keep them safe.

Dafydd laughed at something, another amazing event, and gave Idris more food on his highchair tray. But when Dafydd glanced over and saw Ric, his broad smile was the best thing that had ever happened to Ric. It told him he was welcome, and more, wanted. It might be too soon for Dafydd to use the word 'love', but as Dafydd had said himself, the feelings were there regardless. Ric hurried to join them.

"Good morning." He chanced a quick kiss and was delighted when Dafydd made him linger.

"The food's a bit cold," Dafydd said with a cock of his head at the spread.

"I don't care in the least." Leaning in, he whispered, "How do you feel?"

"Brilliant. You?"

"Well fucked."

Across the table, Mackie giggled.

"That's another stroke of the cane for tonight, boy," Val intoned beside him.

Mackie huffed at his husband. "For what?"

"Eavesdropping."

"I was not! It's not my fault you gave me superhero hearing. It's like he's shouting."

"Hive members learn to mind their own business and give others privacy, regardless of what they actually see, hear or smell. You need to learn that lesson, along with a few others."

Mackie crossed his arms. "Huh, so you say."

"Yup. That's what makes me the Master."

Ric might have been alarmed at his words causing Mackie pain, except there was a wicked gleam in boy's eyes that reassured him those lessons were enjoyed by both of them.

"Well, this isn't a hive," Mackie tossed back, apparently willing to risk another stroke.

Val sipped at his coffee before saying, "Close enough."

He's right, Ric thought as he went to fix a plate for himself. Being with these men and their boys was like living in a family, albeit a weird one. As he sat to join them, he felt welcomed and included. In only a few short months, his life had changed radically — and for the better. With most of his biological family scattered back in South America, it was nice to have a strong bond with people here in his adopted home, even if many of them were from another world.

When Ric was done eating and enjoying his own coffee, Dafydd leaned in, a bit of worry in his eyes. "Can I ask a favor?"

Somewhat alarmed, Ric shot back, "Anything, baby. What do you need?"

Dafydd gestured with his head and stood. "Will you watch Idris for me, Mackie? I want to talk to Ric outside of the range of your big ears." He threw in a grin to show he was teasing. That he felt comfortable both asking for help and poking at Mackie's sensitive hearing were two more signs that he was improving rapidly.

Mackie took the ribbing good-naturedly by rolling his eyes. "Sure. Go ahead and spoil my fun."

Ric followed Dafydd to the far end of the room where the kitchen staff were both making noise and too far away to hear the conversation. "Is something wrong?"

"No." Dafydd put doubt in his answer by twisting his fingers together and looking at the floor. "It's only that there's something I want to do—must do, in order to move past *everything*."

Putting his hands on Dafydd's shoulders, Ric said, "Tell me. I'll help you however you need me to."

Dafydd peeked up at him. "I want to go see Petru— now, this morning."

Ric almost recoiled at the unexpected request. "Why?"

"I need to stare down the monster, to know that I can." His shoulders slumped. "I know it's nothing like facing Dracul, but it's a start. If I don't, I worry that it will all haunt me for the rest of my life. I can still see them in my mind's eye as they were when I was helpless. Confronting Petru when he's without power will hopefully give me some of my own back."

Ric considered the rationale and it did have merit, psychologically speaking. "Okay, although I don't want you facing him alone. I'm going with you."

Dafydd smiled. "I was hoping you would. Will you also come with me when I ask Alex?"

"Of course, baby. I think we should start with Val, though. He's in charge of security. Perhaps his permission and help are all we need. Come on."

He took Dafydd by the hand and returned to the table to stand behind Val. He cleared his throat, and the man looked at them.

When Dafydd remained silent, Ric spoke up for the both of them. "Val, Dafydd would like to go see Petru."

Val stared at them unblinking. He said nothing, although beside him, Mackie murmured something like 'holy crap'.

Val shifted his gaze to look only at Ric. "Do you think that's a good idea?"

"Doesn't matter. Dafydd does."

"Uh-huh." Val pushed back and stood. "Not my call, guys. We need to speak with Alex."

So, they all trooped down to the boss' office and went through the process all over again. With Quinn lounging on his lap, the man took a minute to mull the request over. Standing in front of the desk, Ric felt like an errant school boy. But he worked to hide it because Dafydd needed him to be strong.

"I must say, gentlemen, this request has caught me by surprise." He eyed Ric much as Val had. "I assume you'll be accompanying him?"

"Yes, sir."

Alex waved his hand. "Well, there's no obvious reason to refuse. The fucker is naked, chained and locked in tight as a tick. Have at him, I suppose. Val, you'll go in, as well. There's no sense in taking chances."

"Will do."

That seemed to be that, except that there was one more issue for Ric. While Dafydd went to rescue Mackie from childcare duty by securing Idris upstairs again with Lucien, Ric and Val waited at the locked door that led to the basement. As soon as Dafydd disappeared, Ric turned to the bouncer.

"Quick, before he gets back, bring me a gun. Please," he tacked on when he realized whom he was ordering about.

"You can't kill Petru, Doc. Unless and until we can confirm that Dracul is dead, we need him breathing. Plus, Alex gave his word we wouldn't. It wasn't the call I would have made, but then, I'm not the captain."

"I don't intend to shoot him so long as he doesn't try to hurt Dafydd."

"It's my job to protect you both."

Ric got right into the guy's face, worry for Dafydd making him bold. The size difference between them, since he had to stand on his toes to have a face-off, would have been comical if not for the deadly seriousness of the situation.

"No, sir, it's not. *I'm* responsible for Dafydd from now on."

He wasn't sure what showed in his expression, but Val simply nodded and disappeared a few seconds later down the stairs. He returned almost as quickly and handed Ric a small nine-millimeter.

"You know how to use this, yes?"

Ric took it, checked that the safety was on then made sure the clip was full before tucking it under his shirt and into his waistband. He didn't want Dafydd to see it. This was something his lover didn't need to know about.

"Yes. Duncan taught me in Scotland. I didn't think then that I could use it. I hadn't met Dafydd yet."

That was all the explanation he gave, and Val seemed to accept that as sufficient. By the time Dafydd returned, the evidence of what they'd been up to was well-hidden.

Ric held out his hand. "All set?"

Dafydd took it and nodded. "Yes, let's go."

Val went first and they followed, the stairs just barely wide enough for them to walk side-by-side. At the bottom, Val opened a door and led them through a room laden with the kind of firepower that made Ric's gun seem like a slingshot. At the far end, there was another door. For this, Val had to turn a tumbler, as if there were a giant vault on the other side. Instead, when he pulled it open, a brightly lit, windowless room greeted them.

It was a prison cell. That was obvious, and it was a bare-bones one at that. It contained only a wall-mounted shelf with a thin plastic pallet for sleeping, a sink and a toilet. Lounging on the bed was, as promised, a nude Petru, who was also shackled by both wrists to the wall behind him. Ric estimated there was sufficient chain to make it to the necessary facilities but no chance to reach the door or any visitors. In a war that had led to fatalities on both sides, Alex had nonetheless provided adequately for a prisoner, testament to the kind of honorable man he was.

Petru slowly raised his gaze from the book he was reading to stare at them. That one creature comfort was another sign of the decency of Alex and his crew. Petru smiled like the Cheshire Cat, arrogant even in his captivity. Ric had a sudden impulse to wipe the look off his face. That instinct doubled when he felt a tremor in Dafydd's hand.

"You don't have to do any more than this," he murmured.

Squaring his shoulders, Dafydd stepped forward. "I want to."

Letting go of Ric, the former slave walked boldly, if slowly, toward one of the foul creatures who had tortured him for centuries. Petru watched the approach, putting down his book and swinging his legs to stand as he did so. The chain links rattled with every movement. Ric surged forward at the same time. He didn't care how diligent Val had been with those restraints. He wasn't going to take any chances with his lover.

"This is unexpected, I must say," Petru drawled.

"Your opinion wasn't requested, asshole," Val shot back.

Dafydd surprised him by holding up his hand. "It's okay. Let him say what he wants. His words can't hurt me. Nothing about him will ever touch me again." If there was a slight quaver to the boy's voice, it didn't detract from his firm stance and courageous words.

Petru spread his arms out. "Lo, how the mighty have fallen, heh?"

"You flatter yourself, mun," Dafydd retorted. "You were never that, merely the mud under Dracul's boots."

The insult didn't appear to faze the man. "And here I'd thought that was you all this time." He tsked. "I admit I underestimated you, although not as much as Dracul did. You always were a willful cunt."

Ric bared his teeth at the casual insult and would have marched into the cell if Val hadn't blocked him with his arm.

Petru's gaze shifted past Dafydd and onto Ric. "Is this your new Master? Huh, looks more like a slut to me. I bet you like taking it up the ass, hmm?" The question was aimed squarely at Ric.

He was happy to reply. "Every chance I get, shithead. You should try it. The pleasure of it might improve your disposition." As come-backs went, it wasn't much, but the statement was more for Dafydd's benefit than Petru's. He wanted his lover to understand that being penetrated didn't make anyone less of a man.

Petru merely shrugged. Life with Dracul must have trained him to let things roll off his back. It wasn't worth the breath to speak with him. "You know," he continued, looking once more at Dafydd, "I warned him those first few months when you fought him and tried to run away that he should kill you and find a more biddable toy to play with. Of course, he didn't listen to me."

Ah, and there was the bitterness, finally.

"And what happened? You brought the whole fucking thing down on our heads. After a thousand years of battling our own kind, worthy opponents on this miserable planet, we were destroyed by a mere human." He shook his head. "I'd tip my hat to you, if I were permitted to have one."

"You're lucky to have what you do," Dafydd scoffed. "It's better than what I was often given and without the threat of death hanging over your head."

The man went back to sitting on his pitiful bed. "Is this all? Have you finished gloating?"

Dafydd shook his head. "That's not what I'm here for. I only wanted to see for myself that you truly are nothing. And even if you remained powerful and even if Dracul is really still alive, I'm not afraid."

Dafydd caused Ric's heart to leap by taking a step closer. "I killed Cadoc. Did you know that? My own son. I had to. That's the kind of monster Dracul made of me and him both. I'll kill Dracul, too, and you, if it comes to that."

"Feel free. Dispose of Dracul, I mean." Petru leaned back against the wall. "I don't care, and in fact, I welcome it. That's what I'm doing here. I've had it up to here with his ridiculous ambitions."

"No. That's a lie. You want Andri back." That statement got the first real rise out of Petru. He sat up again. "You'll never have him," Dafydd dug in deeper. "He won't want you again, not after being Dracul's slave. To go back to being a boy for anyone less than the Master of Masters? A step down from occupying the top spot?" Dafydd shook his head slowly. "Never. He always wanted Dracul to notice him so he could trade up from your paltry bed. It's what he was angling for all along, and you were too stupid to see it." He scoffed. "I hope you live a very long life knowing that you were always second best—in everything."

With that, Dafydd wheeled around and marched away from the cell.

Ric puffed up with pride. His boy was not only strong, he had a killer instinct that would serve him well in his recovery and the rest of his life.

He caught Dafydd's hand. "Go on up, please, and wait for me at Lucien's. Then we can get Idris ready for our outing. I won't be but a moment."

Dafydd narrowed his eyes. "Are you sure? What's this about?"

Ric gave him a peck on the lips. "Nothing, baby. I just want to help Val lock this asshole back up. Okay? Oh, and you are *not* a monster." He'd hated hearing his lover speak of himself in those terms, even if it were only for effect, which he didn't think it was. It was important that Dafydd start to feel good about himself.

Dafydd gave him a wan smile. "I can believe that when I'm with you—and that I'm not broken, either."

"You are certainly not that. Didn't last night prove it?" he added in an extra-low voice. He flashed his eyes as he said it, in the hopes of making a clear invitation.

Dafydd rolled his eyes. "Perhaps I'm the one who has created a monster." To be able to joke after such a fierce confrontation was the best possible sign. "All right, then, I'll meet you upstairs."

Ric waited until he heard Dafydd walk all the way back up before heading into the cell. He pulled out his gun and, flicking off the safety catch, pointed it two-handed at Petru. That got another rise out of the man. Petru stiffened, although he didn't cower.

"Jesus, fuck, Doc," Val murmured.

"I'm not going to kill him," he reassured the man, worried that he'd yank him away. "Not yet," he amended.

Adjusting his grip and stance, he worked to ease his breathing. "Listen up, you fucker. I don't care what you say about helping out and going away nicely after we put Dracul down for good. If you ever so much as look at Dafydd again, I will kill you."

Petru opened his mouth.

"Shut up! I don't want to hear your voice. I'm a doctor. Did you know that? First, do no harm. That's what we swear as medical students to become full physicians. And I've lived by that oath my entire career and will continue to do so, except in this one instance."

His heart was beating jackrabbit fast, something the alien could undoubtedly detect. No problem. Yeah, he was scared, but he was also serious. "I know how to draw it out. Death, that is. I will kill you by inches. I'll blow bits of you into dust until there is nothing left." Ric took one more step closer and drilled a hole into the alien with his stare. "Do you believe me? Do you, motherfucker!"

He had the satisfaction of seeing the man startle. "Yes, I rather do. Fortunately, I have no interest in doing anything that would incur your wrath. The boy says I'm nothing to him." Petru shrugged. "I feel the same. He was, and always will be, of no consequence."

Ric barked out a laugh. "See? That right there... That's what fucked you over. By your own admission, you underestimated him. You should have known that he's *everything*."

Lowering his weapon, he backed out then turned away. He re-engaged the safety and handed the gun over to Val as he passed him. Petru didn't warrant so much as a backward glance. Ric waited for Val at the top of the stairs, where Val relocked the entrance to the basement.

"Congratulations, Doc. You made a lasting impression on one of the most dangerous creatures on this planet and managed to scare the pants off me."

Ric raised his shaking hands. "Thanks, but we both know that's a lie."

"Nope. I know you meant what you said and so does Petru, and that's fucking terrifying." He clapped a hand on Ric's shoulder. "Good job. I would have done the same. Now, don't keep your boy waiting. Mackie swears by the aquarium. You and your family will have a great time."

"Thanks, Val. I'm going to do just that."

And he did, spending a glorious day with his lover and their child, the first of what he knew would be many.

Chapter Sixteen

Two Months Later

Malcolm stood up from the co-pilot seat and stretched. "I'll go make sure everyone is properly strapped in for the landing, Will."

"Roger that." His laid-back friend was in work mode, his focus on the instrument panel as he made their approach to Logan Airport.

Being nighttime, the birds-eye view of the city was a pretty sight, although Malcolm would have preferred to yacht-in again. There'd been no time for that kind of leisurely voyage. *More's the pity*. Alex wanted everyone under one roof while they planned how to locate Dracul and defeat him—again. It still rankled that the fucker might have escaped, although Malcolm didn't object to the plan itself. He'd come to the same conclusion independently of his commander, so he was hardly in a position to complain. Speed mattered more than comfort at this point. Besides, spending a couple of weeks even on his large ship with the hybrid hellion he was transporting didn't bear thinking about.

"We're starting our approach to the airport, everyone," he called out when he entered the cabin. "Buckle up."

Brenin headed his way. "Thank God, this has been a terrible ride. Not even the meds Doc MacPhee has me on can dampen the misery."

Concerned, Malcolm cupped his boy's chin. "Did you take one of those short-acting pills she gave you for anxiety?"

Brenin's expression softened. "No, it's not that bad. I didn't mean to worry you. Besides, poor Alun has the worst of it."

"Well, he is the lad's father. It's his job."

"One he's not suited for. You can't know what it was like in that castle. Inside Alun's head, he's a slave without power. And Merlin doesn't see his human father as any kind of authority figure."

"Aye, I ken." Malcolm watched for a few seconds while the poor man pleaded with his son to comply. When that was clearly not working, Malcolm strode down the aisle to deal with it himself.

Alun's low voice reached Malcolm's ears. "Please, Merlin. Does everything have to be a fight? Everyone has to do this. It's basic safety."

The mulish boy, who already had the height of a teenager although willowy with it, sat glaring at his father with folded arms. "It's pointless. I can weather any bumps, and if we crash, a seat belt isn't going to save me. Only the strength I inherited from my father will. There's none of your puny human in me."

Och. Malcolm had heard this refrain over and over since 'rescuing' the lad. The little shit was completely dismissive of his human half. Poor Alun had been so beaten during his captivity that he didn't gainsay any of the insults. He simply sat there, taking them with barely a change in his placid expression.

It was time for Malcolm to bring the hammer down, as usual. He couldn't wait to fob some of this responsibility onto Harry or one of the others. Even Lucien would be more effective at dealing with the unbearable pup than Alun was. Most importantly, he wanted Brenin well clear of the duty. Doc MacPhee had been very helpful once Brenin had been willing to ask for it. Talking, meds and that simple relaxation method that Paz had passed along had all worked well since they'd returned from Boston. Brenin had improved, Malcolm could tell as much. The less stress, the better, though.

Before he could reach his destination, however, his attention was taken by Will's daughter. Annika had come along, naturally. There had been no question of that. There was also no doubt as to her true nature. Malcolm hadn't been privy to the conversation between Alex and Will back at the castle, and both men had been tight-lipped about it. But the sweet wee lassie had aged to pre-adolescence already. What more evidence did one need to understand she wasn't merely human?

She smiled at him as he approached. He could see the stunning beauty that she would become. She'd just finished strapping her white toy poodle into its harness. "Not to worry, Mr. Malcolm, Babette is all set. She knows how to behave. As do I, unlike some people."

She frowned before turning her head. "Put on your seat belt, Merlin. *Now*, if you please."

It was the tone of her voice — which she never raised, not the volume — that had everyone, including Malcolm, freezing for a moment. A shiver ran up his spine, quickly replaced by a sense of calm that he hadn't felt since…well, in a thousand years. In that moment, he let go of the worry and the doubt that he'd been holding inside him since Dracul's treachery had first occurred. The outcome of their internecine war was clear. It might take a few more years, perhaps, yet victory for their side was almost guaranteed. At least that was his assessment. The proof of it would come soon.

Everyone's movement restarted a second later, with Alun meekly looking out of the window and Merlin acting much the same while he buckled up. Having been raised entirely within Dracul's orbit, the lad nevertheless reacted to the primordial instincts of half his gene pool. For her part, Annika returned her attention to her dog. She hadn't waited to see if she'd been obeyed. She knew she had, like all of her kind. Feeling delightfully superfluous, Malcolm turned to go back to the cockpit.

Brenin snagged his hand when he passed him. "Malcolm, is she — ?"

"Aye, laddie, and thank God for it. Settle in. We'll land quickly and be at our new, temporary home shortly." He gave a quick squeeze before letting it go.

His presence beside Willem was also unnecessary, but rules were rules, and the rest of the journey was uneventful. Customs proved a breeze, as well, given the lateness of the hour. Darling's expertly forged passports held up under scrutiny and the only bad moment came when Merlin seemed to be ready to say something inappropriate. A quelling look from Annika did the trick. Really, the girl was a marvel. And with Babette's veterinary paperwork also in order, they were able to make it out to the curb in record time.

The reassuring sight of Val's SUV eased Malcolm even more. The man hopped out of his vehicle and did a double-take when he saw Annika. The reaction would have been comical if the stakes weren't so high. He was alone, given the size of their compliment and the seat count of the SUV. That meant no Mackie to jabber away the tension. The ride to the club was a silent one, except for Annika's chatter to her dog. Because he was sitting in the front, Malcolm saw the way Val's stony expression softened at the sound. Aye, the lassie was going to do them all a world of good, although how Willem had pulled this off was an intriguing question. Likely, the man had no idea himself.

Once they'd arrived and pulled into the underground garage, Val led them not into the club but over to what proved to be a new corridor. It held a big lift at the end of it, and Val took them to the first floor of the renovated building. The doors opened to a single, enormous, wide-open living area. It was dotted with couches, tables and chairs of various kinds, covered with lush carpeting and sported what appeared to be a kitchen and bar combo at one end and an old-fashioned jukebox and video game contraptions at the other. The space had been designed to be comfortable and entertaining for everyone. And it was family-friendly with no go-go boys performing or leering club members prowling.

"Welcome to the new common area," Val said with a sweep of his hand.

Everyone was there, including Duncan and Dr. Paz, engaged in one sort of activity or another. Only Kitty, Logan and Anderson were missing. There was no surprise there, as someone had to mind the club. And where Kitty was, one would find Anderson. Logan, however, was a law unto herself. Given the mental demons she was fighting, it was always a surprise when she showed up. Regardless, they'd all be there when needed. He had no doubt of it.

The room practically vibrated with masculinity at the moment. Mackie and the rest of the lads stopped what they were doing to run and welcome Brenin, in particular. They swarmed around him good-naturedly. Malcolm kept a keen eye out to make sure *his* lad wasn't overwhelmed. Brenin shot him a reassuring smile.

Alex rose from his seat on one of the couches and approached with more decorum. His gaze took them all in with one sweep, although it landed on Annika. "Welcome." He was saying it to her, and he nodded his head with the greeting.

"Alex." Willem stepped up to shake his captain's hand. "I'm afraid I underestimated the growth timetable, as you can see." He nodded at his daughter.

"Indeed. These things are always hard to gauge, given our limited experience. A good thing, as it happens, dear fellow."

"Oh, you've brought a dog!" Mackie squealed. "It's adorbs."

"She," Annika corrected. "This is Babette. Willem got her for me so that I wouldn't be quite as outnumbered with all you boys around."

"Can she do tricks?" Demi asked.

"Of course, she's very smart."

"Let's go over by the kitchen where there's more room," Quinn suggested.

"There's snacks out on the counter, too," Jase added.

"Okay."

The lads crowded around her, even the humans sensing how it should be. But they'd gone not two feet before she stopped and looked over her shoulder. "Come on, Merlin. We're all going to play with Babette."

The hybrid waged an internal battle. Malcolm could tell by the look on his face. Then he gave up and followed in their wake with angry steps. When he passed a spot where Dafydd sat cross-legged on the floor, playing with his son and Paz, his pace slowed. There were a few seconds of surprised glaring before Dafydd returned the look. Paz placed a comforting hand on his lad's shoulder, providing a clearly united front, although it didn't seem to Malcolm that Dafydd needed it. Whatever crossed silently between the Welshman and the hybrid, Dafydd prevailed. Merlin dropped his gaze and continued on.

Lucien walked up with Harry. "It's Alun, isn't it? Why don't we take your bags upstairs and I can show you where you and your son will be staying." When Alun merely nodded, Lucien added, "Are you hungry?"

"No, sir." Alun's quiet reply was in sharp contrast to the noise around them.

"Let's go, then. If you change your mind, there's always food to be had. And, please, call me Lucien."

Harry's husband had such a soothing way about him, not that Alun seemed to notice. He kept his head down, as always, and meekly handed over one of the bags he held when Lucien tugged at it. Then he followed Lucien silently back to the elevator.

"There's no hope for that poor man, is there?" Emil asked no one in particular.

"None, I'd say," Harry answered. "We'll try, regardless, and, if nothing else, give him a safe home for the rest of his life. As for that brat of his?" Harry shook his head. "That's going to be quite the project, but Lucien and I are determined."

"You'll have some unexpected help there," Malcolm said, jerking his chin in Annika's direction.

Alex rubbed at the back of his neck. "Yes, that does seem promising."

It was Val who asked the question they were all thinking. "How the hell did it happen?"

When they looked at Willem, he shrugged. "Don't ask at me. I haven't a clue. I practically fainted when I first saw her."

"I wouldn't have thought it remotely possible," Harry interjected. "Still, life always finds a way, doesn't it? Especially when the hive is in jeopardy."

Malcolm watched the young people playing with the dog, popping snacks into their mouths. It was all very sweet if one discounted the reason they'd gathered together. "What's next, sir?"

"Let's give them some time to enjoy themselves. Then I want to put it to the test tonight."

Willem grunted. "Sir, is that necessary? I mean…so soon? I'd like to wait, please. I am her father," he added with more balls than Malcolm might have had in the situation.

Alex took on his captain's expression. "I'm sorry, Will. I can see no value in waiting, only ever-increasing risk. We'll keep her safe."

"Yes, sir."

Emil clapped him on the back. "Come on. I bet you're hungry. A full stomach helps with everything."

* * * *

"This is really very kind of you, but I don't think I need such a large escort. Willem has always protected me on his own."

Without looking behind him, Willem said, "That's true, honey, but I feel better with all of my friends coming with us."

They marched down into the basement, surrounding the lass like the Pretorian Guard. Not a man among them, even Trey and Paz, thought they were being overly cautious. And while poor Willem had the most to be worried about, none of them wanted to take any chances with this precious life. If this test went as hoped, they'd have their proof of victory over Dracul and what was left of his forces. Excitement mixed with trepidation. Malcolm could feel it in himself and the others.

Only Annika acted unaffected. Alex had been honest with her about what she faced. She didn't appear to be the least concerned and had readily agreed to the short trip over to the club and into the basement.

"Oh, if it's for you, Father Willem, then I don't mind. I do hope Babette is behaving herself. She can be quite a handful, although she seemed quite taken with baby Idris."

"Dafydd is keeping a careful eye on them both," Paz assured her.

The human doctor also seemed unfazed by their adventure. He'd changed in the short time since

Malcolm had last seen him. Not only had the man obviously cemented his relationship with Dafydd, he held himself with more of a warrior's confidence. Malcolm had a feeling that for the next battle, he'd join them in the fight. Plus, of all of them, he hadn't appeared surprised as the conversation about Annika had played out among Alex, Willem and Harry. *Interesting.* The man had proved smart and fearless, and Malcolm was damn glad to have him on their side and in their hive, which was truly what they were becoming, apparently.

As they reached the bottom and waited for Val to open the armament room, Annika said, "I love the music coming from the club. Might we not sit in the pretty room with all those men for a while after this and listen to it?"

"No." The answer came out of every man's mouth.

The lass huffed yet said no more.

The trip over to the far door seemed interminable. Without discussing it, they flanked into a phalanx, with Willem standing directly behind his daughter. He only had to reach out and yank her away if trouble arose. Malcolm held his breath while Val turned the tumbler to unlock the cell door. It opened soundlessly to expose Petru's bright prison. He rose slowly from his narrow, hard bed. Naked.

Malcolm winced. They'd all forgotten that detail. Back home, it wouldn't have mattered in the least, but Annika was a young female of this planet and of European culture. He could tell by the set of his body that Willem wasn't much pleased.

Then, it didn't matter anyway. For, in the next instant, Petru's gaze homed in on the lass. His eyes went wide and his mouth gaped open. There was a visible tremble through his entire body before he dropped to his knees and bowed his head.

The tension in the room snapped. It was as if everyone both breathed a silent sigh of relief and inhaled with optimism.

Paz leaned over to Malcolm. "I'm not sure I understand. Is this what the proof we're seeking looks like? Is he accepting her as a queen?"

"Aye…and more." He grinned broadly at the human. "It means she's *the* queen."

Epilogue

"Shall I fetch you your dinner, Master? Or, would you prefer to *feed*?" The slut's voice was breathless with anticipation.

Dracul didn't bother looking away from the mirror as he backhanded him. With a muffled grunt, the boy sprawled onto the floor. "I'll tell you when I'm hungry."

Really, the impertinence of the stupid creature. Being confined for so long with only the dumb bitch for company was wearing on him. Then again, the slut was a tight hole and totally devoted to his Master, like the dog he was. He would have to do until Dracul had rebuilt his power base and decimated his enemies. Once he was back on top, he'd have his choice of toys. Maybe he'd keep this one, maybe not. Although variety was always desirable, there was something to say for the unusual coloring of his bed-warmer. Plus, loyalty was hard to come by. No one had learned that lesson better than Dracul.

Recuperating from his near-death experience had been more difficult than he'd anticipated. Having only one blood source didn't help matters. His body was slowly coming back to full strength. Waiting for it had been frustrating. Patience had never been his strong suit. He could admit to that one weakness. Staring at himself had become a terrible habit, too. He couldn't quite stop, however. As he gazed into the hand-held looking glass, he traced the scars running down his face with his fingertip. Barely a spot on him had been spared during the fall into the cistern. Grooves lined his face from the rough rock. The tip of his nose was gone entirely, leaving a gaping view of his nasal cavity.

He was hideous.

His pique rose with blinding speed, as always. He threw the mirror across the wall and watched it shatter with some satisfaction. The boy pushed up to kneel in front of him, his bare chest heaving and a trickle of blood running from the corner of his fetching lips. The slut knew better than to lick it or wipe it away. His blood, every drop of it, belonged to his Master.

Dracul crooked his finger and the boy shuffled closer to his side. At first, he ran his tongue up the line of red. The quick burst of flavor made him sigh. Then he latched on to the cut and sucked. Instead of struggling against the assault, the ever-accommodating slave leaned into it. Dracul could hear the boy's heartbeat, quick with his arousal. Although, with his useless little cock caged, there was nothing to be done with it.

Just the way Dracul liked it. There was only one need that counted.

He yanked his slut up by his hair, forcing him onto his lap and onto his cock. That part of him, as well, had been disfigured. He could barely look at the gnarled thing. Nevertheless, it functioned and he'd have to be content with that, not happy. That was an emotion he'd lost forever.

It was disappointingly easy to mount this human. His body gave almost no resistance to the invasion. *Unsatisfying.* To help rectify that problem, he released the lip, twisted the head out of the way and sank his fangs deeply and brutally into the waiting neck. That got a cry out of the cunt, while causing him to clench his hole tightly around Dracul's dick.

Ah, much better.

He drank his fill, tugging forcefully at the artery, and drilled that ass to acceptable satisfaction. Nothing truly pleased him these days. No matter. He would regain his full strength. It was only a matter of time. Plus, his enemies didn't even know he still lived. They had no idea he spent his days tracking them and plotting their destruction. He retracted his fangs once his climax ended, barely bothering to lick the wounds closed, and shuddered out a harsh breath against his never-ending disappointment.

"Idiots." He chuckled. "They think they're safe. I'll show them how wrong they are."

"When, Master?"

Dracul shoved the impudent creature off his lap and onto the floor. "Ask me another question and I'll cut off your balls."

"Yes, Master." The boy dipped his gaze, yet not before his eyes told Dracul how much the threat excited him.

God, where is the fun in all this? Dafydd had given him more pleasure merely by hating his guts and loathing his touch. The thought of what he'd lost infuriated him, chasing away the buzz of his feeding.

"Oh, go fix me some dinner."

"Yes, Master." The human scrambled to his feet and scurried out of the room.

"And don't make it goat again!"

His diminished circumstances really were insupportable. This hideaway he'd created long ago had never been intended to be a place to stay long-term. But it was the best he could reach, for the moment. Gazing around the richly-appointed accommodations, he sneered. No amount of Persian rugs could hide the sand that blew in constantly or the scorpions that dared to slink over his bare feet.

This was all Alex's fault. And Petru's, who'd failed to come to his aid when it had counted most. "Traitor." There would be a special punishment for that perfidy.

But no, the worst of the lot was Dafydd. "I will come for you first, my pet. Oh yes, I will. And the last thing you'll see before I tear out your throat and eat your heart will be my son in my arms where he belongs."

Want to see more from this author?
Here's a taster for you to enjoy!

Alien Slave Masters:
The Inconvenient Pet
Samantha Cayto

Excerpt

Wen's knees hit the hard-packed dirt with a force that reverberated up his exhausted body. His lungs ached with the effort to draw in enough breath to keep from passing out, while his heart hammered so fast he feared it would burst. He couldn't go on. He'd run as fast as his comparatively short Travian legs could manage and still his pursuers were gaining on him. Of course they were. Unlike him, they had a hovercraft. With each passing moment, it got closer and closer. The scrubland around him afforded little cover, and the outcropping of rock that had seemed a manageable distance when he'd started out now appeared farther away. A trick of the sun… He knew that. This damnable planet was hot and hazy and the vast areas lying beyond the human settlement and Travian command center robbed one of moisture and energy.

Accepting defeat, he fell down on his hands and waited to be caught. That was assuming the humans didn't simply blow him to dust from their perch in the sky. How had they come to possess such a craft? He knew his own people's technology, and he'd been on the planet long enough to know humans didn't have anything like it. Not that it mattered. These humans chasing him were not of the farming community — not so far out here. He was sure of that. His human friend Jo-el had told him that his people had been forced to choose less desirable planets to colonize as time had worn on. This most current one — a place the humans called New World Colony Seven and to which Travians simply assigned a number — didn't lend itself to cultivation very well. To succeed, the humans had concentrated their farming efforts on a small patch far from this area.

He drew in a ragged breath then choked on the dust the hovercraft kicked up as it landed nearby. He closed his eyes briefly and thought of his family. He wouldn't get to see them again, and, in all likelihood, they'd never know what had happened to him. There was no chance he'd survive this assault. Even if he'd been armed, he'd spotted at least three humans pursuing him. He was outnumbered and probably outgunned. Besides, he was a scientist, not a soldier. Not really. He'd finished at the bottom of every combat course he'd taken as a cadet. No surprise there. As an almost-runt, he'd been lucky to have been accepted into the military at all.

A sudden silence surrounded him as the craft shut down. He waited with his head hanging, working up the courage to face his attackers. The clomping of their steps caught his attention before three pairs of scuffed brown boots entered his field of vision. With one more fleeting thought of his family, he raised his head. He wouldn't die cowed in the dirt. Slowly, he straightened, throwing his shoulders back and keeping his hands by his sides. If these humans were not inclined to kill him right away, he didn't want to give them any reason to.

He focused his gaze on the nearest set of feet and roamed up—and up. Then up some more as two thick legs planted themselves right in front of him. They tapered in briefly at a waist laden with all manner of weapons before widening again into a massive wall of muscle. Wen found himself staring at the tallest, largest human he'd ever seen. The male looked to be bigger than him, even. Wen had kind of liked working among humans because—for the first time in his life—he hadn't been the small one. This male must be some kind of leader of his race. His vast size surely commanded respect.

The male scowled down at him, his square jaw clenched and his brow furrowed. As different as their two races were, they had similar enough expressions that Wen could easily see how pissed off this male was. He had so little hair on his head that his face was wide open, although his lower cheeks and jaw were dotted with bits of reddish-brown hair. Strange. None of the other humans he'd seen, including Jo-el, had such a trait. Was it natural to some of their species or a sign of something wrong? Regardless, it gave the human an even more menacing look. The male fascinated Wen and scared the shit out of him in equal measure. His gaze was so intense it felt as if his strange eyes—the color of the sky—bored right into him.

"What the fuck are you doing out here, boy?" The human's voice was pitched low and rough. It sent a shiver up Wen's spine.

"He's obviously spying, boss."

"Yeah, of course he is."

The other two humans had come up to flank the obvious leader. The one who'd spoken first was even larger than the head male, scarier and with even less hair. The other was a boy no older than Wen, with a mop of hair the color of a Travian's. He sneered down at Wen the way many of the cadets he'd served with did. The insult gave Wen spine.

Straightening even more, he returned their stares. "I am *not* a spy. I am Wen, a life scientist on a fact-finding mission concerning the natural resources of Planet Three-Five-Dash-Zero-Zero-Five-Triple-Dash-Nine." He was proud of how strong his voice sounded, despite the quiver in his belly. All three humans had weapons strapped to their waists and on their arms. The largest of them and the boy held weapons in their hands, as well. Travian weapons, he realized with a lurch. *How is that possible?*

"Jesus fucking Christ," the leader spat out. "What the hell are we supposed to do with you?"

The larger, secondary male took a half-step closer and raised his pulse rifle. "I have a suggestion, boss."

The leader held out his hand as if to block him. "Give me a break, Branch. We're not killing him."

"Why not, Dax?" the kid practically whined. "They've killed enough of our people."

"As far as we know, they've never summarily executed anyone, and that's what you're talking about here." He blew out a loud breath. "Besides, we're better than they are, right?"

The other two grumbled some kind of assent, yet their expressions trained on Wen remained dark and menacing.

"All right. On your feet, boy." The leader issued the order with a wave of his hand.

Wen stood up carefully. "My name is Wen."

"Oh, yeah?" The human took a step closer and it took all of Wen's self-control not to retreat. "Well, I'm Dax,

Wen. And, if you give me one bit of trouble, I'll let Branch here off his leash. You've led us on a merry enough chase as it is."

Some of the words used made little sense to Wen, almost as if the human were making a joke. But he understood their meaning well enough. "I won't give you any trouble. I have no wish to die."

The human nodded once. "Good. Get moving." He gestured toward their craft, the thing resting idly on the ground. Wen could confirm now that it was, indeed, Travian. They must have stolen it, although he'd heard nothing about theft since he'd joined the garrison. These males didn't strike him as farmers, either. So who were they and what were they doing on the planet? He'd only glimpsed some kind of small settlement nestled among an outcropping of rocks before he'd been spotted himself and chased. He supposed he was about to get all of his questions answered. Whether or not he would live to tell anyone else was the issue.

He climbed into the craft at the silent urging of the leader. Dax, he'd called himself. An odd-sounding name, but then he knew from Jo-el that human names didn't necessarily mean anything in particular. They put him in the back with Dax, while the boy took the helm with the larger male, Branch, sitting beside him. Now that was a name with meaning. It just struck Wen as strange that a mother would give her son such an agricultural one.

Although a fairly spacious craft in general, it felt very small to Wen as Dax's big, hot, hard body pressed up against him. There had been a time not so long ago when he would have appreciated the feel of a powerful male. Since his near-death beating from Merell, however, Wen had become skittish. That was even without factoring in how he was a prisoner, heading to an unknown fate.

"What are you going to do with me?" he blurted out as the craft lifted off.

Through the sudden dust swirling around them, Dax turned his stern gaze on Wen. Those weirdly blue eyes pierced him once more. "I'll let you know as soon as I figure that out, kid," he said over the roar of the engine.

Well, what did I expect? He was their prisoner. The fact that they hadn't killed him yet gave him hope that they wouldn't at all. He knew, though, that they couldn't simply let him go. Whoever they were, they weren't supposed to be out there. Certainly, the garrison commander had no knowledge of them. If he had, Wen would have been briefed on the security situation the same way he already had been concerning the human settlement. Damn him for being an impulsive fool. He should never have given in to the yearning to explore on his own. Because he hadn't filed a report, no one knew where he'd gone.

Despite feeling as if he'd run forever, the journey back to where he'd started, then beyond, took very little time. Wen was acutely aware of every moment, given how often his body collided with the human beside him. As used as he was to hard Travian males, this human felt like one of the rock walls they approached—unyielding. His palms sweated and his heart still raced, even though he'd caught his breath. Fear, of course, drove much of that reaction, but some of it reminded him of how he used to feel being in the presence of an older, enticing male. He silently chastised himself for being so silly. The human had no interest in him that way, and, even if he did, Wen had no interest in the human.

I don't.

All thoughts of desire—or not—fled as they circled for a landing and Wen got his first good look at who populated the rather primitive buildings. Everyone's face was turned up to watch them. There was one human—a female, if he wasn't mistaken—with amazing dark skin. That didn't surprise him, not really. He'd already seen the variety of skin and hair color of that species. It was the Travians around her, both female and male, that piqued his curiosity. *How is this possible?* The Travian garrison living among the official human settlement was set off to one side. It kept the two species living apart, and they gave each other a wide berth whenever their paths crossed. Not so here. Everyone was dressed as civilians, as well, and their stance beside the human implied that they mingled freely.

As soon as the hovercraft landed, the human, Dax, gave Wen a little shove. "Get out."

Wen did as he was told, landing lightly on his feet. He stared at all the people gathering around them. They all wore the same drab, brown work clothes. Many carried what looked like basic farm implements. Some were armed like the humans who'd captured him, including an imposing Travian male, who pushed his way past the others. His gaze homed in on Wen and the menace he saw in the male's expression had him cringing inside. He took an involuntary step backward and bumped into Dax. The human did an odd thing. He put his hand on Wen's shoulder, but, far from frightening him, it oddly made him feel a little safer.

The Travian stopped in front of him. "You caught him, I see."

"Yeah," came that deep voice from over Wen's head. "He gave us a good run. Says his name is Wen and that he's a life scientist. Whatever the hell that means."

The Travian sneered briefly at hearing Wen's name, which only served to make Wen raise his head in defiance. He'd spent his whole life staring down higher caste males who disrespected his humble birthright.

The Travian stepped closer and glared at him. "I am Burrell." Naturally, a higher caste, almost the highest. *Almost.* "What are you doing out here, boy?"

Wen did his best to match the gaze. "Exploring the natural flora and fauna. I am a scientist, as the human said."

The slap happened so fast Wen didn't have a chance to avoid it, even if he hadn't been pressed up against the human. Burrell bared his teeth. "That's Commander Dax to you, runt. Show respect."

The human—*Commander* Dax, apparently—pulled Wen back. "Hey, knock it off, Burrell. He's my prisoner, after all, and I really don't give a flying fuck what he calls me."

Burrell didn't like that. His expression changed in a way that was obvious to Wen. He could see how angry he was, yet trying to rein it in. Wen wondered if the humans could detect it. "Of course, Dax, as you say. These En caste boys, though, need a firm hand or they get above themselves."

"Burrell, please." A rather plump, older Travian woman worked her way past the crowd and joined the male. "Remember what our movement is about. We are not only trying to return to a simpler way of life, but we also want to end the social systems that led to war and rigidity to begin with."

Burrell's expression morphed immediately into one of contrition. "As you say, Clarith. My apologies. I see a boy in uniform and I revert back to my military days without even realizing it. I shall do better."

He sketched a short bow. His words and demeanor were all calculated to placate a female, the kind of things that males said and did all the time. Did the female recognize it for what it was? And, for an Ell caste male to show such deference to a Th caste female struck a discordant tone for him, although no one seemed surprised by it. He started wondering what their Families were and what the mix of females and males might mean in this strange group.

Clarith approached him, a genuine smile gracing her face. "Are you truly out here for scientific reasons?"

Lowering his gaze in a respectful way, he answered, "Yes, ma'am."

"And does anyone at the garrison know where you are?"

Wen considered lying for the span of a few heartbeats. But honesty had been drilled into him since birth, and he'd been told many times that he lacked the ability to fool females. "No, ma'am. I left early on my own without telling anyone. I just wanted to see more of the planet, out of curiosity."

Clarith peered at him closely before nodding. "Well, that helps."

"Has his vehicle been dealt with?" This from Dax, his warm breath teasing the top of Wen's head.

The dark-skinned human female stepped up. She wore her equally dark hair in a long single braid. She looked military, the same as Dax and the other two human males who'd captured him. She had an air of authority, too. The idea of females lowering themselves to handle martial issues still struck him as strange, but the humans didn't categorize roles by gender the way Travians still did.

"We drove it back here. Burrell removed the tracking device and we sent that off on a drone in the opposite direction. It's set to self-destruct, so by the time anyone at the garrison realizes the kid's missing and tracks him, they'll find nothing but scattered, tiny pieces of metal and a mystery."

Hearing this, Wen lost whatever hope had been left inside him that he'd be missed and rescued. He looked over his shoulder at Dax, the one being in the whole damn place that he already trusted to tell him the truth. Although he couldn't say why.

"What are you going to do with me?" he asked once more.

The human rubbed at the back of his neck as he looked past Wen. "Fuck, this is a mess." He shot his gaze to Wen. "We can't just let you go, kid. You get that, don't you?"

Wen didn't shy away. "Yes, I understand." A mewl of distress caught his attention, and he looked at Clarith.

"We're not set up for keeping prisoners." She raised her arms. "This is the beginning of a new way of life. We can't start it by adopting the worst of our culture, either," she added with a look at Burrell.

That male's face took on a gleam that made Wen's stomach clench. "We don't need to kill him. Or keep him locked up as a prisoner. There is a third option."

"I don't understand, Burrell," Clarith said.

"Me neither," the human agreed. "Spit it out, Burrell. What is this third option?"

Wen's stomach lurched even more. He knew the answer already.

"I'll make him my boy."

The subtle leer he'd sent Wen made him flinch.

Dax stepped up beside Wen. "Your *what*?"

A murmur rose from the crowd, and Clarith flapped her arms. "Oh dear. I'm not sure I like that idea any better."

Burrell gave her a slight pat on her arm. "Please don't distress yourself, ma'am. This is a male thing—a military tradition. The boy understands, and he'll agree because it's his best alternative. I assure you the solution is not offensive to him in the least."

That might have been true if Burrell didn't make his skin crawl or if the memory of Merell's beating didn't linger so sharply. He swallowed past the lump forming in his throat, working up the courage to accept his fate as the best possible outcome.

"Will somebody please explain to me what you're talking about?" The human's tone clearly indicated his patience was at an end.

"It's simple, Commander," Burrell began. "In the Travian tradition, males form bonds with junior boys by coupling. The boys appreciate the attention of someone more senior and the males like the release the boys afford them if they don't have access to their mates."

The male shifted to stare at Wen. "A boy in such a position gives his body and his allegiance to that male, utterly and completely. It's a strong bond, and one that can only be broken by the senior male or by the direct order of a male even more senior, such as a commanding officer. As I am the senior Travian male of our cadre, there is no one to interfere with the bond. We won't let him go back to the garrison, of course, where there is someone ranked above me. Simply put, once made, the boy won't be able to change his mind and break off his bond to me."

Unless you try to kill me. Wen would have broken his bond with Merell even if the male had survived the attempted rebellion. Loyalty between males and their boys had their limitations. But Burrell was right. If Wen pledged his body to him, he'd be unfailingly loyal, and that would mean sticking tight to the senior male. There'd be no running back to the garrison telling tales. The tradition was too engrained for him to break his word. Honor dictated that he keep the bond or not agree to it at all. Being killed or locked up for an indefinite period of time were worse choices, by far.

Dax shook his head. "Wait a minute. Are you saying that if this kid lets you fuck him, he'll form a bond with you so tight that he won't rat us out? Reveal our presence, I mean," he clarified.

"That is correct."

"Wow, that is *so* messed up." This from Branch.

Dax glanced at his fellow human. "You got that right. It's a fucking terrible idea. Right now, human boys are being held as sex slaves by Travians. We're *so* not doing that ourselves."

"Commander…Dax," Burrell soothed. "It's not the same thing. I will not force the boy. He will come to my sleeping pallet willingly."

"To save his life. Or to keep himself from being locked up for who knows how long." Dax shook his head. "That's not being willing. That's being desperate."

"We Travians do not see it that way."

"He's right about that," Clarith chimed in. She heaved a sigh. "I can't say we females understand or appreciate male bonding, but, if the boy is willing to agree, I have no objections." She turned her kind face toward Wen.

He looked at her, then at Burrell. He saw the male's interest there and what it would mean for his fate. Then he looked at Dax. The human scowled back. He wasn't happy with the solution. He was worried about Wen, even though he had every right to do what he wanted with his captive. As he stared at the commander's face, Wen felt the first stirrings of yearning that he'd buried as he'd lain recuperating in the medical bay of Outer Ring Station Twelve. There was something strangely appealing about the human, and the male didn't send a feeling of dread through him the way Burrell did. That male reminded Wen too much of his former master.

Knowing there was really only one solution to his plight and determined to take some measure of control, Wen dropped to his knees and gazed up at Dax.

"Please, sir. I'm willing to become a senior male's boy and pledge loyalty to him. But I want it to be you. I know this isn't something your species does or is comfortable with, yet I ask you, please, Commander, will you make me yours?"

PUBLISHING

Sign up for our newsletter and find out about all our romance book releases, eBook sales and promotions, sneak peeks and FREE romance books!

About the Author

Samantha Cayto is a Boston-area native who practices as a business lawyer by day while writing erotic romance at night—the steamier the better. She likes to push the envelope when it comes to writing about passion and is delighted other women agree that guy-on-guy sex is the hottest ever.

She lives a typical suburban life with her husband, three kids and four dogs. Her children don't understand why they can't read what she writes, but her husband is always willing to lend her a hand—and anything else—when she needs to choreograph a scene.

Samantha loves to hear from readers. You can find her contact information, website details and author profile page at https://www.pride-publishing.com